PRAISE FOR

MW01256594

Echoes of Memory

"The protagonist is rife with trouble and misfortune, but, ultimately, she rises to the occasion. Sara Driscoll turns the ordinary into extraordinary in this top-notch thriller."

—STEVE BERRY, *New York Times* BESTSELLING AUTHOR

"After suffering an attack that's left her with short-term memory loss, Quinn Fleming witnesses a murder, one that forces her to recreate evidence through carefully documented notes. Soon, as snippets of her memory solidify, Quinn begins to find patterns and connections in her notes, ones that place her in mortal danger. Driscoll's first standalone thriller delivers a fast-paced, intricate plot paired with a deep exploration of the aftermath of trauma. You won't want to put it down!"

—EDWIN HILL, EDGAR- AND AGATHA-NOMINATED AUTHOR OF *Who To Believe*

"A fascinating and compelling look at memory loss wrapped in an exciting mystery."

—KIRKUS REVIEWS

The FBI K-9 Novels

"Tense and exciting, Sara Driscoll has created a new power couple, Meg and her FBI K-9, Hawk."

—LEO J. MALONEY, AUTHOR OF THE DAN MORGAN THRILLER SERIES

"Exceptional . . . Readers will hope this series has a long run."

—PUBLISHERS WEEKLY, STARRED REVIEW OF *Storm Rising*

The NYPD Negotiators Series

"Tense and tightly plotted, *Exit Strategy* pulls you in and doesn't let go. A compelling page-turner."

—MARC CAMERON, *New York Times* BESTSELLING AUTHOR

"Pulse-pounding . . . Breathtaking panache . . . Driscoll approaches the potentially lurid material with admirable sensitivity, and maintains suspense throughout. Readers will clamor for the next installment."

—PUBLISHERS WEEKLY ON *Lockdown*

BOOKS BY SARA DRISCOLL

Echoes of Memory
Shadow Play

FBI K-9s

Lone Wolf
Before It's Too Late
Storm Rising
No Man's Land
Leave No Trace
Under Pressure
Still Waters
That Others May Live
Summit's Edge
Deadly Trade

NYPD Negotiators

Exit Strategy
Shot Caller
Lockdown
Terminal Impasse

SHADOW PLAY

SARA DRISCOLL

KENSINGTON
PUBLISHING CORP.
kensingtonbooks.com

KENSINGTON BOOKS are published by

Kensington Publishing Corp.
900 Third Avenue
New York, NY 10022

All Kensington titles, imprints and distributed lines are available at special quantity discounts for bulk purchases for sales promotion, premiums, fund-raising, educational or institutional use.

Special book excerpts or customized printings can also be created to fit specific needs. For details, write or phone the office of the Kensington Special Sales Manager: Kensington Publishing Corp., 900 Third Avenue, New York, NY, 10022. Attn. Special Sales Department. Phone: 1-800-221-2647.

Library of Congress Card Catalogue Number: 2025935032

KENSINGTON and the K with book logo Reg. U.S. Pat. & TM. Off.

ISBN: 978-1-4967-4872-0
First Kensington Hardcover Edition: September 2025

ISBN: 978-1-4967-4873-7 (ebook)

10 9 8 7 6 5 4 3 2 1
Printed in the United States of America

The authorized representative in the EU for product safety and compliance is eucomply OU, Parnu mnt 139b-14, Apt 123
Tallinn, Berlin 11317, hello@eucompliancepartner.com

To the April Moms
Because internet friendships can be genuine and long lasting . . .
It's been a pleasure to have you by my side, sharing
all aspects of our lives, since August 1996.
Here's to the next thirty years together!

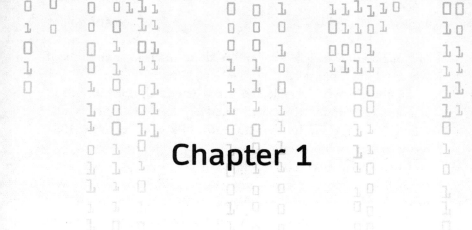

Chapter 1

KRISTA EVANS SLIPPED HER RIGHT hand under the middle-aged woman's sock-clad right foot and her left under her injured right knee. "Mrs. Bowman, we're going to begin with some very gentle range-of-motion exercises today. Ready?"

The fiftysomething woman, dressed in a T-shirt and gym shorts, lay supine on the treatment table. She was two weeks out from knee replacement surgery and was progressing nicely, even if she was a little impatient to move her recovery along like she was eighteen. "Yes."

"Great. Dig your right heel into the table. Just like that . . . Good. Now slowly slide that heel up toward your butt." As Mrs. Bowman dragged her heel closer, Krista gently helped lift her knee. She kept one eye on the long, flexible dressing that rode over her client's knee, covering the healing scar, but it stayed in place with no sign of blood blooming beneath. "That's great. You tell me when it starts to hurt. Remember, we want to stop just short of pain."

"There." The single word was ever so slightly breathy.

Krista halted the movement. "Ninety degrees. That's great. Now, let's slowly lower it down to the table. Then we're going to do it another fourteen times. There's no gold standard to meet. It's just what's right for you at this point in your recovery." Krista assisted the next five reps, then pulled her hands away. "Keep going on your own. I'm right here and ready to jump in at any time if you need the support."

Standing beside the table, her hands extended, ready to slide in at a moment's notice, Krista shimmied her shoulders to the beat as Olivia Newton-John hit the chorus for "Physical" from the Bluetooth speaker behind her.

Mrs. Bowman couldn't help the smile, even if it was a bit strained with effort. "I know why *I* listen to eighties music, given my age—it's the music of my teenage years. But why do you?"

"Because it's the music of my parents' teenage years. From an early age, I was instilled with a love of eighties pop." Krista grinned. "My folks are frozen in time. They may even think Ronald Reagan is president still."

Mrs. Bowman rolled her eyes. "Those were the days." She ran a hand through her short blond bob. "Those were certainly the days when my hair color didn't come in a box with a number." She looked up at Krista. "Not that you have anything to worry about in that respect for a while. Does your hair do that lowlight thing all on its own?"

Krista slipped a loose tendril of her light-brown hair behind her ear from where it had slipped free of its ponytail. "Guilty as charged."

"You must have men knocking down your door."

Krista jerked fractionally, losing the beat, but recovered quickly, pushing her smile wider and leaning on the bright melody to bolster her.

"Look at you with those gorgeous eyes," Mrs. Bowman continued, her eyes locked on the ceiling as she continued her exercises. "Do you do your makeup special so the one seems bluer and the other seems greener?"

"Definitely not. I'm a slug in the morning, and while I won't set foot out of the apartment without my eyeliner, that's about it. And trust me, stick with me long enough, and they won't seem so special."

"Spoken like someone who's naturally gorgeous, while the rest of us have to work at it."

"Nothing wrong with looking your best, for you or for Mr. Bowman. Speaking of which, did you work out that issue between him and your daughter?"

"We did. And you were absolutely right. It was a total misunderstanding. She was trying to spare his feelings, and he was being overly sensitive about something that didn't exist. They've talked it out now, and everyone is on the same page."

"I thought it might be. Just needed a little straight shooting. Okay, that's fifteen. Well done. How's it feeling?"

"A very minor ache, but I'd chalk that up to not using it for a few weeks. And it being a new joint."

"Reasonable." Krista picked up a large foam roller wrapped in a towel from a nearby counter. "Slide your heel back up again to raise your knee. I'm going to slip this underneath. It can go under your good knee, too." She slipped the roller into place. "We're going to work on some gentle strengthening. The harder weight-bearing exercises—squats and the like—will come in three to four weeks depending on your progress, but for now, we want to get those muscles moving. We'll be doing some exercises to isolate certain muscle groups today. Sound good?"

"Absolutely. There's chocolate in my purse as my reward for all this."

"Chocolate?"

"Honey, when you get to be my age with a bum knee, you're not rewarding yourself with sex."

The laughter bubbled up and out of Krista before she could slap a hand over her mouth.

Mrs. Bowman winked at her. "You just wait. You're young now, but later in life, chocolate will seem like the ultimate reward."

She was glad her mouth was covered to hide her reaction—*being young isn't a shield against pain*—but had her smile in place when she dropped her hand. "Chocolate is already pretty close to the ultimate reward now, so that sounds about right for me. The

next exercise you're going to do is to start working your VMO—
your vastus medialis oblique muscle—which is instrumental in
stabilizing and extending your knee." She grabbed a small folded
towel and tucked it in between Mrs. Bowman's knees, then ran
her fingertips from the inside of her right knee up a few inches.
"The VMO begins down here and reaches all the way up to your
hip bone. What you're going to do is squeeze the towel between
your knees . . . That's it . . . Now tighten this area by pulling your
kneecap up toward your hip and lifting your foot off the table,
straightening your leg." She slid her fingers under Mrs. Bowman's
right calf, helping her lift her leg. "That's perfect. Now hold it for
ten seconds." She dropped her hand a fraction of an inch away, so
Mrs. Bowman was doing all the work, but she was there to catch
her if the muscle failed. "That's ten. Now release." Mrs. Bowman
lowered her foot to the table, and Krista pulled her fingers free just
before they were trapped. "Excellent. Look at you go."

"Couldn't do it without you."

"You'll be doing it all without me before you know it. Now, let's
do six repetitions of that, but if you can do eight or ten, that would
be better. I'll be hands-off, but am here to swoop in if needed."

Mrs. Bowman did the first repetition to the beat of the music,
then said, "I mean it when I say that was really good advice. You
could give up your day job and start a column." Mrs. Bowman
looked down at her elevated right knee. "Actually, scratch that.
You stop doing this, and I don't know what I'd do. I'm going to
be selfish and keep you all to myself. As long as I can still ask for
advice on occasion."

"You absolutely can. It's funny you say that, because a bunch of
clients have told me I give good advice . . . so I started a live advice
chat on Twitch."

"On what?"

"It's a live gaming platform on the internet."

"You're . . . doing an advice game?"

"No, just using the platform. Most of what's on Twitch is people playing games. Viewers tune in to watch them play."

"That's fun?"

"Actually, it is. But it's more than that. It's about the people playing the games and the communities that build up around them. My college roommate, Hailey Swanson, she's one of those gamers. She talked me into creating a show on Twitch."

Mrs. Bowman peered like she was trying to see into Krista's head to understand what she was saying. "A non-gaming show?"

Krista grinned. "Now you've got it."

Mrs. Bowman rolled her eyes. "I have an MBA and you've lost me. Explain it to me like I'm five."

"You're sure you want to hear this?"

"It will help pass the time while I'm lying here doing leg lifts a one-year-old could lap me on. And I'll impress the socks off my twentysomething children." Her gaze flicked to the analogue clock on the wall. "You have fifteen minutes anyway. Humor me and tell me about your Twit show."

"Twitch." The opening notes of "Footloose" sounded, and Krista extended her arms and did a quick Kevin Bacon side shuffle, a grin spreading wide. "You asked for it."

"I did."

"In this job, there's lots of time to chat while I work with clients. I like to talk to people anyway, but talking goes a long way to distracting clients who might experience some discomfort." With a quirk of her lips, Krista glanced toward the speaker on the counter beside a bright-green medicine ball. "That's why the music."

"Because of the age of your clients?"

"That helps. Also, I love it, and most of them do, too. Talking helps, and I like hearing about people's lives—the family and personal issues they're willing to share. And I'm nosy and pushy."

"I wouldn't say that."

"Okay, I'm nosy and have opinions."

"*That,* I'd say." Mrs. Bowman gave her a wink. "They're clearly winning opinions."

"That's what I kept hearing. Honestly, for me, it's just common sense. I'm all for standing up for yourself, not taking anyone else's garbage, and communication. Anyway, I made some comments to my college roomie—"

"You still keep in touch?"

"Oh, yeah. When we graduated from Northwestern with our undergrad degrees, we stayed in touch as she got a job as a Web developer and I went on to get my Doctor of Physical Therapy."

"She's a computer geek."

"Totally. And a gamer. We met for dinner one night, and I was telling her all about my clients and talking them through their personal issues, and she said she knew some gamers I could help. And that's how the idea for *A Word from the Wise* was born. We do it together. Hailey set up the channel on Twitch and brought a lot of viewers from her own channel to our new one. From there we started to pick up steam. We broadcast twice a week. Hailey runs it, and sometimes puts in her own ideas. Otherwise, she's a great sounding board for me. People ask me questions and I answer them on the fly. If it's a really complicated issue, I'll think about it and answer it in the following stream."

"It's totally interactive? You're talking to people in real time?"

"We interact through a chat window. There's always a slight delay, so relying on a verbal conversation would be challenging. This works for us, and it's a really fun community. We have subscribers and regular viewers and chat in-jokes. We call them our 'Apples.'"

Mrs. Bowman's eyes narrowed to a squint. "I don't follow. 'Apples'? Like the fruit?"

"No, like 'wise apple.' Because we're called *A Word from the Wise,* and they contribute to the conversation. For a while, they were the 'wise asses,' and then someone pointed out that's a name for irritating people, whereas 'wise apple' denotes smart alecks. Wise Apples as the community name. They liked that better."

"Thus . . . 'Apples' as a short form."

"That's it. And that's them. They're an irreverent bunch. Unless it's a serious topic, then they're surprisingly supportive of the person who raised the issue."

"No one causes any trouble?"

"Of the base community? No. Once or twice, there's been the occasional viewer who swings by to cause trouble, but I wouldn't call them part of the community. By and large, we're still pretty small, and we're not a gaming channel, so we haven't attracted a huge amount of attention. If things do go sideways, we have moderators, who keep things sane, so if anyone acts out, they can be banned."

Mrs. Bowman's snicker turned into a low groan as she lowered her leg one last time. "People behave that badly?"

"They can. So far, it hasn't happened on this channel. It helps that the community is familiar with the platform and general community rules. At the beginning, it was mostly a gaming crowd asking questions about how to involve their partners in gaming or how to deal with them when they nag because of too much time spent gaming. But it's branched out to all sorts of advice about kids, in-laws, spouses, work environments, and so on." She laid a hand just above Mrs. Bowman's knee. "That's good. Our next exercise is to work on the quads and glutes. I want you to tighten your butt muscles, then tighten the front of your legs to push the knee down into the roller. Do this one with both legs to keep you balanced." She watched as the older woman tightened up, slightly tilting her hips off the table. "Even tighter . . . That's it. Good. Hold for ten, then relax, and we'll do ten reps of that."

Mrs. Bowman did a full rep, then said, "You sound like a busy girl—here five days a week and doing that on two evenings. You must love it."

"I have to admit, I didn't think I'd enjoy it, but it's turned out to be really fun. And it's starting to make some money."

"You get *paid* to do this?"

"That was the cherry on top for me—earning a little mad money. But eight months in, it's becoming a little better than that. You get paid through donations and as a cut from subscriptions. If you get huge, you can make deals to get paid to push brands. We're not that big, and I don't want to move in that direction. The original idea was to help people who needed it. Pushing a product at them doesn't feel right to me—like it's undue influence. Money coming from people who value our content is one thing, but hawking a product? That feels like profiting off someone's misery. Maybe someday a mental health sponsor might be okay. But for now, I like that we're our own channel with our own rules, answering to no one.

"For me, it's all about the community—the viewers who show up week in and week out to be a part of the discussion and to offer their own advice. People say internet friends aren't real friends. They're totally wrong." She checked the time. "And now you've listened to me prattle on about my night job and we're just about done. How does the leg feel?"

"Almost like I'm not so old I needed to have a joint replaced. *Almost.*"

"We'll get you the rest of the way. Just give it a little more time. You're doing great." Krista stepped back and lifted a hand to indicate Mrs. Bowman could sit up so Krista could strap her back into her soft knee brace.

"Next week?"

"For sure. And I'm going to give you some new exercise sheets for you to do at home. Am I there to police you? No." She gave her a bright smile. "Will I know if you likely aren't doing them? You bet."

"I'll do them, I promise."

"Knew you would. Make an appointment with Melanie at the front desk for next week. You're already really coming along. Do the exercises at home, and soon you won't need me at all."

"Now you're making me sad. I'd miss our chats."

"Get one of your twentysomethings to set you up on Twitch to-night. We stream Tuesdays and Fridays. *A Word from the Wise.* You don't even need an account to watch the fun. Or if you can't make it live, we have video on demand, or VOD, as the techies call it. You'll never miss me again." She finished fastening the brace and stepped back. "All set."

Mrs. Bowman laughed as she carefully got down and picked up her purse from the chair by the door. "Somehow I doubt it. See you next week. And have fun tonight."

"I will."

Krista turned away to make her notes in Mrs. Bowman's file, al-ready looking forward to the night's stream.

Never dreaming her life was about to change forever.

Chapter 2

KRISTA CAREFULLY SET HER FULL mug of tea down on the coaster behind her keyboard, tucking her bottle of chilled water behind it. When you talked almost nonstop for an hour, hydration was key.

She did a quick camera check of the image she projected—a bright-blue V-neck that made her bicolored eyes pop, with her honey-brown hair down in loose waves over her shoulders, her key and fill lights picking up both blond and copper streaks. Behind her, mounted on a pale-aqua wall, was a pattern of six wooden hexagons, each about twelve inches across, mounted together like a honeycomb. Inside and on top of the hexagons were a number of potted succulents, funky white animal statuary, a brass steampunk Ferris wheel, and a flickering LED candle. On the other side of the screen was a tall, slender-leaved, three-branched "not-a-palm"—as Hailey coined it—which was, in reality, a dracaena in a heavy teal pot. While Hailey's setup was purely technical, with electric blue lighting, framed gaming posters, and her collection of gaming action figures, Krista preferred to project a soothing peace. People came to their channel for advice because they were confused or distressed. She wanted to be the calm they needed.

Ready to go. She clicked over to the *A Word from the Wise* Discord voice channel the group used as video chat for meetings and to input video into the stream. She maximized the window to go full screen on her left monitor.

As if the thought traveled halfway across the city, Hailey jumped into Discord.

A petite and proportioned five-foot-four, Hailey was all in black tonight in leggings and a crew-neck, long-sleeved tee. Her shock of poker-straight, electric-blue hair, the dark roots just beginning to show at the edges of her side part, fell in a dramatic ombré waterfall almost to her shoulders. She sat in a high-backed electric blue and black leather gaming chair, lit by bright-blue LEDs. One ice-blue eye partially covered by a swoop of hair, Hailey grinned at Krista's image. "Hey, Ziggster."

"Hey, Hail. How are things?"

"Great day today! You know that back-end code giving me fits? The one with the four-dimensional data structure with bidirectional constraints running in three of the four dimensions?"

Krista nodded, hoping that Hailey wouldn't ask anything specific about what she remembered, because most of Hailey's technobabble sailed straight over her head. This certainly did. "I remember."

"Finally got that baby nailed. Hands down the most complex problem I've ever had the misfortune to deal with." Hailey raised a tall, slender teal-and-white beverage can in a toast. "May I never meet its like again." She took several long gulps from the can.

Krista stared at her in horror. "You're drinking double espressos at this time of night?"

"You bet your ass. And that's a double espresso martini, I'll have you know."

"Maybe the booze will counteract the caffeine."

"And what are you drinking tonight? Some kind of stewed grass?"

She lifted her mug. "My banana bread chai and I salute you."

Hailey shuddered. "You gotta live a little, and I don't mean with another one of your crazy teas. It's Friday night, the end of a long week. You could at least have one of your fruity girly drinks."

"Only if you want me to doze off partway through the stream. Caffeine will keep me up, but the tea will be perfect for settling into the conversation." She took a long sip. "Feeling Zen." She closed her eyes and wobbled her head like she was in a trance.

Hailey snorted a laugh, then took another drag from her can. "You're old before your time. I have another one lined up right behind this one."

"I have no idea how you'll sleep tonight."

"I'll take the edge off later with one of my special gummies." Hailey winked into the camera. "We ready to roll?"

"I'm ready whenever you are. Emily has done her usual magic and has me set up with a question and a comment from Tuesday's stream to run with until the chat gets rolling. Fire it up when ready." Krista's gaze slid to her right monitor where Twitch Mod View was displayed—the control panel for all the moderators that showed the stream, the chat, and all moderator actions taken during the broadcast.

It didn't seem so long ago they'd done their first show with less than a hundred of Hailey's viewers tuning in. And now look at them, about to start episode sixty-five, with over 34,000 followers and more than a thousand viewers tuning in for each stream to listen to her. *Her.* It still blew her mind anyone would come to her for advice, let alone several thousand people.

Their broadcast went live. In the video panel of her Mod View monitor, Krista saw the stream as it was presented to their viewers— two landscape video feeds overlaying a pale-aqua background, a neon border in green and blue framing each video feed. Just below their video feeds lay their logo: *A Word from the Wise*, with "Word" and "Wise" in large stylistic letters, in green and blue, respectively. The remaining words were in a smaller black type, and every word glowed neon white. Two comment bubbles, blue below Krista, and green below Hailey, each pointed in toward the channel name to complete the logo. The overall effect was bright, light, and cheerful.

When they were looking for channel colors, they'd had to go no further than Krista's eyes and Hailey's hair. Everything about their channel was in tones of blue, green, or their combination of aqua. And everything related to the channel, from their subscription badges to their chat emotes, stayed on theme.

"Welcome to *A Word from the Wise*—real advice from real people." As always, Hailey was the first to speak. The technical end of their partnership, she ran both the Discord video chat she input to the broadcast feed, as well as the broadcast itself. She was the one who could see all the details of the feed, as she had it set up inside her OBS Studio streaming software—the controls, audio mixer, sources, scenes, and transitions.

Krista grinned into her camera. "Hey, Mortie. How's it going?"

Hailey threw up a hand in a wave. "Hey, Ziggy. I'm still waiting on a perfect hair day, a 1956 white-on-red Corvette, and world peace . . . not necessarily in that order. And for Timothée Chalamet to return my calls, which, strangely enough, never happens."

Some people had no problem being real-life celebrities on Twitch; everyone had screen names, but often those people used their own names or a similar screen name. Both Hailey and Krista had opted to keep their identities secret. There were simply too many people out there who felt entitled to the attention of a perceived celebrity and who would stomp on an individual's rights to get that attention. So they both used screen names to keep their true identities hidden. Krista was ChiZiggy, a nod to both the city she grew up in and called home as an adult, and the nickname Hailey had called her since college—Ziggy for Ziggy Stardust, the alter ego of David Bowie, who also was born with heterochromia. Hailey was Dumortiere—or, more familiarly, Mortie—a short form of dumortierite, a gorgeous blue semiprecious stone, a reference to the blue hair she'd had for years.

"I'm keeping that flame of hope alive! Timothée doesn't know what he's missing . . . yet." Hailey's eyes briefly dipped down from the camera. "Hey, Apples! I see we already have a good turnout to-night. Let's get that chat rolling!"

Her suggestion was only for show, as the vertical black box on the right side of Krista's Mod View screen was already streaming with comments in bold white type, each line preceded by a number of colorful badges—each member's subscription or loyalty status—usernames, and comments.

> 🐢💬laterweirdo: 💬 I could be out drinking, but
> I'm here instead! 🍺🍺
> 🐢 bisquebroccoli: 😌 lookin good mortie 🐱 💬
> d1lobaj0le: 💜💜 Let's do this!
> 🐱✅hatingdawall: 😌 TGI AWFTW! ⟨WOOT!⟩⟨WOOT!⟩

The phone lying in front of Krista's monitors showed their channel in the Twitch app. A quick glance showed the viewer numbers jumping from hundreds to just under a thousand. "Let's begin with a question I couldn't get to at the end of Tuesday's stream," Krista said. "Joulenocturne has a question about what to do about their partner, who seems to be addicted to games on their phone, and how to get their attention." As always, unless the person asking the question outwardly expressed their pro-nouns—and many did, because it helped Krista clarify her thinking—Krista tried to keep things gender-neutral, unless the people involved clarified later. "There's no doubt games are inten-tionally built to be addictive so you spend more time gaming. That's the whole point, as far as the game developers are con-cerned. It's like social media. Why do you think the algorithm keeps pushing content to upcycle your outrage? Because it lights up the same centers of your brain that activate if you're taking an addictive substance, which keeps you coming back for more and more outrage. Same thing with gaming. It can be an addiction, so handle it as such. Now, that doesn't necessarily mean it's a hard-core addiction. I, too, have succumbed to the time suck of *Candy*

Crush occasionally. But your partner may need a wake-up call. Mortie, what do I always say?"

Hailey didn't miss a beat. "'Communication is key'!"

"You guys know how I can't stand movies or books built on the premise of a stupid miscommunication when the whole thing could be solved in two minutes if the people involved actually talked to each other. Drives me crazy. But without that dysfunctional miscommunication, no movie, no book. Joule, don't be that dysfunction. Talk to your partner. Don't accuse—just state your concerns. Work together with them on a mutual contract. What goes for them also goes for you. At least to start, don't ban solo gaming time, but limit it and see if you can both work within those constraints."

"What about writing the contract down and sticking it on the fridge?" Hailey suggested. "Make it official and totally transparent."

"Love it. Solid suggestion. Another angle on this is, what if their gaming time was mutual gaming time. Joule, you described the issue is too much time gaming on their phone, but what if some of that time could be spent as something you two do together? Mortie, you're the gamer. Suggestions?"

"Absolutely!" Hailey, in her gaming element, smiled enthusiastically. "I'd rec starting a quest game like *Stardew Valley* or *Baldur's Gate*, or if you like larger groups, do a multiplayer game."

"Make it about the two of you together, not them on their own," Krista continued. "See if that helps you, and let us know how it goes."

The chat filled with encouraging words of agreement, happy emotes, and more game suggestions.

Successful Twitch channels had custom emotes to express chatters' emotions—happy, sad, angry. Hailey had created a number of custom emotes for the channel—comment bubbles in the same tones of blue and green, but filled with "Hi!", "Woot!", or "!!!", among others. Emotes helped them take the temperature of the community and, especially at the beginning, gave Krista a much-needed shot of encouragement whenever she was insecure about her ability to advise on demand.

"I also wanted to congratulate Cambridgeshiredill. In reviewing Tuesday's chat, I saw they posted that they finally started their own stream highlighting their maker skills. If that interests you, like it does me, be sure to check out their channel. Now, Emily, I see we have some questions already, so shoot them over to me."

Moderators were a must for most Twitch streams. Someone to watch the chat, to moderate the conversation, and to deal with anyone who didn't follow the channel's rules. The two mods who assisted Hailey and Krista—both originally viewers of Hailey's gaming channel—were long-term, dependable community members who had proved their worth time and again. They were instrumental in keeping the chat moving smoothly on a channel where people, even if anonymous behind a screen name, bared their souls about some of their deepest problems and insecurities.

Emily—screen name emily_brontesaurus—was the mod who took the lead on managing the questions for Krista—filtering comments and sending questions through the channel's Discord chat, where they showed up in a vertical scroll window on her left monitor; whereas Rob, known on Twitch as RobBot_Tinker, was the more technically inclined. He took on more of the content moderation and stayed on top of viewers who might need a heavier hand. Krista and Hailey were also both mods, but Krista let the others take the lead so she could concentrate on the content. Hailey also helped moderate; initially she'd been the only one to fill that role, but their channel had since outgrown having only one mod.

Krista picked what seemed like a softball for the first question from the Discord chat. "Basistfireclan asks about how to deal with her partner. They've recently moved in together, but it's not going smoothly. Every time she asks him to do something, or comments that something needs doing, he stops whatever he's doing at the time to do whatever she pointed out, but is snippy about it. Or he tells her he can't do two things at once and she'd already asked him to do the first job. She'd like some advice on how to keep things from getting confrontational." Krista looked directly into her web-cam, trying to make a connection with an unknown person out there who had come to her for help. "Hating to flog a dead horse, but communication is key. Only you can tell me if you think this is what's going on, but it sounds to me that when you ask him to do something, he sees it as an immediate and direct order. Not as 'Hey, honey, we need to add cleaning the ceiling fan blades to our weekend to-do list,' but rather 'Thomas, *you* need to do this *now.*' He may see this as you pushing him around or may see it as an un-equal distribution of labor. Do you both work full-time outside the house?"

Krista paused and watched the chat for about ten seconds, knowing that there was always a slight delay that could sometimes be longer than ten to fifteen seconds between her speaking and the broadcast of her statement. Then Basistfireclan's comment ap-peared in the chat. "You do both work full-time. Well, if I can make a suggestion," Krista said. She quickly scanned the chat, a smile curving her lips as the conversation exploded with multiple messages of **Communication is key!** accompanied by emotes of danc-ing animals, fireworks, and pompoms. "I'd say, 'Say it with me now!', but chat has beaten me to it, so you already know what I'm going to say. You guys need to sit down and talk this out before any more hard feelings come from it. You need to be really clear what you're asking for. Is it 'Can you please hand me that glass so I can wash it right now?' or is it 'I noticed the upstairs window tracks need cleaning, so can we put it on the list to do sometime this weekend?' You also need to be clear when you think a job can be done together, or if you're asking him to do it solo. If you are— and maybe that makes sense because it's in his skill set and not yours—make it clear that while he's doing X, you're going to be doing Y. Clear communication and a fair-and-balanced workload means he won't have anything to be upset about."

Chat rolled with words of encouragement for Krista and for Basistfireclan, as well as words of commiseration or alternate suggestions.

Community—it was her unexpected gift from *A Word from the
Wise*. Viewers showed up once, sometimes twice a week, like
clockwork. They sent words of encouragement or gentle teasing.
They bought subscriptions for themselves or to gift to newcomers
to the channel to draw them in or to encourage them to stay. They
used in-jokes, tossed out different techniques that had worked for
them, and suggested self-help book titles if Krista was having trouble finding just the right support. There was the occasional troll,
but she and Hailey had a double-barreled support there—first from
the community itself, who would pile on anyone who gave Krista
and Hailey a hard time, and second from Rob, and occasionally
Emily, who would swoop in to clean up any remaining mess. It
left Krista and Hailey free to carry on with the discussion and to
never have to climb into the occasional mud fight.

On those evenings when her apartment felt particularly empty,
her community buoyed her, as it did this night.

The stream continued, with Krista fielding question after question. As was their habit, Hailey mostly stayed in the background,
occasionally chipping in with her opinion, but overall letting Krista
take lead. This setup worked well for both them and the community—Krista had the human connection skills, whereas Hailey had
the technical skills and knew the gamer mindset inside and out.
Sass might be Krista's go-to response to much that happened in
her life, but she was careful to never let it intrude into her advice—
once she took on a question, she dialed the sarcasm down to zero.
How else could the community trust her if they couldn't tell if she
was joking? For Krista, this was an ironclad absolute. Even Hailey
knew her job was perhaps to lighten the conversation, but never
to let it appear like she was making light of the original poster of
the question.

"We'll do one more question tonight, and I'll hold any remaining
questions for the next stream. I have a comment here from Chase547,

who writes about a woman he really likes. He's attentive to her, doing little acts of kindness, like complimenting her on her outfits, commending her on work tasks well done, and always being interested in what's going on in her life. But she keeps giving him the cold shoulder. He wants to know what he could do to get her to notice him." Krista turned as if she was looking toward Hailey, who wasn't in her apartment, but halfway across town. The two women used this as a trick to shape the intimacy of their conversation, to look like they were conversing side by side. "Mortie, have you ever had a guy you didn't know well show you special attention?"

"Sure have." In the Discord window on Krista's left monitor, Hailey angled to her right.

"How did it make you feel?"

"Honestly, kind of uncomfortable. And he acted like I was lucky to be getting his attention." Hailey swiveled toward the camera. "I'm not suggesting that's what's happening here."

"Not at all." Krista turned back to the webcam, making "eye contact" with Chase547. "You need to be a bit careful here. Maybe she's a little shy and you need to give her some space to be comfortable around you, but it sounds like you don't know her that well. Maybe she's in a relationship already, so she's uneasy about being, or even just seeming, disloyal to her partner. Or, if you work with her, maybe there's a power imbalance. If you're in a more senior, supervisory position, she may feel you're pressuring her and she can't speak out because you have all the power in the relationship and her job could be on the line. My advice to you here is to consider all that and either step back if there's a power imbalance or lighten the romantic pressure and just get to know her as a friend, if she's amenable to that."

"Chase has clarified they don't work together, so there's no power imbalance." Hailey had her eye on the chat and called out Chase547's update. "Their connection is merely social."

"That's good, and also simplifies things. But let me reiterate that you need to be careful. Some women are flattered by attention, some are annoyed, and some are scared by it. There are two ways to go here—you either straight out ask her out for coffee or to some mutually enjoyed activity, or you back off completely and friend-zone yourself until you get to know her better. If you do the former and she turns you down, take 'no' as the answer it is and back off. If you don't want to take the chance of slamming that door closed immediately because she doesn't know you, then you may up your chances of a 'yes' by letting her get to know you as a friend first. Be sure to let us know how it goes." She flashed an encouraging smile. "And that's it for us. Everyone, have an amazing weekend and we'll catch you on Tuesday."

"Don't forget to give us a follow or subscribe if you haven't yet," Hailey added. "Remember, subscribers get our sweet custom Apples badge in chat. Thanks for getting wiser with us!"

Then the feed ended, and Krista was looking at the Discord chat.

Hailey sagged into her gaming chair, a satisfied tilt to her lips. "Another good one."

Krista let herself relax, suddenly feeling drained. "Yeah, pretty smooth sailing."

"I gotta run. Meeting Aiden. He's amped to show me some new club he found. Got plans?"

"It's a toss-up between continuing my work on the cure for climate change or strengthening my case for the Nobel Peace Prize with my plan for Middle East peace."

"That's a tough one. Let me know next week which one you went for." Hailey tossed her a grin and a hurried wave and ended the Discord video chat.

Krista dropped back in her chair, the apartment jarringly silent and still after the whirlwind of Hailey's energy.

"I'll do that."

Chapter 3

KRISTA ROSE FROM HER CHAIR, grabbed her near-empty mug of tea and her half-empty water bottle, and walked to the doorway, pausing with her hand on the light switch, looking back into her office.

Not seeing what was there, but what might have been.

Not the long desk tucked against one wall of the narrow room holding her PC and double monitors. Not the aged brown-and-buff brick wall below the exposed ductwork, interrupted by a single wood-framed double-hung window, its soft Roman shade permanently raised to both let in light during daylight hours and look out at the opposite brick wall, only a handful of feet away. Not the pale-aqua walls, camera ready with her shelving, plants, and knickknacks.

Instead, she saw the room as it was originally meant to be, as they'd planned—soft green walls, a white crib with a curving headboard, and the matching dresser and change table. A rocking chair filled with stuffed animals and perhaps a handmade quilt. A matching shelf full of board books and toys, some of which spilled onto the soft area rug that covered the aged oak-plank floor.

She blinked, and reality returned. With a quiet sigh, she flipped off the light switch and turned away from what might have been and into her great room.

When they'd bought the condo a few years ago, one of the things they'd loved about the space was the exposed brickwork.

Situated on the second floor of a 1924 six-flat, an eminently Chicago architectural style, the space consisted of two bedrooms, a full
bath, a hidden stacked washer and dryer, and a U-shaped kitchen
that opened out into the larger living room. The long wall of the
living room was entirely composed of the same brown-and-buff
brick, with a flat-screen TV hung in the middle of the wall, surrounded by angled steps of floating shelves. A long, padded navy
couch sat opposite, while its matching armchair angled to face the
screened patio door at the end of the living room. Beyond the glass,
two cushioned chairs and a small round table looked out onto the
autumnal splendor of the leafy courtyard and the facing balcony
about forty feet away.

At close to nine-thirty, on a late-September evening, it would
be a bit chilly to sit out on the balcony with a book, but it was one
of her favorite activities on a warm summer evening. Now, long
past dusk, the courtyard lights only barely highlighted the brilliant
yellow leaves of the green ash trees.

Moving into the kitchen space, enclosed by two walls and a
long counter that doubled on one side as a breakfast bar, with twin
tall stools, she dumped out her water bottle, rinsed her mug, and
set both in the sink. She started out of the kitchen, then changed
her mind, went back, and flipped on the kettle.

She was itchy and restless. Maybe another cup of tea would
soothe her.

Her eyes found his picture on the top right-hand shelf from
across the room.

A framed eight-by-ten photo, it showed herself and a man of
the same age with windblown blond curls. They both wore wind-
breakers—his red, hers hunter green—and were framed by a
backdrop of blue sky, wispy white clouds, and stunning peaks. She
walked over and picked up the photo, staring down into Lincoln's
laughing green eyes. She remembered the trip they'd taken to the
Black Hills of South Dakota, a spur-of-the-moment trip to celebrate his official remission from brain cancer. He'd still been

healing, still strengthening muscles grown weak from months of treatment, but he'd managed every trail they'd attempted.

She sat down on the couch they'd picked together when they moved in, so perfectly situated between her physiotherapy clinic and his investment company, with the extra bedroom they planned to set up as a nursery shortly after their wedding.

She smiled down at the photo and touched her fingers to his beloved face. So much love, so much joy, just overflowing in this quick selfie at the summit of one of the lower peaks. They'd felt great that day, alive and hopeful. For so long, they'd put off the conversation because of the uncertainty, but they'd actually started talking wedding plans again.

He would be gone nine months later when the cancer came roaring back and there was nothing the doctors could do this time to stop it. They gave him two months; he didn't even last six weeks.

She still lived in their condo alone, even though the internal argument—to stay in the last place Linc had lived so she could feel close to him, or go because it was time to move on—hammered in her head on a weekly basis.

Krista knew she was lucky. She had loving parents, who had moved to Seattle for her father's job, but who stayed in touch regularly and frequently traveled home to Chicago for visits. She had her brother, Zach, who lived only a half hour away in the downtown center. He was eighteen months older, and while they'd always been close, he'd been the solid rock she leaned on during Linc's illness and following his passing. She had good and dependable friends, a great business partner, and what was becoming a lucrative side hustle with a supportive community. But even a little less than two years after his death, Linc's loss was still a gaping hole in her life. Talking to him helped, eased some of the ache, and kept him alive, even if only in her own head.

"Today was a good day." She usually talked to the photo she still kept by her bed—a nighttime shot taken the evening they got engaged—telling him about the day's activities while she changed for bed. Tonight she opted to share her day with happy Linc on the mountaintop. "Busy day in the clinic. Saw Mrs. Bowman again for her knee. She's really coming along. Mr. Peterson was in this morning. This is visit three . . . no, four. He's now ten weeks out from his stroke and his strength is improving nicely. His balance is still a bit wobbly, but he swears to me he's still using his walker and will continue to until I tell him it's time to graduate to a cane and then hopefully to independent movement." She chuckled as she remembered. "When he wasn't paying attention, he hummed along to 'Eye of the Tiger.' When I was surprised he knew it so well, he said his kids used to listen to the radio all the time and he never had them turn it off, even learned to like some of it. Gave him a connection with them." She nodded in approval. "Smart man. Really nice man. Determined too. Wants to stay in his own home with his wife and will do the work to stay there."

The kettle boiled, then clicked off, so she brought Linc with her to the kitchen as she selected new tea—lavender for a quieter sleep—spooned leaves into a strainer, and then poured water over it into her mug. She leaned against the counter as it steeped, her eyes still on his smiling, youthful face, where the frame stood on the counter, pushing aside the thought that he'd forever be youthful in photos because his life was cut so tragically short.

"Spent some time talking through a case with Kyle." Her business partner, Kyle Blackburn, was their sports injury specialist. "One of the guys on the Rockford IceHogs completely ruptured his ACL. Guy is a real star and one of the top prospects for the Blackhawks, so they want him back in fighting form ASAP, because who knows when he might be called up. Kyle and I were discussing strategies to get him there. Then after work, Hailey and I streamed again. It's really taking off, Linc. It took me a while to settle in—I was so nervous and scared I'd make a fool of myself— but it's finally happening. And I think I'm really helping some of them." She pushed off the counter to strain the leaves from her tea and add just a touch of honey.

She carried both mug and photo to the couch and set the mug down on a coaster on the coffee table. Then she crossed back to the shelf, setting the photo in its proper place, running her thumb over his face one more time. "Love you. Miss you."

She turned away, grabbing the remote from the coffee table before flopping down on the sofa, propping her feet up on the table, staying well clear of her tea, and crossed her ankles. She turned on the TV and navigated to the next episode of *Friends,* which she was currently bingeing for the fourth time because feel-good TV never got old. Especially on nights when you felt alone and could pretend those six vibrant personalities were your friends, too.

She grabbed the gray, white, and black stuffed husky tucked into the far corner of the couch and nestled it into the crook of her elbow. "It's you and me tonight, Balto." She looked down at the toy, remembering the warm summer evening at the county fair when Linc had won it for her at the carnival ring toss. It was only their third date, but he'd completely charmed her with his determination—and surprising success—to win something. The stuffed toy continued to bring comfort years later. It had kept vigil in or by Linc's hospital bed as he'd unsuccessfully tried to claw his way back from death, a piece of Krista she'd left with him when she couldn't be there herself. Balto had been there when Linc had finally let go. Had come home with Krista that night, had absorbed the wild storm of her weeping as she'd cried herself to sleep with him in her arms, instead of her fiancé.

He was one of the tools in the toolbox she used to bolster herself against Linc's continued loss. Additionally, her constant contact with her family was a bulwark against depression. They understood her sadness, and their steadfast presence—Zach in person on a regular basis, her parents via phone and text nearly daily—kept her from sinking into depression, even in the earliest days. The persona she projected at the clinic was another tool—the music and the dancing were there to cheer and distract her clients, but were for her as well, to raise her spirits when they wanted to sink. She was careful about her playlists—emotional songs like Elton John's "Empty Garden" or a-ha's "Hunting High and Low" were never included. Instead, only bright, poppy tunes that stirred the impulse to hum along or to even dance were her stock-in-trade.

It was only here, in the privacy of her own space that still hummed with Linc's presence, even all this time after his passing, that she allowed her often-exhausting protective shell of performance to fall away. Here she could be herself, here she could let herself feel.

She picked up her tea and settled back as six friends celebrated Thanksgiving with a game of football. Finally, she allowed herself to relax after a long and busy day, and tried not to think of how the weekend yawned, directionless, before her.

Chapter 4

"ACCORDING TO YOUR FILE, YOU'RE four weeks postsurgery." Krista stood in front of Micah Lamond, who, she estimated, was in his late forties. Lamond had come dressed in a suit and tie, with his left wrist secured in a structured Velcro splint. He exuded displeasure at being there, as demonstrated by his clothes—Krista knew very well Melanie, their receptionist, made sure every client was told to come to their appointment in comfortable athletic clothing to allow for easy movement. It wasn't as crucial for this appointment, as it could be for a shoulder, hip, or knee injury, but at the very least, he'd need to remove his jacket and tie and roll up his cuffs.

"This was the earliest appointment I could make. I'm a busy man." As if counting the seconds, Lamond's gaze shot to the clock and then narrowed on the Bluetooth speaker playing "Shout" by Tears for Fears. "Can you turn down that racket? Don't you have anything soothing, like classical?"

"I can do classical." Krista set the file folder down on the therapy table beside Lamond's hip, pulled her phone from her side pocket, opened Spotify, and pulled up a Bach playlist. *Can't go wrong. Granted, this one might still find fault with it.* The quick and cheerful opening strings of the Brandenburg Concerto No. 3 in G Major filled the room, though at a slightly lower volume.

"Better." Lamond looked slightly less aggrieved.

You're welcome. "I need to do a full examination of your left arm. If you could please remove your coat and tie and roll up your sleeve. I can help if you require assistance."

"Why would I need that?" He shrugged out of his suit coat awkwardly, barely using his left hand, but instead keeping it curled in toward his body, as if afraid someone might accidentally bump it. He dropped his coat in a pile on the table beside him, then loosened his tie, though not removing it as she requested, and unbuttoned the top button at his collar. Then he unfastened his left cuff, going no further than turning the cuff back.

Definitely aiming for bare minimum only.

"Thank you, Mr. Lamond. Tell me about your injury, please."

"Isn't it in the file?"

"It is, but sometimes I hear helpful information when a client describes what happened themselves."

"Not much to tell. The deck around our pool has a topcoat sealant to keep it from getting overly hot in the sun, but that tends to make it slick when it's wet. I slipped on it and went down. Put out my left hand to catch myself, and broke my damned wrist."

"Your radius, one of the two bones in your forearm, more specifically, but the far end of it, so part of the wrist complex."

"As I said, my wrist." He gave her a look that said she was too stupid to live.

You've dealt with bigger idiots than this one. Krista pasted on a bright smile. "Exactly. The radius was broken in two places. They did surgery the next day, put in a plate and screws. It looks like surgery went well."

"So, why am I here? The surgery fixed the problem."

"The surgery tackled the worst of the problem, but my job is to get you back to the strength you used to have. I'd have liked to have begun two weeks ago, but we can definitely start now. We'll just hit full motion and strength a little later. I'll work the wrist with you now, and I'll give you exercises to do at home to slowly strengthen the muscles."

"You think I sit at home all day with time to waste on hand exercises?"

"Certainly not. Whether you do them is up to you." She met his gaze full on, meeting his resentment—that *she* would dare to ask this of *him*—with her own determination. "Do you want to regain full use of your hand?"

"Of course."

"Then I'd recommend following my instructions." She met his pinched gaze. "The only one you hurt by not doing the exercises is you."

Lamond exhaled loudly, but extended his left hand toward her.

"Thank you." Carefully cradling his left hand in hers, she pulled back the first Velcro strap. "Let's remove this and see where you are at baseline."

Forty-five minutes later, Krista held the door open for him. "You have your exercises. Please do the full list daily to make the most use of our time together. I'd like to see you later this week, if possible."

"It's not."

She kept her face in smooth, relaxed lines. "Then next week. But I'd recommend at this stage not making appointments further than one week apart."

The look he threw her clearly showed he thought this was a moneymaking scheme, then he slinked out, head down, with a sheaf of papers covered in exercise diagrams in hand and without a single word of goodbye or thanks.

He stepped out of the private treatment room and into the larger central gym area. The clinic had four treatment rooms for private patient examinations, ultrasound, and treatments to assist with post-injury healing—lasers, transcutaneous electrical nerve stimulation, interferential current therapy, and electrical muscle stimulation. The four rooms branched out from a large central exercise area, complete with dumbbells and stretch bands, BOSU balls, yoga balls, a weighted pulley system, a leg press, both upright and recumbent bikes, two treadmills, and a set of three steps flanked by railings. Two treatment beds sat against the far wall. Tracey, one of the practice's two assistants, was working with a client on a set of mats; the client was flat on his back, with his hips bridged up and his heels dug into a yoga ball, bending his knees to curl the ball in and out.

Mr. Westhausen is coming along nicely after his knee replacement.

Lamond tossed an irritated look at Westhausen, then stalked down the short hallway toward the reception area.

"Don't let the door hit you on the way out," Krista murmured. She propped one shoulder against the doorjamb, waiting as he stopped at the receptionist, pulled out his wallet, and struggled with one hand to extract his credit card.

She waited until his transaction was complete and he'd left, then she strolled down the hallway to their bright reception area. Melanie sat inside their records room, a wide window opening out to the small cheerful seating area, circled with padded chairs, with a tall, leafy rubber tree in the corner and a rotating magazine rack standing opposite. With actual magazines. It never failed to amaze Krista how Melanie always kept the rack stocked with recent magazines—from *Better Homes & Gardens,* to *Southern Living,* to *The New Yorker,* to *Time,* there was something for everyone. Krista had even heard one of their older clients mention once she didn't mind if her appointment was late because it was her only chance to read a magazine these days.

Krista leaned on the windowsill and looked down at Melanie. The clinic had a young staff, and Melanie was only a year younger than Krista. But her age didn't denote her experience or capabilities—the woman was a whirling dervish who kept every one of them organized. From appointments, to billing, to dealing with HMOs that wanted to argue every last aspect of coverage, Melanie did it all. And kept her sense of humor through the chaos.

Dressed in mint-green scrubs with her brown hair in a ponytail, Melanie looked up at her with light-blue eyes. "Well, he was a treat."

"Sorry."

"What are you apologizing for? Did you put him in a mood?"

"Who's in a mood?"

Kyle's voice from almost directly behind her made Krista jump, slapping her palms down on the counter. She turned around and fixed him with a beady stare. Considering that he was substantially taller than her own five-foot-nine inches, she had to fix that stare up high. "How many times have I told you not to sneak up on me?" She looked back at Melanie. "Bells."

"Bells," Melanie confirmed with a conspiratorial smile.

"What do you mean 'bells'?" Kyle asked.

Hands on hips, Krista looked up into amused brown eyes, under heavy brows, below short-cut brown hair spiked skyward with his ever-present gel. In all the time she'd known Kyle—which was years at this point, as they'd been in the same Doctor of Physical Therapy graduating class from Northwestern before buying this practice together—she'd only seen him twice without his hair gel, and both times he'd been hungover the morning after a night of exuberant drinking. Her gaze traveled down over his athletic tee and loose-fit running pants. He, like Krista, wore athletic wear for appointments because theirs was an active profession working with patients. Her gaze stopped on his cross-trainers. "I mean bells. You know—those little metal spheres with a ball inside that jingle when you shake them?" She nudged the toe of his shoe with her own. "You need a set tied to your gym shoes so you can't sneak up on anyone." Her gaze shot back up again. "Don't you have a client?"

"Running late, apparently. Who's in a mood?"

"My last patient. Comminuted distal radial head fracture. Should have been seen two weeks ago, but waited to come in because he's 'busy.'" She leaned into the last word, then rolled her lip. "He complained about the music."

"No!" Melanie laid a hand over her chest in mock astonishment. "The nerve!"

" 'Shout' is a classic. Though apparently not classical. So we switched to Bach."

"The man needs a drink to relax."

"With a Valium chaser."

Kyle leaned one elbow on the counter, settling into the conversation. "Did he lighten up once you changed the music?"

"He might have, except we were actually working on his wrist. He says the pain is about four most of the time, but goes to about a seven by the end of the day. Incision is healing well, with the expected collagen remodeling, but there is decided muscle atrophy and postural imbalances in both the wrist and hand. I think we're looking at restrictive adhesions in the volar soft tissue of the radial side of the wrist."

"If you strengthen the ulnar wrist extrinsic muscles, that should restore the synergistic balance."

"That's my thought. I'm also thinking the median nerve is irritated. We need to get the inflammation down and work on increasing nerve gliding. We worked it today, and I sent him home with a bunch of exercises to do daily."

"Think he will?"

"Let me guess," Melanie interjected. "He's going to be one of the clients who comes in here once a week, you guys do all the work, and they expect to be magically cured with no work on their part."

"He was definitely leaning that way, but I stomped all over it. Made it clear his success rested greatly on whether he did the exercises as required at home. We can't strengthen those muscles in once-a-week sessions, because he says he's too busy for twice-a-week sessions this early in his recovery."

Melanie consulted her computer screen. "Especially when he booked an appointment for two weeks from now."

"He did?" Krista rolled her eyes and groaned. "This one's going to be a total joy. He'll be complaining in a month about how useless I am, and it's his fault he won't be progressing."

"Want me to take his next appointment?" Kyle asked. "Do the good cop, bad cop thing? You know that works."

"Yeah, it works. But why am I always the bad cop? Let's leave it for now, but I reserve the right to be the bad cop at a later date."

"Deal."

They all turned when the front door opened and a petite brunette in her thirties dressed in workout clothes stepped into the waiting room.

"Ms. Turner," Krista said. "How's the back?"

"Really coming along. And what did I say about Ms. Turner? It makes me feel ancient." Her smile was self-deprecating. "My back is already doing a good job there. Don't join in. It's Sophie."

"Sorry. Force of habit." Krista met Sophie's smile with her own. "Definitely don't want to do that. Come on back, and we'll get started." She tossed a look at Kyle. "Hope you didn't get stood up."

He shrugged. "I'm beginning to wonder."

Krista led Sophie down the hallway. "How do you feel about Tears for Fears?"

"Fantastic choice. Crank it."

"Excellent. You're a palate cleanser after my last client." She held up a hand before Sophie could ask. "Can't tell tales out of school. Let's just say it's a lot lighter in here now that he and his dark cloud have moved on." She led Sophie into her therapy room.

The day was definitely turning around.

Chapter 5

"WE'RE GOING TO BEGIN TONIGHT'S stream with a question we didn't have time for on Friday," Krista said after Hailey launched the evening's stream of *A Word from the Wise.* "Notrumpets here asked about her partner, who she calls 'Bob.'" She made air quotes around the word "Bob," making it clear it was a pseudonym, then turned back to finish reading the message Emily had loaded into the Discord chat. "'Bob' was cheated on in his last relationship. Notrumpets says, 'I've been faithful, but I've caught 'Bob' going through my phone several times, looking for evidence of cheating. He's taken innocuous texts from a coworker asking for a quick meeting as evidence of infidelity when it's a discussion over business finances. It's ripping us apart. What should I do?'"

Krista stopped and looked up into the camera. "First of all, Notrumpets, I'm sorry you're dealing with this. From what you've outlined here, you haven't done anything wrong. Any of us who have had relationships know if you or your partner have had past relationships, especially if those relationships imploded, baggage is brought into the current pairing. That's normal. But it doesn't mean it's okay if that baggage impedes the current relationship."

Krista picked up her mug and took a quick sip of her tea before setting it down carefully between computer components. "I hope you've already sat down with 'Bob' and made it clear you're not unfaithful. In fact, I'm going to assume you've done that. If you haven't, that's step one, and that might be enough to make him feel better. Assuming you've done that already, and he's demonstrating that he doesn't believe you, you have a larger problem on your hands. On *your* hands, but the basis of the problem isn't you; it's 'Bob.' I try not to recommend therapy as the all-purpose magic fix for all problems, but in this case, I really think 'Bob' needs to talk this through with someone besides you. The problem isn't your behavior, it's his. You're not doing anything wrong, but if he'll never trust you, you won't have a future together. More than that, 'Bob' needs to work through this so he can be happy. He can't be happy if this is the suspicious life he's leading. You say you've seen him scrolling your phone, but what haven't you seen when you're in the shower or just left your phone in the other room? I think you need to talk to 'Bob' now about saving the relationship and making him happy. Mortie, thoughts?"

Hailey had been sitting with her eyes diverted, watching the chat, but she looked up at her name. "I think you're right on the money. I had a friend once who had a partner who was like this, but more aggressive. He wouldn't hear of it when she tried to talk him into therapy. He started gaslighting her about how others saw her behavior, so she began to close herself off from anyone but him. Luckily, she had a very sticky friend group, and when one of us heard about how he flipped out when she tried to lock her phone so he couldn't see her emails and texts, we intervened."

"The friend group pulled her out?"

"Yes. And I don't think I'm exaggerating when I say it might have saved her life. Or at least her sanity. Notrumpets, I'm not saying this is the direction you and 'Bob' will go—he may not have that kind of personality at all; he might just be majorly insecure—but it's something to guard against. You have a right to your privacy. You have a right to make your own decisions. And you have a right to leave if you're unhappy."

"Not that I'm suggesting Notrumpets will need it," Krista interjected, "but it feels like a good time to remind people of the
National Domestic Violence Hotline." She glanced at the phone
number on a sticky note attached to the bottom of her right-hand
monitor. "If you're concerned about your safety or question
whether you should be, call them at 1-800-799-SAFE or text 'start'
to 88788. Notrumpets, please come back and let us know how
things are going, okay?" Krista took a quick sip of her tea, cradling
the mug for a minute in her cool fingers. "Mortie, Emily says you
have something for us?"

"I have an update from Chase547. We talked to him on Friday
about the woman he likes and is paying attention to."

"The one in the nonwork relationship. I remember. How are
things going there?"

"He's trying to follow your advice of letting her get to know
him, but she doesn't seem interested. He'd like to do some kind
of grand gesture to get her to really notice him on a personal
level. He's thinking some kind of gift and is looking for suggestions. Something out of the box. Not just flowers or flashy
jewelry."

"Chase, when I suggested getting to know her, that really meant
to back off, to give her space, to win her trust. This idea seems
kind of in your face. My advice is to not go for the over-the-top
gesture. Less is going to be more in this case."

> Chase547: 🙍 ive tried to just be friendly
> Chase547: she basically ignored me 😕

Krista, keeping one eye on the chat for an interactive response,
beat Hailey to reading it out loud, but paraphrased it for anyone
listening via the podcast without the advantage of seeing the chat.
"Chase says he tried and was ignored. This is never the response
we want, but sometimes it's the response we get and we have to
respect it."

Chase547: she doesnt know what shes missing
Chase547: she just needs to gimme a chance 😠

The first stirrings of unease shot through Krista. This guy didn't
know when to quit and could be the kind who was a threat to
women. She needed to talk him down, make him realize this
woman had a right to choose her own partner. "Chase says she
doesn't know what she's missing and she just needs to give him a
chance. I have to hard disagree with you here, Chase. You don't
know enough about this woman. Maybe she's in a steady relationship and is turning down every man, but the one she loves. Maybe
she recently had a bad breakup and has sworn off all men for the
time being. The bottom line is, you can't force her to like you."

Krista waited for a few seconds, watching the chat, knowing
the Twitch broadcast would need to catch up. Unsurprisingly,
Chase547 shot back.

Chase547: whos talking about force
Chase547: i want to give her a gift! 😠😠

Krista could feel Chase547's anger rising and her own caution
with it. "Chase says he wasn't forcing her; he just wants to give
her a gift." Time to swing this another way. "Mortie, have you ever
had someone surprise you with a gift you didn't want?"

Hailey's disgruntled expression answered her question before
she spoke. "Oh, yeah."

"How did that make you feel?"

"Uncomfortable. Put upon. Required to accept whether I
wanted to or not. Especially since the giver of the gift was *right
there*. It's not like it came in the mail. He handed it to me and
watched with those expectant eyes as I opened it."

"And as a woman, you were raised as the peacekeeper, the nur-
turer. Your gut instinct was to make sure the giver of the gift felt
good, even if you didn't."

For a moment, Hailey's jaw sagged as her eyebrows shot together. "How did you know?"

"Because I was raised the same way. It's a traditional way many women are raised. Men are leaders, women are nurturers." Krista raised a hand, palm out. "Hang on, chat, before you flip out. I said it's a *traditional* way many women were raised. I'm not saying it's the *right* way or the *only* way. That's way too black-and-white. Many women are leaders, many men are nurturers. But it's really hard to break out of that stereotype. And, Chase, you might not mean to do it, but that's how you'd be pressuring her. Any gift you'd give would come with the pressure to not only accept the gift, but to like it. She may not be willing to do either."

Chase547: you dont know her like I do
Chase547: i can make her happy 🤑🤑🤑

"Chase says I don't know her like he does, and he can make her happy. But do you really know that? You don't seem to know her current relationship status, so I don't think you know her that well. I think you're making assumptions that put the two of you together in a favorable light. You need to be careful here."

Chase547: i know what im doing

A quick glance at the chat told her the community was doing as it so often did—chiming in with opinions on what Krista and Hailey discussed. However, this time, Chase547's attitude was prompting both protective community members, as well as those who got a thrill from fanning the flames of dissent.

casseristen77: Don't be a dick 🍆🖕🙄
equationknown: carpe diem! DO IT!
gritrowdy: she has it coming 😎
XxsequincedgownxX: Ur a creep ☠️💀☠️
cranberriespagophila: Yo mama raised a 😈

The chat inputs streamed by faster and faster as people posted their thoughts. A quiet ding brought Krista's attention to a Discord message from Hailey. **Close this out. Move to another question.**

Krista put on a smile. "Hey, all, stand down. You know the rule around here—all questions and comments get considered fairly. If we only want questions that follow a certain moral code, we'll drive people away. Chase, I'm going to move on to the next question, but I want you to think about what we talked about tonight. You might not mean to pressure this woman, but could do it unconsciously with your gift. Let her get to know the *real you*. People love to talk about themselves, so that's a good conversation starter. Be genuinely interested in her life—her family, her work. Let her lead the conversation, then offer something of yourself afterward. Good luck with it." She turned back to the Discord chat to pick up the next question. "Wharfinger858 writes in about the D and D games they run, where they're having some group dynamic issues."

The rest of the stream was uneventful. The comments settled into their usual flow, and Hailey signed them off at the normal time.

Hailey leaned her elbows on her desk, her eyes angled down to where Krista's face was on her monitor. "Things got a little salty there."

Krista took a sip of her tea—cold now—and made a face. "I'll say. That guy's a problem."

"To the woman he's stalking?"

"You think that's what it is?"

Hailey shrugged. "I honestly don't know. He doesn't give off a good vibe."

"Agreed. Not just with respect to that woman, whoever she is. To us. I thought we might lose control of the chat for a minute."

"You know how some of them love to pile on."

"A little too much. But you were right—changing gears at that moment calmed things down and let the community concentrate on something else."

"And Chase547 buggered off. Or at least shut up."

"I hope he buggered off and that's the last we'll see of him. Clearly, he's not getting the answers he wants from us. If he wants someone to support his obsession, we're not the team for that."

Hailey's grimace reflected her disgust. "Hell no."

"You know, when you first sold me on this idea, the whole real-advice-from-real-people thing, I thought it would all be at arm's length. I'd do what I do at the clinic—give my pithy advice, then hear back later about how it all went. No one's ever given me push-back like that before. They usually think it's good advice."

"Different group here. For starters, in the clinic, you have an aura of professionalism. You're an expert in the kind of physical therapy they need, and that bleeds over into the relationship advice you also hand out, whether it's deserved or not. You don't have that here. Everyone knows you're not a trained therapist. You're a real person giving real life advice—"

"And referring them to professional therapy, if I think they need it," Krista interjected.

"Absolutely. But you have to know you're coming face-to-face with a bunch of biases from people who hide behind their screen names and feel free to be as racist and sexist as they really are be-hind the security of anonymity. They get to say the things here they'd never say if they were standing directly in front of you."

"You're right. Of course, you're right." Krista reached up and rubbed at the back of her neck, where the muscles felt more like stone. "Sometimes I need to be reminded."

"Is it just me, or are you also desperate to know who this wo-man is?"

Krista dropped her hand into her lap. "Find out who she is so we could warn her? Totally. That guy and his entitlement gives me the creeps."

"We women need to look out for each other." Hailey's shoulders rose and fell on a sigh. "We don't even know what country she's in, let alone what town. All we can do is hope she has a backbone and knows how to use it. Also, a knee to the balls helps out in a pinch. You okay?"

"Yeah. Just unsettled by his attitude, I guess. I also had a real pain-in-the-ass client earlier today, so maybe I've just had it with men at the moment."

"Time to run away and organize that all-women commune?"

Krista chuckled. "It might be. See you on Friday?"

"You bet. Till then." Hailey gave her a cheerful salute and signed off.

Krista pushed back from her desk and rose, deciding she deserved a nice glass of white wine and some Netflix to unwind from the day. Chase547 might have simply been trying to get a rise out of her, and maybe none of it was real. Or maybe he was speaking his truth, and she'd given him reason to think about what he was doing. Either way, she wouldn't give him another thought.

If only it was that easy.

Chapter 6

"Hey! Where'd you go?"

Standing in the kitchen, fishing the tea bag out of her mug, Krista could hear Hailey's call from her streaming studio. "Hang on!" she called. "Tea run!" She power walked back to her desk and sank down in her chair, sliding the mug onto its coaster in front of her water bottle.

"And what mad concoction are we drinking tonight?"

"A nice little blend of apple and almond. Like actual apples and actual almonds, with just a touch of cinnamon."

"That's not tea. That's trail mix."

Krista laughed, picked up her mug, and sipped. "I assure you, it's not."

"It's what happens when you steep trail mix. Anyway, you're weird." Hailey gave her camera a sunny grin. "And I've loved that weirdness from the first moment you walked into our dorm room. Come to think of it, even back then, you loved those weird teas."

"Now, why would I have needed a soothing blend like that back then? I mean, college wasn't stressful at all."

"You're not stressed about tonight's stream, are you?"

"Nope. I decided on Tuesday I wasn't going to let that moron put me on edge. He probably won't be back anyway."

"Probably not, but I messaged Emily and Rob. They'll be watching for him to appear and disrupt the stream."

"Maybe he'll be back to tell us she's married and he's moved on."

"That would be great. But if he comes back to cause trouble, we'll put him in time-out."

Krista paused with her mug partway to her lips. "'Time-out'? Like you'd do with a preschooler?"

"Just like that. It will keep him out of the stream for a certain time period. Maybe ten minutes, at first, to give him the message to behave if he wants to continue to interact as part of the community."

"How have I missed that we could put someone in time-out?"

"Because I'm the tech end of the team and I don't think we've ever had to do it on this channel. That's the advantage of starting small and working your way up. You don't get the trolls until you become better known."

"Is this your way of telling me we're popular?"

"In a roundabout way, yeah. Anyway, one of the three of us modding tonight will deal with Chase547 if he shows up and causes trouble."

"Good." Krista hadn't wanted to admit it to Hailey, but, despite her outwardly blasé attitude, dread had been slowly building in her all day that Chase547 might return in the stream to upset their flow. As the day went on, anger grew to swamp dread as her annoyance built that one person had the power to push aside her enjoyment in helping people. But nagging quietly behind both the dread and the anger was concern that some woman might be in danger and not be aware of her jeopardy. "I guess I'm concerned for the woman he's targeting. We've been there, you and me—maybe not in actual danger, but we've had guys we didn't want come on too strong. You know that feeling in the pit of your stomach you get when you know you have to tell a guy to back off, and you don't know how he's going to take it."

"Some take it like gentlemen. Others definitely don't."

"I'd include Chase 547 in the 'definitely don't' crowd."

"Me too."

"I just wonder if we should be continuing to try to talk him down."

Hailey looked off to one side, her mouth tight, her expression saying she was bracing for resistance. She turned back to the camera. "Do you remember when we began, and I told you the first rule of doing this was that we weren't responsible for any outcomes? From the beginning, we were clear we weren't trained therapists, but were a welcome ear for someone to bounce ideas off? That we weren't responsible for what people took from our advice."

Heat built in Krista's cheeks. "Yes."

"I know you, Zig. I knew at some point you'd start feeling responsible, so I wanted to make it crystal clear we aren't responsible for what happens outside the stream. We've been honest with the Apples from day one. This is exactly why."

"You're telling me we're not responsible for what happens to that woman."

"Exactly." Hailey's tone carried a thread of resignation. "In fact, if anything, we might be protecting her. Without us telling him to stand down, he'd have just gone ahead and done something already. We've made him think about his intentions and her reactions. But even if we hadn't, that's why we have the disclaimer on the channel. Just like the slogan says, we're real people giving real advice based on the limited information we're getting in a chat message, based on our own experiences. How many times have we been successful in helping people?"

"More often than not."

"Much more often than not. Don't let this one jerk get into your head so you stop helping those who want it."

"You're right."

Hailey's grin was smug. "I'm always right."

"Like when you decided to get clams from that tiny clam shack during our Massachusetts road trip and spent the night puking up your internal organs?"

"That's the one and only time I wasn't, I swear to God."

"Had a clam since then?"

"God no." Hailey shuddered, disgust carving deep grooves around her frown. "Never again. Projectile vomiting aside, you ready to start?"

"Yup."

"Excellent, because it's time. Here we go." Hailey's gaze dropped for a few seconds, and when she looked up, her eyes were as bright as her smile. "Welcome to *A Word from the Wise*—real advice from real people."

And they were off.

Krista felt a little hesitation at the beginning of the stream, as if she were bracing for attack as she dove into several questions from the previous stream and then into current questions.

Forty minutes in, the attack hadn't come and she'd settled into the normal rhythm of the show. "We have an update from Arvensisrusticolus. If you remember, Arven told us about her husband, who made a cross-country move with her when she took a major promotion at her job, but to be able to do it, he gave up his stable job to look for a new one in their new location. But he couldn't get moving on the job search and seems generally stuck. I advised that while they both lost the home they loved, friends, and possibly family from the old location, she had the security and the challenge of a brand-new job and he had nothing already set up. They sat down and talked it out. Arven herself has done a mental reset and is giving him space to grieve what he's lost, while her husband has agreed to give himself until no later than the six-month mark to get rooted in his new location. Well done, both of you!"

strikingmyfangs: licious! 👍🏆
hatingdawall: WTG! 📷
dumetellavee: good compromise!
loafenheid: Just make sure he sticks to his deadline.
Chase547: youd be a moron to trust this advice
Chase547: they dont know anything

Krista blinked and read the lines in the chat again, her smile melting away at both the appearance of Chase547 and his message. And then those that followed . . .

hanji4501: 👍 Fuck you
d1lobaj0le: wanker 😤 😾
misnomerpersist: U don't have to take her advice. It's good advice and ur an idiot, but U don't have to take it
Chase547: these bitches are probably too hard up to want anyone else to get some
emily_brontesaurus: Community rules, guys. Don't make the mods take action. We will.
Chase547: 👍 back atcha 🖕🖕🖕🖕
hopelesskitchen:
Chase547: they give shitty advice
Chase547: you fuckers think theyre right about everything
Chase547: theyre not
Chase547: your just too stupid to see it

It was happening. Everything Krista had worried might transpire was flying by in the chat before her eyes. She needed to cool the temperature. "Guys, let's cool it down. Everyone is entitled to their opinion."

"Even if it's wrong." Hailey's head was down, her eyes fixed on her Mod View window as she worked on moderating the chat, but her murmured comment was still fully audible.

Not helping to calm the waters. "Chase547, I'm sorry you feel that way. The advice we give isn't one size fits all." Chase547 wasn't only ragging on herself and Hailey—they could take it—but his abuse spewed over everyone in the community. The piling on was happening before her eyes as the chat streamed fast and faster.

"We believe it's the best advice, but if you don't like it, you don't have to listen to us." She kept her eyes on the chat as it moved faster and faster, but caught a flash of Chase547's retort before it disappeared in the flood of incensed comments.

> Chase547: she can take what i give and like it 😈

Panic sliced through Krista like the icy swipe of a blade. "Chase, think about what you're saying. Clarify it for me if I have this wrong, but it sounds like you're not giving her any choice in the matter. She deserves the freedom to make her own choices."

> Chase547: whores dont make choices
> Chase547: they take what we give them

On-screen, Hailey glanced up, then went head down again over her keyboard. Then a new entry appeared in the Mod Action panel in her Mod View window.

> ⏱Chase547   now
> **Timed out** by Dumortiere

Not able to post in the chat, but maybe still listening. "Chase547, I'm imploring you." She went back to using his full username so there could be no mistake who she was talking to. "Don't do anything rash. This woman has a life. She has family. She has the right to decide on the people she's intimate with. Forcing yourself on her is a crime. Don't do it. If you need to find someone to talk to, reach out to friends or to a therapist. Take some time, cool down, and think this through rationally. You have interests and skills. If this woman isn't the right one for you, you can find one who is. Give it some time." A quick look at the chat showed it had completely blown up, messages flying by, almost too fast to read.

They needed to stop this.

"Mortie, I think that's enough excitement for tonight."

"Agreed." On-screen, Hailey nodded vigorously. "Thanks for coming out to *A Word from the Wise,* folks. Have an amazing weekend, and we'll see you on Tuesday."

The channel's broadcast window closed, and before Krista could take more than one shaky breath, Hailey was speaking to her through the Discord video chat.

"You okay?"

"What the hell was that?" Krista sagged back in her chair. "Is he insane?"

"Pissed off, at the very least." Hailey picked up a small plastic action figure of a woman, with blue hair and elven ears, wielding a rapier. "What's his issue?"

"Male superiority complex? He seems to feel entitled to this woman he talks about."

"Nice attempt at the end there to calm him down."

Krista gave her a half smile. "Thanks. He entered the chat with his aggression dialed up to eleven. There was nowhere to go but down. Then once the community jumped all over him, we definitely lost the overall thread. Putting him in time-out dealt with him this time, but it did damage. I think we need to seriously look at banning him for good." When Hailey stayed silent, her eyes on the plastic figure she turned over and over in her fingers, Krista pushed a little harder. "You disagree?"

"I'm not sure that's going to be a good look for the channel. It's going to look like we can't take criticism, but simply knee-jerk jump to banning someone because he says we don't know anything. We, who state, up front, it's advice based on our experience, and not a four-year degree? One strike and you're out with no notice?"

"He caused chaos in the chat. We can't allow that kind of free-for-all again. If that happens, we won't have a channel." Krista recognized the wrinkle across Hailey's brow—she was digging in. She tried another tack. "Honestly, he makes me extremely uncomfortable. We've never talked about this, because we've never had a problem, but I think we need to put some more solid community guidelines into place. Draw everyone's attention to them at the beginning of the next stream. The key is to not let one bad apple spoil the whole bushel."

Hailey set down the figure with a snap. "We're not just dealing with him; we have to take the entire community into account. If we're looking at new guidelines, we have to stick to them, fine, but they have to be reasonable. We're in the process of building up this community. We want interaction, not to be booting people out. We're still just starting out here."

"And popularity beats safety? Or sanity?"

Anger flashed briefly in Hailey's eyes before she tamped it down. "I'm not saying that. I want us to do well, but not at the expense of anyone's safety. We're making up the rules as we go. If we're going to add new guidelines, we need to put them in place, have everyone agree to them, and then we can act on them."

Krista cut off a biting response. From the beginning, she'd harbored the concern Hailey had talked her into this channel for strictly the popularity aspect, rather than Krista's focus on helping people. But Hailey came from the gaming world, which was the majority of the content on this platform. She shouldn't fault Hailey for doing what every other creator on the platform did. "You know more about this than me. What do you suggest?"

"New, expanded rules starting next stream," Hailey said. That gives us a couple of days to work them out and agree to them. Then we'll state them at the beginning of the broadcast."

"What if the chat blows up from the first minutes of the broadcast?"

"We'll set the chat to emote-only mode."

Krista froze for a moment in surprise. "We can do that?"

"There are a number of options for controlling chat. Setting the chat to tiny, goofy images-only mode makes it difficult for harassment to happen. When we start the broadcast, we'll make it clear the chat will be emote-only as we explain the new rules. Then I can turn that feature off and we'll be back with the usual chat platform. Everyone will have to manually accept the new community rules and then they'll have access to the chat."

"And if Chase547 starts making trouble?"

"He'll have one chance. He makes one comment we find inflammatory, overtly antagonistic, or promotes violent behavior, he'll get one warning, then I'll ban his ass myself." Hailey loosed a small sigh, braced her elbows on her desk, and propped her chin on her linked hands. "We maybe should have thought this through a little more carefully. We have community rules already, but they're not robust enough to handle this kind of situation. Live and learn. We'll fix it, and we'll make sure it won't happen again. Then no one will say we're just overly sensitive and can't take a little criticism. This channel is supposed to be a community with give and take, not an autocracy. We can't randomly ban anyone who makes a snarky comment about our advice—unless it's construed as a threat."

"We need standards. I hear you." Krista was left feeling slightly unsettled, but at least it was something. "Let's do that. Do you want to draft something stronger than what we have and run it by me tomorrow or Sunday?"

"That works for me. Gotta run. Talk soon."

Then Hailey was gone.

Krista grabbed her mug and rose from her chair. They had a plan now, one that would protect them, as well as the other community members.

She tried to ignore the tightness across the back of her shoulders that said it wouldn't be enough.

Chapter 7

KRISTA SPENT THE WEEKEND FRETTING.

Normally, she loved the quiet of her weekends. She worked long hours at the clinic, taking her turn to man the late shift until seven-thirty on Wednesday and Thursday evenings, to work around her Tuesday/Friday streaming schedule. Saturdays and Sundays were hers to rest, read, shop, or binge a TV show. She was surrounded by people all week—in person at the clinic, with patients and staff, or online with the *AWFTW* community—so this was her chance to recharge and get ready to hit the ground running at nine o'clock, Monday morning.

This weekend was different because she simply couldn't settle. She woke early on Saturday, but the tone for the weekend was set when she fumbled her first cup of coffee, shattering one of her favorite mugs on the ceramic tile in her kitchen. Once that was cleaned up and she had a fresh cup of coffee, she settled on her couch with breakfast and a book. But she couldn't concentrate on her novel and kept having to go back and re-read the beginning of the chapter, until she finally slammed the book shut in exasperation. She flipped through show after show, but wasn't interested by anything on any of her streaming services. She went out to do her groceries but found herself impatient with jammed traffic and packed stores. She came home and took her lunch out onto the balcony to sit with her book in one of the comfy chairs on what felt like it might be one of autumn's last temperate days. However, her mind kept drifting, and in the end, she spent most of her lunch picking sunflower seeds out of her multigrain bread and tossing them to the sparrow darting about at the far end of the balcony.

On Sunday, she took hours to clean the apartment, which was already clean and organized and could have been spot-cleaned in about a half hour. Still, Krista spent the whole day feeling twitchy, her mind constantly wandering. She thought about giving Zach a call, seeing if he wanted to grab a coffee, then remembered he was out of town with the guys at an NFL game. Blah blah, fantasy football league, blah blah . . . She tended to tune out his football talk.

Her mind wandered back to some innocent woman who might be under threat.

She woke Monday morning before the alarm even sounded. She hadn't bothered to change it, but today she was working the late shift as a favor to Kyle, who needed to help his sister move, in exchange for her Thursday shift. Normally, she'd be up, showered, breakfasted, and ready to leave for the clinic by eight-thirty, but now she was hours early for her eleven o'clock shift.

Her unending weekend continued to roll on at the pace of a tortoise into the workweek.

She flopped down on the couch, but didn't reach for the remote. Instead, she simply cupped her mug of coffee between her hands, warming her chilled fingers as her mind whirled.

Someone's in danger. You can help.

How? We don't know who she is. Or where.

You don't, but who knows what the cops can do?

You'll waste their time.

She took another sip from her mug as her mind circled the critical point.

How will you feel if something happens to her?

Remember what Hailey said. You're not responsible.

Sure. But how will you feel?

She sat bolt upright, the coffee in her mug sloshing dangerously close to the rim as everything coalesced around the answer—she'd be devastated if something happened and she hadn't done everything in her power to stay Chase 547's hand.

Worst-case scenario—she tried and nothing came from it. But at least she'd be able to live with herself.

She picked up her cell phone from the coffee table, opened the phone app, and froze. How to contact them? Calling 911 seemed to be overkill. Anything else seemed like underkill.

Call 311. It's the middle ground. Let law enforcement shoot it up the chain.

She placed the call, sitting forward on the couch, her elbows braced on her knees.

"Thank you for calling Chicago 311." The voice was flat and electronic and dragged her into automated phone system hell, where none of the options suited her issue. She didn't need vehicle services, city alerts, or a service request. She finally opted for a police search, because that, at least, sounded like law enforcement, and then the cycle continued. Finally she reached a human being.

"Chicago 311, can I help you?" The voice was young, male, and harried.

Krista was willing to bet most people getting through were already aggravated before they even got to him. She took a breath, trying not to be that kind of caller. "Hi. I'm not sure if I'm in the right place. I need to report someone being threatened."

"Is the individual in immediate danger?" The voice suddenly sounded alert. This clearly wasn't a call about a pothole.

"I don't know. That's why I didn't call 911."

"What is the name of the individual?"

"I don't know."

He paused for a long moment before speaking. "But you think they're being threatened?"

"She, and yes. I know this is crazy, but I run an advice show on the internet, and someone had been threatened on that show."

"A Chicago resident?"

"I don't know."

Another long pause. "Let's do this. I think you need to talk to an officer. Let me take down your contact information and I'll have someone call you."

"That would be great, thank you." She provided her name, phone number, and that she was only available for the next ninety minutes.

"Please stay available. I'll try to have someone call you during that time. Thank you for calling Chicago 311." Then he was gone.

Krista tossed her phone onto the couch cushion beside her and dropped her head in her hands. "That went well." She collapsed back into the cushions with a groan, her cheeks warm with embarrassment beneath her palms. "Of course, they don't know what to do with you. You have absolutely no information for them."

No point in sitting around just waiting for someone to return her call. She picked up her mug, walked to the kitchen, and dumped the remaining coffee in the sink as the cup-and-a-half she'd already drunk slowly hollowed out her stomach. She walked to the door of her streaming studio. One look inside had her spinning away to the living room. She plucked her tablet off one of the floating shelves and settled in the armchair, propped her feet up on the coffee table with the tablet on her lap, and booted up. She checked her personal mail, ignoring the notifications from Twitch, then opened her work mail and got lost in it. This was what she needed—something to keep her mind occupied when it had been marching to its own beat, one she seemed to have no control over, all weekend.

She jumped when the phone rang, just barely catching the tablet before it slid off her lap and crashed to the hardwood floor. Checking her phone, she saw **Chicago PD** displayed as the incoming caller. Taking a deep breath to calm her suddenly galloping heart— part shock, part dread at the response she anticipated—she accepted the call.

"Hello?"

"This is Officer Doug Green with the Chicago Police Department. Is this Krista Evans?"

"Yes."

"You called 311 this morning to make a report?"

"Yes."

"I don't have a lot of details on the matter, but it was referred to me as a criminal offense. I'd appreciate it if you could start from scratch with me."

"Sure. I just want to say that I didn't know what to do with this information. I'm cognizant of wasting CPD's time, but at the same time, I don't feel I should keep this to myself."

"It's always better to make a report than not. Worst-case scenario, it takes a little of my time. Best-case scenario, we can do something about your concern. And your concern is a woman has been threatened, is that correct?"

"Yes."

"But you don't know her name or location."

Krista let out a frustrated laugh. "That pretty much sums it up. Let me spell it all out for you." She took Green through their experience with Chase547, right up to Friday night's broadcast. When she wound down, Green stayed silent as the muscles running up the back of Krista's neck wound more and more tightly. She badly wanted to prompt him, for him to tell her she'd done the right thing—or she was completely nuts—because the silence was killing her.

"I can see why you wouldn't know what to do with this information. There's a lot you don't know about this situation—the identities of either people involved or their location, for example. But I don't think you're reading too much into Chase547's threats."

Krista hadn't even realized she'd been holding her breath until he spoke and she relaxed her lungs. "Thank you. That makes me feel better. I've been going back and forth on whether to call law enforcement or not."

"I always encourage people to call. Better that we have a chance to look at a situation than for you to assume you know what's best. But from what you've told me here, we don't have enough to go on. We assume he's referring to one specific person, but we can't say for sure. And his threat . . ." He paused and she assumed he was reviewing his notes. "'She'll take what I give and like it.' I agree it could be a threat of violence. It could also be argued he's talking about the gift he's been trying to give her since your very first conversation."

"But—"

"I know." Green cut her off. "When taken in context, that's not the way I take it, either. But you have to look at it from a legal perspective. Even if we knew the principals involved, this would be conjecture because the threat itself is implied and could mean something else. And there's one other thing you need to think about."

"What's that?"

"The internet gives people an anonymity to ignore their filters."

"You mean the ones in our head telling us not to say something."

"Exactly. Sometimes it's easier to be cruel when someone isn't standing in front of you. You might say something online you'd never say to someone's face. Additionally, in this scenario, you have someone hiding behind a screen name. You can't see them, you can't hear their tone, and you certainly have no idea who they really are. That kind of anonymity gives people permission to follow their worst impulses. To be the worst sides of themselves."

"You hear stories, but this is the first time it's happened to me on this channel. I'm kind of new at this. Hailey is the one with the creator experience."

"I appreciate you reaching out, but the bottom line here is there isn't enough to petition a judge to get a warrant to go to Twitch and try to dig into Chase547's identity. I couldn't even say he's in our jurisdiction—forget that any violence has happened or is imminent. There's just not enough here."

Krista stared down blindly, frustration crawling up her spine. "I suspected that might be how this went."

"For now, yes. There's also a chance this is some jackass just trying to get under your skin. Remember, you're on camera and he
can see your every reaction. He may be a sicko who gets his jollies
freaking out other people, while he stays safe and anonymous behind his screen name."

"We haven't banned him yet. He has one more chance before we
do that. If he comes back and starts trouble again, what do I do?"

"You're already recording your sessions, so that's good. I'm going
to give you two things—a reference number for this report and my
phone number here at CPD. If it happens again, call me and we'll
see if it's enough to move forward. Let me give you my direct contact information."

Krista put the phone on speaker and quickly opened a new contact card. "Go ahead." Krista added his phone number, email
address, and the report number before saving the information. "I
appreciate your time, Officer Green. I also appreciate you didn't
make me feel like calling the CPD was a mistake."

"We'd rather have too many reports than not enough. Thank
you for your time, Ms. Evans."

Krista ended the call and sat staring at the information in the
contact card. She'd done all she could do at this point. Now they'd
all have to see if Chase547 returned. Annoyance flickered that
someone could suck her joy out of her role in *A Word from the Wise*,
but there was no doubt about the apprehension that skittered across
her nerve endings.

Tomorrow could force their hands.

She wasn't looking forward to the confrontation her gut knew
was coming.

Chapter 8

"Mr. Tobin?" Krista leaned around the corner of the records room and into the waiting room. "I'm ready for you now."

A man looked up from the magazine he was reading. In his early thirties and with a wiry build, he was dressed in gray track pants, with a navy crew-neck athletic shirt under a matching zippered fleece hoodie. His strawberry-blond hair—what he still had—was cut extremely short, a concession made to his early progressive baldness. He grinned up at her. "Just when I was finding out about what Harry and Meghan are up to now."

She matched his smile. "Pretty sure they'll still be up to it when we're done."

He laughed and stood, holding his left arm protectively close to his body. "No doubt. And it's Jason, remember?"

"Of course, Jason. Come on back."

She waved at Melanie as they left the waiting area, and she led Jason down the short corridor and through the gym area and into Exam One.

"When do we get to work on the fun exercises using all this equipment?" Jason asked.

"When you're ready and not a second sooner. How have your at-home exercises been going?"

"Good. Shoulder's not as tight as it was last week. And I think my range of motion is expanding. I just don't want to push it and take a giant step backward. I'm really careful about this injury. Wore the sling for the full six weeks after surgery, even though my surgeon said I could take it off at four weeks if I was comfortable. I'm doing the exercises three times a day, and I'm being careful not to overstress it. Using hot and cold compresses, as you suggested. So far, I'm hopeful."

"Do they have you back at work yet?"

"Still on leave for now. I got a lump sum from workers' compensation that will keep me going for a while yet. My employer wants me back and is holding my position, but I'm delaying him for now. I want to make sure I'm not going to reinjure it by rushing back and getting in over my head."

"Let's see how the range of motion is coming."

Jason slid his jacket off, revealing a long-sleeved athletic shirt, and laid it neatly over the end of the treatment bed. "It's so quiet in here. What's with the silence? It's unnerving."

Krista laughed. "I was working with my last client out in the gym. I'm always happy for tunes."

"Me too. Takes my mind off the discomfort." He held up a hand before Krista could speak. "No pain—you know I'll tell you if there's actual pain. But as you've said before, sometimes there's some discomfort when we're challenging the muscles and the joint. So music is good."

Krista pulled out her phone and brought up Spotify. "Any requests?"

Jason grinned. "You know the eighties guilty pleasure you turned me on to."

"My work here is done." Krista's smile was sly. "Culture Club it is. Get up on the table while I get this going. On your back. We'll start with forward elevation." Within seconds, Boy George was singing "Karma Chameleon" as Krista danced back to the table.

"Let's see how you're doing for passive range of motion. You're doing this with your wife?"

"Yes. Jacquie's been a champ through this."

"I'm sure she wants you fully recovered as soon as possible. You're going to ninety degrees with her?"

"Yes."

"Comfortably?"

"Yes."

"Then we're going to push it a little farther. Remember, I'm doing all the work. This is passive range of motion. Keep your muscles relaxed."

"Yes, ma'am."

Krista gave him a look. "Don't call me *ma'am*. It makes me feel old."

"Makes you feel old? Look at me. I'm only thirty-two and my shoulder imploded. It's like I hit thirty and my body fell apart."

"You're not falling apart. But you've worked a repetitive-motion carpentry job framing houses for the last decade, and you're not made of steel." Krista grasped his left wrist and cupped her other hand behind his elbow for support. She slowly raised the arm off the table to ninety degrees. "How's that feel?"

"Good. Jacquie is really good with me with this. But we stop here."

"As you should. Now, stay relaxed. We're going to carefully go farther. You tell me when it starts to hurt." She gently guided the arm back a little more, then paused. "You're tightening up. Stay loose."

"I guess I'm anticipating it's going to hurt."

"You're going to tell me the instant there's any pain, which means we've gone too far." She eased his arm a little farther back. "How's this?"

"Okay. No pain."

Another ten degrees. "Now?"

"That's pulling a bit."

"Then we stop here. For a count of ten." She slowly counted off the seconds, then lowered the arm, let him rest for a count of ten, and repeated the motion a total of fifteen times, quietly singing along to the music, purposely keeping his attention fixed on the upbeat melody rather than their activity. "Your mobility is really coming along. You could only just go past ninety last week. Sit up and let's look at your external rotation."

Jason sat up and swung his legs to the side of the table, his left arm bent with his fist, thumb up, resting on his thigh. Krista cupped his elbow again and supported his wrist as she rotated the arm outward. "That's good. You've been stopping at thirty degrees at home?"

"Yes. I thought we could do better than that, but Jacquie is super strict and your word is the law."

"I like this Jacquie of yours."

"Me too. Okay, that's starting to hurt." He relaxed as Krista eased inward a bit. "Better."

"That's about fifty degrees, which is great." Fourteen more repetitions of the external rotation followed.

"Am I healing too slow?" Jason's voice was low, as if embarrassed to ask the question.

"Not at all. Everyone heals at the speed that's right for them. Now, you're not going to heal like you're eighteen, but you're going to likely heal faster than your average sixty-year-old. Our goal is to get you fully functional and back to work when you're ready. If we send you back too soon and you try to . . . What did you say you were doing when you injured your shoulder?"

"Framing a new building in a housing construction site. We'd put the wall together flat, and four of us were lifting it to stand in place, when all of a sudden my shoulder gave and I was in agony."

"That kind of over-the-head lift is what got you where you are today, and could put you back here. We're going to make sure you're ready before you return, and then you're going to protect against it happening again. You work the kind of job where repetitive-strain injuries like this occur. You'll want to be careful going forward, or think about how to be a part of the company without being so hands-on. A man of your experience could maybe find his way as a supervisor of some sort."

"I've been offered the foreman job a few times, but turned it down because I didn't want to deal with all the pressure, paperwork, and frankly, the BS." He glanced darkly at his left shoulder. "Maybe it's time to think about that again. I don't want to repeat this kind of injury."

"Still being a part of the crew without the same physical toll? It might be an idea to think about."

"Yeah." Jason grinned up at her. "I might not have thought about it that way. Good suggestion."

"Thanks. Always happy to offer advice." She studied his shoulder. "Are your incisions healed nicely at this point? You had four?"

"Yes. Extremely small, all things considered, but four. All well healed, though I think the scars will stick with me. It looks good externally, but do you think I should have the shoulder imaged again to see why it seems like I'm recovering slowly?"

"No, because you're not. Remember at the beginning when I told you everyone recovers at their own pace? I meant it. And imaging won't tell us the whole story at this point. What looks like severe damage on an image can lead to mild symptoms and vice versa. We'll work with you at your own speed. Now stand up and let me see your shoulder shrugs and shoulder blade pinches, just like in the at-home exercises. If I like what I see, we're going to move into active-assisted motion." She studied his form as he cupped his left wrist in his right palm and did a full shoulder shrug, holding them high for five seconds before lowering. "That's good. Now repeat that ten times. I'm going to run out and get the TENS machine to give you a short treatment before you go, because if we're going to push things a bit, you may be a little sore. Some transcutaneous electrical nerve stimulation could really help minimize that. Be right back."

She jogged out of Exam One in search of the small handheld TENS device. She found it in Exam Four and jogged back with it in time to catch his last shoulder shrug. "Looking good. Now let me see your shoulder pinches."

Jason brought his shoulder blades together and held for five seconds as she circled him, studying his form. "Looks okay?"

She set the TENS unit down on the counter beside her keys. "Looks great. Do another ten reps."

"Can do." He did the motion again. "Any big plans for the week?"

Besides hopefully not hosting a Twitch stream that devolves again into chaos? Not something she wanted to discuss. "Nothing much. Hoping for an easy, stress-free week."

"You deserve it."

She certainly hoped so. Tomorrow night's stream would set the tone. She could only pray it went better than the last one.

Chapter 9

"WE'RE ALL ON THE SAME page?" Hailey asked. "Everyone understands the changes?"

Krista studied the three faces in the Discord video chat. Hailey was in the top left window, wearing a hunter-green top that made her blue hair extra vibrant by comparison. Her face was set in serious but confident lines. She was in her element—in control of the platform she loved, talking tech issues with the moderators.

Krista herself was basically there as support. She didn't tinker in the technical aspects of their channel; not only was it not her forte, it was clearly Hailey's. They were in good hands.

"Got it." Emily was in the window beside Hailey. Petite and blond, her hair pulled into a high ponytail, she wore a white crewneck sweater with a flurry of bright geometric shapes. Behind her, a wide shelf was crammed full of books, knickknacks, framed photos, and tiny models of spaceships. Emily had her own channel and streamed occasionally with friends, but her real skill was as a moderator and chat organizer. She was fast, fair, and their viewers considered her one of them, as she'd been in the chat since almost their first stream.

"Me too." Rob almost appeared otherworldly. He was in a dark room, wearing all black, and the effect was one of a floating pale face, lit by the illumination of his monitors. Rob wasn't a content creator himself, but was a solid moderator and faithfully showed up to all of their broadcasts. "We'll be on the lookout and will send out warnings. One warning. Second offense and they're gone."

"That's it," Hailey said. "Zig, anything else to add?"

Krista shook her head. "You've laid it all out really well. I hate that we got to this point, but I guess it was bound to happen sooner or later."

"A lot of channels have issues with trolls. We were maybe overly optimistic about a channel where people open up about personal issues, that we wouldn't have some idiot picking on them. We're ready to begin. When I fire up the broadcast, we'll be in emote-only mode in the chat, and I won't flip it back to regular mode until the new chat rules have been discussed. Rob, Emily, we'll let you go so it's just Krista and me. Thanks for your help on this."

"You're welcome." With a wave, Emily disappeared.

"We got this," said Rob. "We'll keep things tamped down." He left the chat, leaving only Hailey and Krista on-screen.

"You feeling okay about this?" Hailey asked.

"It's this or nothing," Krista replied. "We can't go on like that last stream."

"Firing it up now."

The broadcast started, with Hailey, as usual, taking the lead. "Welcome to *A Word from the Wise*—real advice from real people. I'm Mortie"—Hailey motioned with her right hand to where Krista would appear in the window beside her in the broadcast— "and this is Ziggy. Before we begin, we want to review some new ground rules for participation, so while we're doing that, you'll notice the chat is set to emotes only. We'll be back to our normal chat functions shortly, but we've put some new chat rules in place, and we wanted a chance to review them with you."

As Hailey talked, Krista watched the viewer count for the stream as it climbed from several hundred to over a thousand, and then rolled over two thousand and kept going. A quick check of their follower count gave her a jolt as she marked the difference

from the last time she'd paid attention, only a few streams ago—
it had jumped from 34,500 to 39,200. In the eight months since
the channel had debuted, their follower count had been a slow
but steady growth; it was a point of pride for both of them. Word
was spreading, and their community was growing. This kind of
bump, though, meant word of another kind was spreading—not
of sensible and helpful advice, but of an exciting, no-holds-
barred chat.

That would end today.

Krista forced her attention back to Hailey, who was finishing
with the new guidelines. "Each of you will have to agree to the
new guidelines before entering the chat. And once you do, there
will be a single warning of an infraction only, and then you'll be
banned following a second. Ziggy, anything to add?"

"Yes, thanks." Krista held her gaze steady on the camera. "This
is a place where people come for advice. You only do that when
something in your life isn't working. No one comes here because
their girlfriend accepted their proposal of marriage or they're em-
ployee of the month at work. They come because their girlfriend
doesn't want to settle down or they're clashing with a coworker.
People come to reveal the hidden parts of themselves, even if it's
behind a screen name. We'll respect those brave enough to come
forward, and we'll respect each other in the chat." She paused for
a moment, glanced at the chat—which was full of happy emotes
and symbols of love and support—then decided to go all in.

"I love this community. I love how you all support each other,
no matter what the issue. And last Friday's stream really upset me,
that this great community could be poisoned by a few bad apples
so quickly. Many thanks to all who stood up for us. And I'm sure
you all understand we needed to take these steps to keep the community strong. Now, enough of this serious stuff." She turned to
her left, to Hailey, and grinned. "Let's get this stream started!"

"You got it!" Hailey's gaze dropped to her keyboard as she
opened the chat, and suddenly there was a stream of supportive

comments—words of approval from regular viewers, introduction and engagement from new viewers. "Ziggy?"

Krista had handpicked the first question herself from the previous chat, looking to set the mood for the stream, but they'd loaded it into the Discord chat to look like any other typical question that would have been new to her. She'd purposely selected a question with a technical angle that could interest the tech geeks in the stream, as well as one she could draw Hailey into, based on her experience, as they presented a united front.

"Ethelinda1998 writes in about how to handle a work problem. She's been unhappy in her current job as a programmer and started to look for other opportunities. She interviewed and was offered a new position for more money, but it would require a move, and she's not sure what to do. Mortie, this isn't exactly your wheelhouse, but I'd love to hear your angle on this as someone inside the tech community."

Even before the channel launched, Hailey was known to the Twitch community as a Web developer, though who she worked for and where they were located was a secret. "Oh, yeah, I know the tech community," Hailey said, and they dove into a conversation about salary, benefits, pensions, the devil-you-know, and the risks and benefits of pulling up stakes.

As Hailey talked, Krista picked up her mug and sipped her tea, some of her jagged edges smoothing out. Tonight's stream felt totally normal, and picking an issue with a positive spin started the broadcast off on solid footing. The chat was rolling with lots of useful comments, many from personal experience, adding to the conversation. Ethelinda1998 was active in the chat as well, answering questions and thanking viewers for their help.

"Andrastianmonk has a good point," Krista said. "Don't get so blinded by the salary you don't consider things like the company culture. Some tech companies have a history of being toxic to female employees. Making twice what you're making now might not be worth it if you dread going to work every day."

"And if you don't know the culture," Hailey added, "it would be worth checking out sites like Glassdoor.com to see how the company is reviewed. Have you done that already?"

Krista's gaze dropped down to the chat, waiting for Ethelinda1998 to answer in real time after a few seconds' delay.

> evil4hire: If the job is mostly remote that could minimize a bad culture fit if teh job is really what you want
> Ethelinda1998: I haven't checked out Glassdoor. Thanks! Will do that. 👍
> Chase547: i killed her 💀 shes dead

Krista's heart stuttered, and she blinked twice and then had to search for the message, up the chat, as more messages flew by. Surely, that's not what she'd just read.

But it was.

He'd killed her?

Others were reacting faster than Krista could as the comments shot by nearly too fast to read.

> notrumpetshere: not funny dude
> rhythmburst: WTF 😧 😧 😧
> Chase547: she didnt deserve to live 😼

In her window beside the chat stream, Hailey was head down over her keyboard, and then the Mod Action panel in the Mod View window shifted with a new action.

> ⊘**Chase547**   now
>   **Banned** by Dumortiere

But the damage was already done. As Krista's gaze slid to the stream, the chat was a flurry of comments—some disbelieving, some angry, some despairing. Emily and Rob were working hard, giving out warnings as the mood spiraled into outrage, fury, and condemnation.

Her breath caught in her lungs, Krista knew she looked stunned and horrified, but she couldn't form any words. From the activity in the Mod View window, the mods were being forced into the nuclear option by a number of viewers who had ignored their warnings.

⊘**vesworried**   now
    Banned by RobBot_Tinker
⊘**geotekker**   now
    Banned by RobBot_Tinker
⊘**ceintetrabb**   now
    Banned by emily_brontesaurus

Krista looked back at Hailey. It was as if they locked gazes, even though they were half a city apart. Krista nodded, and Hailey's jaw firmed.

"We're closing the stream down for tonight, guys. See you at our usual time later this week." Hailey terminated the broadcast, then slumped back in her chair, staring at her lap. "Holy shit." Her gaze rose. "Do you think that was real?"

Krista tried to draw breath, tried to form her lips around words, but remained frozen.

"Krista? Talk to me."

Krista dragged in a ragged breath, then expelled it on a whisper. "We killed her."

"We did not." Hailey's words were full of vehemence.

Krista could barely hear Hailey over the roaring in her ears.

i killed her
shes dead
she didnt deserve to live

Someone was dead because she told some maniac to back off.
Someone paid because of her advice.

The monitors in front of her faded behind a patchwork of
green and black dots.

"Oh, God." Krista rolled her chair back until the casters hit the
baseboard, and then she bent forward to put her head between her
knees while her breath sawed.

"Krista? *Krista!* Are you all right? Did you pass out? Answer me!"

Hailey's words penetrated, and Krista realized she'd dropped
from view and Hailey might assume she was lying flat out on the
floor. She gripped the corner of the desk with one hand and pushed
herself upright. "I'm here."

"Where did you go?"

"I was feeling faint, so I put my head between my knees. Give
me a second to get it together." Silence lay heavy for a long stretch
of seconds before Krista pushed off her thighs to sit straight. "Shit,
Hail. Did we do this?"

"You know how I feel about the whole responsibility thing."

Krista knew very well, but something in Hailey's expression telegraphed that the shock of the evening was making her unwillingly
second-guess herself.

"What do we do now?" Hailey asked.

"I need to call CPD."

"*You* need to call CPD?"

"I didn't tell you, but after the last stream, I called their nonemer-
gency line because I didn't know what to do with Chase547's
threats. They didn't know, either, so they referred me to an Officer
Green. He was a good sport and took down the full report, but was
honest there wasn't a case there. We don't know who Chase547 is;
we don't know the woman; we don't know that he's not just trying
to yank our chains—"

"If he is, he's doing a good job," Hailey mumbled.

"And we don't even know if they're in this area. They could be
in Istanbul, for all we know."

"You're going to contact him again?"

"He gave me his phone number and the report number. Told me to call him if we learned anything else. Apparently, we have."

"You're going to call him now?" Hailey pressed.

"Yes."

"Ask him to come to your place."

"Why?"

"I'm coming over. That way, he can talk to both of us."

"You sure?"

"Yeah. I'm tired of just sitting here and taking this. Time to be proactive."

A zing of adrenaline pumped through Krista as the surety in Hailey's tone kicked free some of Krista's guilt and despair. She sat a little straighter, her head clearer. "Yeah, let's do that."

"Call him. I'm on my way." Hailey ended the call.

Krista picked up her phone, opened her contacts, found Green's number, and placed the call.

A man picked up on the third ring. "Officer Green speaking."

"Officer Green, it's Krista Evans calling. We talked yesterday about the person on my Twitch channel who was threatening a woman. I'm sorry to call you outside of business hours."

"That's okay. The CPD is always open."

"You asked us to call you if something new developed. It has. He came back tonight to announce he'd killed her."

Krista took Green into the details of the night's broadcast.

Chapter 10

W‍HEN THE KNOCK CAME AT her door, Krista rose from the couch where she sat with Hailey, who had arrived ten minutes earlier with her laptop. "That took longer than I thought it would." She crossed her living room to the front door. A quick look through the peephole showed her a dark-haired man wearing a charcoal trench coat.

She opened the door. "Officer Green?"

A man she judged was in his early forties stood a good six inches taller than Krista. His medium-brown hair was neatly cut, and he had hazel eyes, fair skin, and a strong jaw. A navy suit with a white shirt and patterned blue-and-gold tie lay beneath the open trench coat. He opened a flip case and held it out to her—one side held his star-shaped gold badge and the other his department photo identification.

"Detective Simon Miller, Chicago Police Department, Homicide. Officer Green referred your case to me."

Homicide. A shiver ran down Krista's spine. *Of course. You reported a potential murder.*

She stepped back and held the door open. "Please come in. My Twitch cohost is here as well."

"Saves me running around. Thanks." He focused on her face momentarily before his gaze shifted away to scan the apartment behind her, but then it snapped back to her.

This happened often when she first met people. *Noticed the eyes.* "Can I take your coat?"

"Thanks." Miller slipped off his coat.

Krista caught a glimpse of his service weapon in a shoulder holster under his suit jacket and was struck with another wave of unease. How had her life devolved into police reports and armed detectives?

She accepted his coat, hung it in the front closet, then led him into the living room.

Hailey rose from the couch. "Hi."

"Hi." Miller showed Hailey his ID, sat down in the armchair, and pulled out a notebook and pen as Krista settled beside Hailey. "Officer Green talked to me and sent me a copy of the report. I've reviewed it, but I'd like to hear what happened from both of you, in your own words."

"Would you rather see it?" Hailey asked.

"You have copies of the streams?"

"Full copies of all, including the chat, are uploaded as video on demand on Twitch." She tapped the closed lid of the sleek black laptop on the coffee table. "I know the times for each of our interactions with Chase547, so you'll see for yourself what happened, with no bias from us."

"Thanks. I'd like to see that, and I can ask questions as we go, if needed."

Hailey pulled her laptop toward her on the coffee table, opened the lid, brought up Twitch, and navigated to their channel. She angled the laptop so everyone could see it. "That good?"

"Yes."

"Hang on a second." Krista lay a hand on Hailey's arm as she reached for the trackpad to start the first on-demand video. "Officer Green said there were no leads to follow. No specific threat, no identities for either party, no location. What changed? I know Chase547 said he killed her, but we still don't know who she is. Who he is. Or where they are."

Miller laid his pen and notebook down on his knee. "That may be true, but if she's dead under suspicious circumstances, it will come to someone's attention. We have no idea if his statement is real, or, if it is, where it took place. But police forces don't work in a bubble. The file we build here could be useful to someone else, even if it's not useful to us. It's worth an hour of my time. I'd like to hope if this was one of my cases, someone else would do the same for me."

"Cosmic karma," Hailey said.

Miller's lips twitched. "Not a typical cop outlook, but I guess that's one way of putting it. Let's review it, and we'll go from there."

"Here's the first time he showed up." Hailey opened her phone, flipped to her notes, found the exact time code, and advanced the video to just before. "We host an advice stream. People ask us questions in chat, and we answer them. Well, really, Krista answers them, though I sometimes pitch in. I'm mostly the tech half of the partnership and Krista is the human relations half. In this case, the question came in as usual through the chat, which is this box here on the right-hand side of the screen."

"Our show also gets released later as an audio podcast, so I always read the question out loud for those who aren't seeing the video," Krista clarified. "Also, sometimes the questions fly by so quickly in chat, not everyone has time to read it."

They ran Miller through the stream segments as Chase547's rhetoric built, until they got to that evening's stream.

Embarrassment wormed through Krista's gut as she watched her owned stunned reaction after Chase547's announcement. She should have been calmer, been more decisive, but it had been up to Hailey to do everything while she sat there frozen.

The video ended, and Miller was silent for a moment, staring at the screen, idly tapping the end of his pen against his notebook above his page of notes.

As the silence stretched longer, Krista's gaze stayed fixed on the screen, not wanting to see what she assumed would be the condemning expression on Miller's face. She skimmed past the follower count on their channel, then snapped back to it, stared.

"What's wrong?" Hailey asked.

"Our follower count."

It took a few seconds for Hailey to find it. "Holy—"

"What's happening with it?" Miller asked.

"It's gone up," said Krista. "Way up. I don't usually note what the count is, day in and day out, but I happened to note it earlier this evening. It was just over thirty-nine thousand. Now it's almost forty-seven thousand, barely three hours later." She turned to Hailey. "How would it go up this fast?"

"When something happens in a stream, word spreads on other sites. Reddit, Discord—hell, even Facebook. And when there's any sort of incident, people show up to watch. Someone admitted to committing murder on our channel. It's going to attract attention."

Krista rubbed the heel of her hand over the headache pounding behind her forehead. "This isn't the kind of publicity we want."

Miller's sharp gaze fixed on her. "What does this kind of publicity get you? Is this a paying gig?"

"Yes."

"And this kind of attention means you'll make more money."

"I would assume." Krista looked up when Hailey's hand landed on her forearm, but Hailey's attention was fixed on Miller.

"This isn't something we did." Hailey's words had an edge of bite to them. "This happened on our stream, but we didn't do it."

Krista stared at Hailey in shock, reading both suspicion and temper in her tight expression. She swiveled to face Miller. "Wait. You think *we* did this? Why?"

"You just said the attention would bring in more money. More eyes, more followers. Do the people who watch the stream pay you directly?"

"Everything goes through Twitch," Hailey clarified, "but yes, people can subscribe to our channel, or make donations through bits—the Twitch equivalent of virtual currency." When Krista stared at her in horror, Hailey snapped, "It's not a secret, Zig. He can do a little research and find all this info. It's how the platform works."

Krista surged to her feet, slipping past Hailey to stride to the balcony's sliding door. She hadn't drawn the curtains yet to the darkness of evening beyond. Ground-level spotlights illuminated the trees outside her balcony, and through the incandescent branches, lights twinkled from the flats opposite. She took a deep breath, searching for calm, before she spun to face them. "I went to the CPD in good faith. I didn't know what to do with the information we had, but it didn't feel right to ignore it. If someone was in danger, the responsible thing was to let the authorities know. I'm in health care. I take care of people, so I couldn't turn my back on this. But because of that, our actions are suspicious?"

"I have to look at this from every angle."

"And your angle is this was never a real threat, but was our attempt to attract attention to make a fast buck?" Outrage rang in Hailey's tone. "If that's what we wanted, why would we come to you?"

"*You* didn't. She did. You've already said you're the tech half of the partnership. Sounds like you know the system better."

"Are you implying I had someone pose as Chase 547 to stir up trouble and attract attention? Or maybe you think I did it myself."

"No. You can tell during the stream when you're typing. Those times don't line up. Did you know Krista reported these threats to the CPD?"

"No, she didn't," Krista answered for Hailey. "I spent the weekend stewing about it and couldn't stand leaving it so someone who maybe could help was being kept in the dark. Looks like that was a mistake."

Miller kept his gaze on Hailey. "Did this backfire on you? Did you set this up to bring the channel a little fame and fortune, but then your partner took it to the CPD and it got out of hand? Did either of you have a reason to bring in some extra income?"

Ruddy color suffused Hailey's face, right up to her hairline. "How can you even ask that? We all have financial responsibilities, but that doesn't mean we'd fake someone's death to rake in the cash."

"Some would."

"This is unbelievable." Krista strode back to stare down at Miller. "We were concerned someone was in danger. We wanted to help her if it was true. That's all. I don't want this kind of publicity. It won't help the channel. We work best as a slightly smaller, intimate group who can actually talk. We don't game, we don't perform. We have actual relationships with our followers. This could make the group unwieldy and, in the end, lose us even our long-term followers, leaving us with less money in the long run. In the end, this could ruin our community. Why would we do this to ourselves?"

Miller stared up at her, unblinking, as the seconds dragged on. Then he nodded and wrote briefly in his notebook. "You wouldn't. I believe you."

"You . . . what?"

"I believe you. I had to test the theory to discount it. Both your reactions and your reasoning about why this wouldn't improve your channel in the long run make sense to me. They also ring true."

The wind sucked from her sails, Krista circled the coffee table and sank down next to Hailey, who simply stared at Miller, mouth agape. "You believe us."

"Yes. I'm sorry if I was rough on you, but I'm not here for you. I'm here for the person this has been about from the start—the woman in jeopardy. She's what matters."

"Yeah, she is."

"Hell of a way to prove a point," Hailey muttered.

"We've run through what Chase547 has done. What can you tell me about him? What kind of information is listed about him on Twitch?"

"I've looked. Not much." Hailey brought up their creator dashboard and then clicked through to their follower list. "He's here

somewhere in this list of now nearly forty-seven thousand followers, but I can use a specific Twitch tool to track him down."
She brought up a Web page, filled in the username as Chase547,
authorized the tool's use on her Twitch account, and ran the search.

Chase547's Twitch page appeared. At the top of the page,
Twitch reported Chase547 as off-line. Below it, his home screen
was entirely blank.

"There's nothing here, because he's never streamed." Hailey
clicked on the About tab, where it showed Chase547 had 863 followers; besides that, there was no information about him. "Even
though he's never run a single stream, he still has over eight hundred subscribers, most of which are probably following him
because of the crap he pulled on our channel. Otherwise, most
people wouldn't know he exists on the platform. Other than that,
there's no information here." She let her hand drop from the trackpad. "That being said, Twitch knows more about him than we do.
When you sign up, you have to provide your phone number and
a birth date to prove you're over thirteen."

"Can't that be faked?" Miller asked, looking up from his notes.

"Sure, it can. So can the phone number. Or he could have used
a burner phone that's entirely untraceable. Can you get a warrant
for more information from Twitch?"

"Can I get that kind of information from Twitch with a proper
warrant? Yes. Can I get a warrant with what we have now? No.
There's just not enough information for a judge to sign off on this
kind of invasion of privacy. Not when we don't have a target name.
Or a jurisdiction. Or evidence of an actual murder." He dug into
his jacket pocket, pulled out two business cards, and handed one
to Hailey and the other to Krista. "For now, we're building a case.
Chicago averages between one and two homicides a day, so if it's
here, we may be able to tie one of them to this. If either of you
think of anything you want to add, or if something new happens,
I want you to reach out to me. Don't try to decide if it's useful information or not. Let me make that call." He closed his notebook,

and tucked it and his pen into the breast pocket of his suit jacket. "Hailey, can you email me the links and the times to those videos?"

"I'll send you the times, and I'll send you links to an FTP site to download the videos so you have a permanent copy." Hailey looked sideways at Krista. "I'll cc you as well. You should have copies, too."

"Are you worried Twitch might take them down?" Krista asked.

"At this point, I'm not taking any chances. Better we all have our own copies." Hailey turned back to Miller. "I'll send you links to the channel page and to the individual videos as well, just so you have them."

"Thank you." Miller stood and held out his hand to Hailey, prompting both women to rise. "I'm sorry if I seemed aggressive before. I had to be sure of who I was dealing with. If someone has really died . . ."

Hailey clasped his hand. "I get it. Glad you're on our side, rather than against us."

"Ditto." Krista shook his hand next.

"I have your contact information and will be in touch if I need anything. You get in touch if there's anything new. Have a good night. I'll grab my coat and see myself out."

The two women stared after him until the front door thumped closed behind him.

Hailey collapsed backward into the couch cushions. "I thought we had a problem for a minute there."

Krista sank down next to her. "You and me both." She sat back, tipping her head against the cushion to stare up at the curving S of the track lighting fixture above. "Are you mad I didn't talk to you before I contacted the CPD?"

There was a pause and then the sound of Hailey blowing out a breath as the couch cushions shifted beside Krista. "Initially, yeah. But I see why you did it. And once tonight happened, you were right to do it. I just wish we could be more helpful. Give them more information."

"We're giving them everything we have. They know what we know."

"Which is frustratingly little."

"Sure is. What's our plan?"

"We keep going. Chase547 is banned, so he won't be back. Let's think about making a statement at the beginning of the next stream so it's clear we're back to business as usual. I'm going to change the chat to verified accounts only. We may be getting new followers, but I want to make sure they're all real accounts, not a bunch of throwaway accounts used just to continue to stir up trouble. If that doesn't work, we have other options, but let's start there."

"Sounds good to me. What time is it?" Krista struggled upright to check the time on her phone on the coffee table. "Nearly midnight."

"Time for me to head out." Hailey pulled her computer bag out from under the coffee table and packed her laptop away. "You okay?"

"Yeah. I mean, not great, but okay. You?"

"Same." Hailey gave her a hug, then headed for the door, Krista in her wake. "Talk tomorrow?"

"Definitely."

Krista closed the door behind Hailey and then shot the dead bolt home. But that security didn't make her feel safe. She turned and looked at her unlit studio.

The threat still lay there in the dark, just waiting to leap out when she least expected it.

Chapter 11

KRISTA KEPT BUSY ALL DAY at the clinic, even offering on her lunch break to give Melanie a little help with the filing. How could one clinic doing its best to be entirely paperless still have so much paper? As a goal, achieving a fully paperless office was one they were still striving to reach. However, helping Melanie do the filing kept Krista focused on the task at hand—her practice—and off the evening's scheduled stream.

Yet her feeling of foreboding never fully disappeared.

She tried to give herself a pep talk, but her own perky enthusiasm was nothing short of annoying.

She sent off a quick text to Hailey, just to check in. It took Hailey a full hour for a hurried and harried reply about a code glitch from hell and seeing her that night. Clearly, Hailey had her hands full with a coding issue requiring her full attention, with no time for chitchat.

Lucky girl.

Clients coming in gave her renewed focus all day, but she dreaded the lulls, thus the filing on her lunch hour. And that was after running next door to Starbucks to buy everyone coffee, which had eaten up about six minutes. Not nearly enough time.

When they closed the clinic at six o'clock, Kyle headed for his car, Melanie for her Chicago Transit Authority bus, and Krista started her walk home. It was a brisk twenty-minute walk from the clinic to her six-flat building. Most of the time, she enjoyed the fresh air and exercise, especially at this time of year, with its moderate temperatures; whereas in the deep winter or in inclement weather, she could opt to take her car.

She slipped her headphones in, cranked up the tunes, and power walked home, singing to the Cutting Crew in her head the whole way, because if she concentrated on the lyrics, there was no room for anything else.

All through dinner prep, she kept up a running commentary that she was letting Chase547 get to her, which meant he'd won. And that rankled. As Detective Miller said, there was no guarantee he wasn't just trying to stir the pot, to make trouble, to sow chaos and throw her off her game, all for no better reason than his own entertainment. The more she thought about it, the more the tiny flame of her anger grew into a blaze.

She wouldn't let him win. She wouldn't give him the power to frighten her off her own show.

She made dinner and ate in front of the TV, firmly putting the man and his chaos out of her mind.

Well . . . mostly out of her mind. He had an annoying tendency to sneak in at odd moments, but whenever he did, she firmly shoved him out again.

Now she was pumped to take on the stream. Hailey had called another meeting for just before stream time to go over a few things, and Krista was primed and ready to go.

Krista settled into her desk chair, more than five minutes early for the meeting, and entered their Discord voice channel to find no one else was online yet. She turned to the group chat to review the three questions left over from Tuesday that Emily had listed.

Krista knew it must have taken Emily considerable time to comb through the chat, especially by the end, to find any legitimate questions from viewers, as the chat had exploded with

attacks both on and from Chase547 before Hailey had shut it all
down. She picked a question with a number of points she could
speak on, grabbed a pad of paper and pen, and jotted down her
thoughts. She was on point number three when Emily popped
onto Discord.

"Hey, Krista."

"Hey. Thanks for compiling the question list. How hard was it
to dig those out of the chat explosion?"

"Wasn't that bad. Slowed the stream down to a quarter speed
and combed through that way, so it wasn't horrible."

"You're being generous."

Emily shrugged. "No biggie."

Krista hesitated for a moment, then asked the question spinning
in her brain. "How bad was it?"

"The chat?" The way Emily's body tightened, paired with the
sudden stiffness in her shoulders, answered the question before she
put words to it. "It was . . . a lot. But he's banned now, so hopefully
that will be the end of it."

"Did you see our numbers?"

"Yeah. Apparently, you girls have attracted some attention. It's
been going up all week. There's a whole thread on the Twitch subreddit about it."

"Ugh." Krista's whole body sagged like she'd popped a valve and
the air was leaking out of her body. "Really?"

"You had to know it was going to attract attention." Hailey's face
popped on-screen as she joined the video chat, and Emily waved.
"Hey, Hailey."

"Reddit isn't even our platform." Krista continued. "Hi, Hailey."

"What's this about Reddit?" Hailey asked, her gaze fixed off to
the side at the equipment around her.

"There's a Twitch subreddit thread about Tuesday's stream,"
Emily said. "I believe the term 'murder' was used in the subject
line. It kind of took off from there."

"Oh, God," Krista groaned.

"Yeah, it's not great. The r/Twitch subreddit has millions of sub-scribers, so it could have been seen by a lot of people. It certainly explains the jump in followers."

Krista picked up her mug and wrapped her suddenly cold, nerveless fingers around it. "I haven't looked since Tuesday, when we were just under forty-seven thousand. What is it now?"

Hailey's gaze shot sideways. "Sixty-three thousand, eight hun-dred, and fifteen."

"In three days?"

"Less than," Emily interjected. "That Twitch subreddit post went up Wednesday afternoon."

"Two days. This is unbelievable."

Rob, once again cloaked in darkness, appeared as the fourth window in the video chat.

Emily laid her hand over her chest and fanned herself with her other hand. "Rob, you have to stop scaring us like that. Don't you own a lamp?"

"I do. I just like it like this."

"We were discussing the new follower count."

"I saw that. I also saw the subreddit thread that likely pushed it that high. Word is spreading. We're going to have a possible chal-lenge on our hands. If we were gaming, it wouldn't matter, but we actually need to be able to read the comments, interact with them, and police them, not just watch them fly by. Do you think we need to add another mod or two?"

"I think you guys have it," Hailey said. "If we need anyone else, I have someone in mind. You've seen him before in the commu-nity—Logjammer."

"Yeah, I've seen him."

"I went to college with him, and then he was an early follower of my gaming channel. He's at almost all of our streams. If we need another mod, I'd ask him, as a known commodity I can trust, but you guys do such a good job, I'd rather leave it to just us unless we really can't handle it."

"I think we can manage," Emily said. "We'll just need to stay on top of things."

"And then some," Rob stated. "Hailey, we'll do our best to keep you free to concentrate on the stream. We want to make it look like it's a totally normal stream."

"Maybe if we're really dull and boring, people won't stick around," Krista suggested, only half-joking.

"You do realize having people watch is the reason we're running this, right?" Hailey's tone carried a sharp edge.

Irritation frizzled across Krista's nerve endings. Clearly, Hailey had missed the fact Krista was joking...mostly. "Of course, I know that. But we want followers who are here for the content, not to rubberneck at a train wreck." She forced herself to pause, to take a breath and let go of annoyance. "We just need to get back on track with a normal stream. Back to normal, starting now. Are we ready to go?"

"Yes," Hailey said. "Also, so you know, I've activated Shield Mode."

That was a new term for Krista. "Shield Mode?"

"It's a way to add extra security through a couple of different features. For instance, we can use AutoMod to ban all users who use specific words or phrases, if we need that. If tonight doesn't go smoothly, it will allow the next step—a follower-only chat. Rob did a great job last time of staying on top of the harassment, while Emily was trying to keep the rest of the show running normally, making sure you had questions and so on. But we need different tools. Currently the chat is set to verified accounts only, so that will limit some of the newcomers who are just being lookie-loos. Let's see how that goes."

"Good. Also, when you throw it to me, I want to say something about the last stream."

"You think that's a good idea?" Rob asked. "Would it be better to just keep your chin up and proceed as usual?"

"Honestly, I don't know. My gut says, especially with this many new people watching, we need to make it clear to them who we are and what kind of community we are. That they're welcome to join us, but we're not here for the drama that may have brought them in the first place. Hailey, that okay with you?"

"Sure. Just keep one thing in mind. Chase547 could still be watching."

"What? How? I thought you banned him."

"I did. And that means he can't chat or interact with the community. But there's no way to block him from seeing the channel, especially if he's not signed into his account. Or if he's watching the stream later as video on demand, or on YouTube, or listening to the podcast. If all he wanted to do was mess with us, he's no threat. And maybe he's buggered off. I just want you to be aware that he might still be watching or listening." Her mouth took on the mulish set Krista recognized as Hailey digging in. "I actually kind of hope he *is* watching or listening, so we can show him he's nothing and we're going to completely forget about him."

"As soon as I finish this intro, that sounds absolutely perfect to me. Emily and Rob, do your thing." Krista waited as Emily and Rob left the call. "Fire it up."

"You got it."

Then they were live, their two screens highlighted by their cheerful aqua backdrop and their neon *A Word from the Wise* logo.

"Hey, Ziggy! How are you?" Hailey's smile was broad, her tone chipper, entirely void of her earlier harshness.

Putting on the armor, setting the tone. "Hey, Mortie, I'm great." Krista looked right into her webcam. "Before we start today, I wanted a quick word." A quick glance at the viewer count gave her another jolt as the number ticked up in real time as people signed on to the stream. Normally, they'd have been lucky if they had 1,500 viewers. Now they were already at 10,577 . . . 10,591 . . . 10,649—*Stay on track.* She looked away from the viewer count and fixed her mind on what she needed to do.

"First of all, welcome to all our new viewers. We've caught some inadvertent notoriety lately because of one particular individual in our chat. I just want to make sure everyone knows that individual has been banned. We have no cause to believe anything he said was real, and he had no reason to be here except to cause trouble and mess with our heads. He's now banned from our channel. Chase547, if you're here watching, you won't be chatting with us again. You're not a part of this community."

The chat was full of messages of greeting to the channel and good riddance to Chase547. The camaraderie warmed her. She knew she was in this with Hailey and the mods, but the community phalanx lining up behind her gave her a boost.

"Apples, we see you, and we want to thank you for the way you stood up for Mortie and me last stream. We may have created this channel, but the community is really about you. About the hive mind who offers advice in chat, or who comments on YouTube for a particular stream. Who protect the vulnerable and raise up those who are feeling down. You make this a fantastic community, one we're happy to be a part of and share time with. We're not going to let one literal bad apple spoil this for us. To our new followers and new viewers to the stream, we're happy to have you. If you've come to take part in our discussion, if you have questions or insight, we welcome you. But that's what we are—an advice stream. We're not here for melodrama or for anyone to be hurt. Mortie and our other mods are standing by and will remove anyone who doesn't follow the guidelines from the chat. To enter the chat, you'll need to have a verified account and you'll need to sign off on our community guidelines." She picked up her mug of tea and raised it in a toast. "Then welcome to the community. The Wise Apples, Mortie, and I are glad to have you." She took a sip and set down the mug.

"Solid!" said Hailey, raising her own drink, some sort of energy concoction in a neon-colored can. "Let's hit our first question."

"You got it! Our first question is from TintaTurnter, who was told as a child her stepfather wasn't her biological father, but her mother didn't know her father and she was a result of a one-night stand in college. But she stumbled across some old paperwork of her mother's proving her mother *did* know the name of her father, and she'd been hiding it all this time. A little internet research allowed her to track him down via his online presence. He's married with two children, the oldest of which appears to be only a few years younger than her. She confronted her mother with this information, and her mother doesn't want her to contact the bio father, but Tinta wants to. What should she do?"

Hailey winced. "That's a tough one. And for more than just Tinta."

"You just nailed one of the major points. When deciding what to do about this information, you need to consider your father. Does he know about you? He may have been out of your life all this time because he never knew you existed. You're an adult, not looking for child support, just looking for a family connection, but you'll still be a shock to him and to his family."

"Tinta is in the house," Hailey said. "She says her mother wasn't totally clear, but Tinta doesn't think her father knows about her."

"You need to take that into account. I'm not saying don't contact him, but keep in mind the shock factor for him. Also, it sounds like he's been married, or at least been with his partner, possibly for almost as long as you've been alive, if not longer. When he had this one-night stand with your mother, was he cheating? Was he 'on a break'?" Krista made air quotes around the phrase most people her age knew as a reference to Ross and Rachel in *Friends.* "Or maybe they were just about to meet. You don't know the story from his perspective, so give him space to take care of others in his own life, including his children. You have half siblings, and it's hard to say what their reaction will be. Mortie, put yourself in their shoes. How would you take it?"

Hailey looked thoughtful, leaning her elbows on her desk, intertwining her fingers and tapping her thumbs together. "A lot would depend on my mother in this situation. If my parents were together, he cheated on her, and a child was the result, I'm probably going to look at that child as the physical representation of that infidelity. If they hadn't met yet and this was a dumb-ass college move, having unprotected sex, assuming I'm about that same age, I might be more understanding, knowing how these things can happen. I might even find a new sibling to be kind of exciting. Either way, making contact with Dad on the quiet is going to be necessary. Give him time to absorb the shock about the situation all those years ago, then let him make a call about if he should tell his family."

"Or *when* he tells them," Krista suggested. "In this current age of online genetic databases, people are finding relatives from infidelity all over the place. People might lie, but DNA doesn't. Once he finds out he has a child he was previously unaware of, he'll need time to process it himself, even before he figures out how to deal with his family. Contact him privately and give him that time. This will likely upend his world. Be prepared, at least initially, that this might not seem like great news to him. Give him time for that, too, and don't be disheartened if he doesn't initially welcome you with open arms."

Krista glanced at the time, then the chat. Lines of text were moving fast, but what she saw as it flew by was advice about how to handle her mother's secrecy, suggestions about how to reach out to her father to start off on the right foot, different points of view about how her half siblings might feel. Everyone was settling into a perfectly normal stream, so she'd give this one a bit more time.

"Your other consideration is how to deal with your mother. Understandably, you could be feeling a lot of anger toward her. She outright lied about your father's identity and denied you both the opportunity for a relationship in your formative, growing years. But was there a reason for her deception? It certainly made it harder for her to raise you alone. It also meant no child support, so unless your mother was independently wealthy, you may have struggled financially, yet she never reached out to him. You need to consider why she didn't. Was the one-night stand nonconsensual and she's lived with the trauma of rape all these years? Was she worried she'd lose you in a custody battle? Or was she simply embarrassed? You need to try to put any anger you have for her on hold until you know the real story. You may be about the age now she was then, so you know how complex relationships can be. Give her a chance to explain what happened and why she did it. Your future relationship might depend on it."

Krista took a deep breath and blew it out. "That was a heavy one. Let's aim for something a little lighter." She checked the group chat to find a few questions from Emily. "Andrastianmonk wants some advice dealing with a neighbor who's gone overboard with the Halloween decorations, turning the street into a local landmark with constant car traffic and people coming through to rubberneck at the display at all times of the day and night."

The stream continued. Krista was deep into her rhythm, and Hailey was right there with her with bright quips and her characteristic offbeat suggestions. This was when they were at their best—Krista more grounded, seeing a situation from all sides; Hailey thinking outside the box, giving suggestions that never occurred to Krista.

It renewed her faith in what they were doing.

"Thegoodhippogriff, you know I'm not a medical physician, so I strongly advise you to make an appointment with your general practitioner. The kinds of chronic sleep deprivation you describe can be due to chemical imbalances in the brain that can lead to depression. Go in and talk to your doc. If they suggest meds, don't be embarrassed to try them. Too many people have mental illness medically in its own category. No one thinks twice about a diabetic replacing the insulin that's missing from their system. Why is taking meds that make brain chemicals more available to the cells there not exactly the same thing? If that's what your doc recommends, give it a try."

"Excellent advice," Hailey chimed in. "Just remember, brains are complex and it can take time to find the right meds." She wagged her index finger back and forth, so on-screen it was clear she was including Krista in her statement. "We went to college with someone who started depression meds. The first couple she tried were a disaster. One made her a rage monster. The next made her so manic, we found her frantically reorganizing her room at three in the morning. The next one was the winner and made a huge difference in her life. Don't give up if the first one you try isn't the one. It's worth the time and effort to find the right fit."

"It sure is." Krista took a quick look at the chat to see it still moving quickly, but the tone had changed, making her realize she'd missed something. The emotes that streamed by had taken on an angry edge. Then two messages appeared, catching her breath.

> Tracker3199: you didnt believe me
> Tracker3199: that was a mistake 😠

By the time she'd blinked to see if she'd really seen the messages, they were gone, scrolling off-screen.

Then a new message appeared.

> Tracker3199: will I have to kill again for you to believe?

If she'd harbored any belief this wasn't Chase547 in disguise, it was instantly obliterated with that last message.

Chase547 had a second verified account?

In her Mod View window, the Mod Action panel shifted, adding two new lines.

⊘Tracker3199   now
Banned by RobBot_Tinker

As promised, the mods were on top of things, but not fast enough to keep the chat from spinning out of control again as messages flew by telling Tracker3199 exactly where he could go in no uncertain terms.

> rhythmburst: @Tracker3199 👍 Fuck off 👍
> 🍎jO1ntcOh3r3nt: @Tracker3199 Eat shit & die 💩
> 🐱Hunter68: youll never get rid of me 😼
> 🐱Hunter68: you can try
> 🐱Hunter68: youll fail 👍 😫
> 🖼️🐱RobBot_Tinker: @jO1ntcOh3r3nt Warning issued. Comply with community rules or you will be banned.

Krista knew she had to be staring blankly, like a deer in the headlights on camera, unable to react physically as her mind spun.

Chase. Tracker. Hunter.

A predator was in their community.

> 🍎Hunter68: maybe youll be next 🔪 🩸

A killer was in their community.

It had never occurred to Krista that the person behind Chase547 could have planned ahead, knowing he'd be banned at some point. But he clearly knew the platform and had made contingency plans, having new accounts ready to flip to as soon as one account was banned. Perhaps not for their channel specifically—maybe he had a history with the platform. Either way, he'd come prepared.

Log out of the banned account, log into a new account, return to the stream, enter the chat, continue the attack.

Because that's what it was.

Lines shifted in the Mod Action panel again, two new lines appearing, care of Rob.

> ⊘**Hunter68**   now
> **Banned** by RobBot_Tinker

He was gone, until he came back again with another account. Each account would need a different email, but how many free email services were out there? Or how many accounts could he have on each one? He could keep it up forever. And what would his screen name be next time? Stalker? Trapper? Pursuer? His intent had been crystal clear from the start. She just hadn't seen it.

She could certainly see it clear as crystal now. However, she'd be damned if she'd allow him back in her chat. At least for tonight. Soon they'd have to figure out a long-term solution. They couldn't turn off the chat function—it was integral to the community interaction on the channel. At the same time, they couldn't allow it to be hijacked on a nightly basis.

That discussion would have to happen later. For now, she was going to cut him off at the knees.

She fixed a steely eye at the camera. "I think that's it for today. Say good night, Mortie."

Hailey didn't miss a step. "Good night, folks."

The screen went blank.

youll never get rid of me.

you can try.

youll fail.

maybe youll be next.

Krista sagged back in her chair, and dropped her face into her hands, her scream of frustration bouncing back at her off exposed brick and drywall.

Chapter 12

KRISTA LAID HER FORK IN the empty bowl that had held the remains of her chopped salad, then pushed the bowl away a few inches over the wooden surface of the table. She looked over the dishes at Hailey, similarly perched on top of a high steel-and-wood stool, still working on a giant cheeseburger and a plate of fries. Lit by the warm glow from overhead recessed lighting, the lines of stress had finally eased from Hailey's face over the course of the meal and conversation that touched on anything but their Twitch channel.

Last evening's righteous anger had dissipated during a night of tossing and turning, and then, when Krista finally dozed off, in the lines of chat and flying emotes filling her nightmares. She'd jerked awake, exhausted, her limbs feeling weighted by lead, her head aching for coffee.

She'd texted Hailey that morning, asking if she'd like to meet up for dinner so they could chat. Krista needed to hear what Hailey thought about how to handle their current position and what could be accomplished from the technical side to stop this maniac. But more than that, she wanted her college roomie, the woman who had been there for her every step of the way through the worst of Linc's illness and especially after he passed. The one she'd naturally call if she was having a bad day. The one who'd call her to complain about her blind date the night before or an idiot coworker who harbored the incorrect assumption that women couldn't code . . . until she'd shown him in no uncertain terms that she could code circles around him. She wanted her best friend.

Hailey was also unsettled by yet another stream terrorized by some guy who felt it was his right to keep them on the ropes. They needed a defensive plan and only had three more days to get it put into place before they were live again.

Hailey set down her burger. "That's all I can manage."

"Take the rest home for lunch tomorrow?"

"Yeah."

"Too stuffed for dessert?"

"I couldn't eat a whole one."

"Want to split a slice of the dark-chocolate tart?"

Hailey's eyes brightened. "That, I can do."

Krista waved at their server, who came and took their order for dessert, plus an herbal tea for Krista and an espresso for Hailey.

"I don't know how that doesn't keep you up," Krista said, watching the server walk away. "I'd be wide awake and staring at the ceiling at three in the morning." She stared down at the table, her lips twisted in a sour line. "Though maybe that would be better than the dreams I had last night."

"You seemed pretty pissed last night when we signed off. I thought that would keep you going for a while."

"It did. Though my subconscious apparently thought it would be amazing to take everything churning in my head and turn it into a series of nightmares." Krista rubbed the back of her neck with one hand. "Being kept awake might have been better." She dropped her hand back into her lap. "We've avoided it all evening so we didn't ruin our dinner, but we need a plan after last night. When we banned this guy the first time, I naively thought that would be it. But he had us figured out long in advance."

"Yeah, we definitely have a problem."

"I was a little slow on the uptake, but even *I* figured that out last night. Do I have it correctly that he could have any number of free email addresses leading to any number of free, verified Twitch accounts?"

"Yes."

"And we have no idea how far back those accounts could go."

"Correct. I could put a limit on chat, maxing out the restriction so only accounts following us for more than three months can enter, but we have no idea when he made those accounts. And as we've been around for eight months, we don't know that every one of those accounts haven't been with us that long. I'm gonna do it anyway. I plan on slapping a bunch of restrictions on the chat." She looked up to meet Krista's eyes, deep unhappiness shadowing her own. "I'm doing this because I think we have to, but I really don't like it. This is going to hit our viewers hard. Some who have recently joined, and have been a great part of the community, will have their hands slapped because of this one guy."

"I'm sorry for that. You really think he'll be back."

"I do, yeah."

"I can talk to the community at the beginning of Tuesday's chat. Smooth the way a bit."

"You took the community discussion last night. This is a technical restriction, one I'm initiating, so I'll explain it this time." Hailey searched the room for their server, her gaze almost frantic. "Where's dessert? I *need* chocolate for this conversation."

"She's coming. So the chat will be only verified accounts"—Krista counted points off on her fingers—"and accounts who have followed for more than three months. What else can we do? We can't do emote-only mode for a full stream, or we won't get any new questions and it will basically kill community interaction."

"Agreed. We could do a non-mod chat delay so the mods could see each message for up to six seconds before it posts and delete before it goes up."

"How would that work with this many participants?"

"It wouldn't. We'd have to have a stable of mods to manage it, not just the two who have been sufficient up to now—three, if you count me. Alternatively, we could do slow mode so any one user can only send messages up to once every two minutes."

"That could work."

"It could. Drawbacks—it could really annoy the followers we want to keep because they'd be blocked to any active conversation for two minutes after a single comment, and then by the time they could chat again, the conversation would have moved on. Here's another thing—we know he had multiple IDs because we've already met them. What if he has more that get through all the other blocks? All he needs is to sign in from multiple browsers on his computer to be able to comment from different IDs. Add in the potential of logging in from his phone or a tablet, and maybe he could have five or six IDs going at one time."

"You're saying he could get around slow mode by simply using multiple IDs at the same time."

"It's a possibility. We'd keep blocking the IDs, but it could be chaos." Hailey's eyes lit up. "Ah, there it is. Suddenly I'm hungry again."

Their server arrived with a laden tray. "Here you go." She set a plate down in the middle of the table. Centered in an artistic zigzag of chocolate sauce and flanked by two forks was a generous slice of creamy chocolate custard on a chocolate wafer crust, sprinkled with flaked sea salt and topped with a dollop of whipped cream. "Dark-chocolate tart to share. Tea"—she set a cup and saucer and a diminutive silver teapot in front of Krista—"and an espresso." She transferred the tiny mug and matching saucer from her tray to the table in front of Hailey. "Can I get you anything else?"

"This is great for now," Krista said. "Thank you."

"Give me a shout if you need anything, or when you're ready for the bill." The young woman flashed a smile and turned to address the waving hand of another diner.

Krista picked up the fork facing her and cut off the tip of the slice of tart. "So, do we have any other options?" She took a bite of the tart, and chocolate exploded on her tongue—silky, earthy, a little smoky, without even a touch of bitterness. "Oh, this is excellent. We chose well."

Hailey set down her cup and cut off a piece for herself. "What do you mean?" She took a bite and hummed with approval.

"Are there any other tools we can use?" Krista felt a little kick of alarm when color flooded over Hailey's cheekbones. "What?"

Hailey made a show of repositioning the cloth napkin in her lap. "I applied for us to be a Twitch Partner earlier this week."

This was new terminology for Krista. "What does that mean?"

"It's for Affiliate streamers who are ready to level up their efforts. It's a real status symbol if you become a Partner. Out of fourteen million streamers, only about sixty thousand are Partners, and that group includes all the top broadcasters."

"Why would we want that?"

"Because it would give us additional security tools. More importantly, it would give us priority support access, the kind of support that not only gets a response, but actual assistance. Depending on how things go for us, that could be extremely helpful. Then there's other handy stuff, like the ability to delay broadcasts if needed, keeping our on-demand videos on the site for a longer period of time, early access to the newest features, and transcoding—the ability to convert files from one format to another so we have the top quality possible for all streams. We'd also get better promotion on the Twitch homepage, which could bring in new viewers."

The first frizzle of suspicion snaked down Krista's spine. "And more viewers means more money because we make money based on the follower count."

"Well, sure. But there are lots of reasons to be a Partner. The channel customization is another big plus. We talked before about custom apple emotes for the group, and how to celebrate those who have subbed us for different periods of time. If we get Partner, we get to unlock more emote slots based on sub numbers, which would be fun." Some of the brightness left Hailey's eyes. "After this last week, we could use some fun on the channel. And so could our viewers." She finally looked up and met Krista's flat stare. Surprise and defensiveness shot like twin lightning bolts over her expression, and then were gone just as fast. "This is a good thing."

"I'm sure it is." Krista calmly cut off a piece of tart, carefully slipped it between her lips, chewed, swallowed, and washed it down with a sip of tea. "Two questions. When did you apply for the channel—for *us*—to be a Twitch Partner?"

"It must have been . . . last weekend. Not just anyone can apply, or they'd be inundated. You have to meet a certain block of standards called the Path to Partner. Basically, it's a combination of audience and engagement stats. Once you reach that level, a new button appears on the channel's Achievement Dashboard."

"It sounds like a big deal to meet those standards. I guess we got there?"

"Yes. It's partly about stream time—how long and over a certain number of days—and staying above a particular average of viewers, all within a set time period."

"I see."

"Why are you being all stiff about this?"

"I'm not being stiff."

"I've known you for nearly a decade, Zig. I know the ice princess routine when I see it."

Krista's eyebrows shot skyward as her temper flared, but she kept her voice level. "Last question—how much extra money will this make us? I assume it's more lucrative to be a Partner than an Affiliate."

Hailey put down her fork and sat back in her chair, crossing her arms over her chest. "That's a perk, yes."

Oozing defensiveness. "A significant perk?"

"It can be. It depends on the channel."

"Anyone who makes a living doing this is a Partner, I assume?"

"Yes."

"You applied for this without us discussing it first."

"We agreed at the beginning I'd be running the technical aspect of the channel."

Anger bloomed hot and raw. In the back of Krista's mind, she recognized that while Hailey deserved some of that anger, there were other aspects of the situation driving it. Still, the quiet voice of reason was quickly drowned under a vicious red wave. Krista leaned forward, bracing her hands on the tabletop. "This isn't a technical aspect, and you know it," she hissed between gritted teeth. "Last weekend makes it after Chase547 appeared in the chat. We were already getting attention and our numbers were going up. Not as high as they are now after he announced the murder, but still up. Or has it always been about the money for you?"

"No!" Hailey managed to keep her voice down, but anger flowed over the whispered word.

"Then why was the application a secret? Better still, why wasn't it up for discussion? At its heart, becoming a Twitch Partner is an income issue. A fame issue. We went into this together as a team. Why wasn't this discussed?"

"This is why." Hailey wagged an index finger between them. "I knew you'd balk at it, but it's what we need to continue to grow. To continue to protect ourselves and our followers."

"When you completed the application, that's not what you were thinking. You thought we had a pain in the ass in the chat we'd have to ban as a worst-case scenario. You also saw the numbers going up and thought to use it to our financial advantage."

"Believe what you want, but Chase547 was a wake-up call, at least for me," Hailey bit out, clearly struggling to keep her voice low. "The channel had been slowly growing and everyone was playing nice, but there isn't a single channel that doesn't eventually have some sort of problem with a viewer. The anonymity of the internet gives people the freedom to be abusive. We need to protect our followers."

"I agree, one hundred percent. The nature of our show means people are baring their souls as they ask for help. We have to protect those people from abuse. We have to protect *us* from abuse. But you did this before we really had an idea of what we were facing. It should have been something we discussed."

"You object to making more money?"

"I object to taking this nightmare of a situation—a situation where a woman has possibly died—and using it to our financial advantage. It's not right."

"We didn't kill her to make money." Outrage undergirded Hailey's tone.

Krista simply stared at her for a long moment. *What's going on?* This was not the Hailey she'd known for years. That Hailey would never put financial interests above the safety of the people around her. This hard edge felt extremely out of character. "Absolutely not. But it could still look like we're taking advantage of the situation."

"By people who don't know the whole story."

Krista laid her hand over Hailey's wrist, where her clenched fist lay on the table. "Hail, what's going on? Is everything okay? You know there isn't anything you can't tell me."

Hailey opened her mouth on a breath as if she were about to speak, but then closed her lips, firming them for an instant in a thin line. "No, it's all good." She tugged her hand free, tossed back a few long swallows of espresso, and set the cup down in the saucer with a little too much force. Twisting her hands in her lap, she looked over Krista's shoulder toward the bar running along the far wall behind their table. Closing her eyes for a few seconds, she blew out a long breath through pursed lips. When she opened her eyes, the fire within had dampened. "Look, I'm sorry. I shouldn't have done it without talking to you first. When I saw the button, I was just so excited. This is what Twitch streamers do." She met Krista's eyes. "And that's what I am. I'm a streamer. You're not."

Krista forced herself not to snap back a response, and instead listened as her own catchphrase echoed in her head: *Communication is key. Shut up and let her communicate.*

"I've been running my gaming channel for two years now, but my channel has never taken off like this one has, even though I'm playing *Hades 2,* which is super hot right now. I've been an Affiliate for over a year, but I can't push through to the point where I could apply to be a Partner. And here I am, on this second channel, one put together for fun, with someone who isn't a gamer and has no ambitions of success on this platform, with no expectation of success, and it's the one that's taken off."

Krista's anger at the situation dissipated slightly, but enough remained to make her a little snappy. "Chase547 is responsible for most of that."

"I disagree." Hailey's lips twisted as her shoulders slumped as if in defeat. "Sure, he's maybe had a part, but I think most of it's you. You know how to talk to people."

Hailey was putting up a good front, trying not to look disappointed, but Krista had known her far too long to be fooled. "How *we* talk to people. It's not just me. Your story about the surprise gift and how it made you feel is only one example. You put an additional face to what women can experience in their interactions with a partner. When we're looking at chat messages talking about people only they know, there's no face to a viewer's issue. You give it one."

Hailey's expression brightened, animation creeping back into her eyes. "You think so?"

Krista pushed down on the wave of irritation that rose at the hope in Hailey's eyes. At the need for validation, when Krista was the one doing the hard work on dealing with the issues brought to the table. *Be nice.* "Yes." The niceness slipped fractionally. "You didn't need to apply to be a Twitch Partner. We were doing fine."

"We could be doing better." As if finally noticing Krista's bristling, Hailey quickly added, "If it makes you feel better, the chance of being accepted as a Partner is astronomically small. It will probably never go anywhere."

That might have been true when Hailey applied, but now, following an admission of murder in one broadcast and a stream of abuse in another, Krista wasn't so sure. As far as she was concerned, she didn't want any more notoriety. If they became Twitch Partners, that's all there would be—more promotion, more viewers, more chaos. It would ruin the show.

It might already be too late. The charming community they'd tended was becoming an unruly mob, and Krista didn't see a way to get back to where they'd been.

Hailey was staring at her, waiting for her forgiveness.

Forgiveness would come later. Right now, she was still angry, but at the very least, she could put up a good front. "You're right. It will probably never go anywhere."

They could only be so lucky.

Chapter 13

Krista stumbled out of her bedroom, still rubbing sleep from her eyes as she made a beeline directly to her kitchen. Evenings were for tea, but mornings were definitely for coffee.

She needed it this morning. After her dinner with Hailey the night before, her temper had burned at a low ebb for hours. She hadn't bothered to go to bed right away, but had stayed up late watching TV, curled on the couch in the dark with Balto, finally going to bed after two o'clock in the morning. Which explained why she'd overslept and why she was dragging herself around the apartment like she was sleepwalking.

She needed caffeine.

She staggered to the kitchen, grabbed the coffee carafe, rinsed the last of yesterday's coffee dregs from it, and filled it with fresh water, which she poured into the reservoir in her coffee machine. She measured beans into her grinder and turned it on, wincing slightly at the racket, glancing upward at the ceiling and wondering once again if the noise bothered her neighbors. "Sorry," she mumbled. She turned to her pantry, pulled open the bifold door, and reached for her box of coffee filters. Then stood blinking at it dumbly.

It was empty.

How did she let that happen? She always put items on the grocery list when they were getting low. She'd never let something like that run out. Especially not when she needed caffeine in the morning. She turned to the fridge, where a magnetic shopping list pad showed a number of items—paper towels, salt, butter, cinnamon—but no coffee filters.

"Damn." The grinder whirled to a higher pitch, indicating it was done, so she flipped it off and stared glumly at the pile of grounds in the glass collecting jar. "So much for fresh. You'll have to wait until tomorrow. Tea it is." She filled and flipped on her kettle, then turned to the pantry for her English Breakfast tea, her highest-caffeine blend. She pulled out a tea bag and one of her bigger mugs and then leaned against the counter, waiting as the kettle boiled.

Leaving her tea steeping to make a good strong brew, she pulled out eggs, cheddar, and a skillet and set about whipping up some scrambled eggs with multigrain toast. When it was all cooked and steeped, she carried her plate and mug over to the couch, set both down on the coffee table, and flopped down on the couch, leaning the stuffed husky against the couch cushions so it was almost like they were breakfasting together.

She flipped on the TV, found her next episode of *Friends,* and dove into her breakfast. She set down her fork just as Ross and Rachel were breaking up for the first time. "That's not going to last," she said to Balto. She picked up her mug of tea, took a sip . . . and then froze. "What the hell?"

She'd been so absorbed in making and eating breakfast, in watching the dramedy on her screen, that she hadn't noticed Linc's picture. Well, she had, in her bedroom as she said good morning to his photo on the bedside table, as she always did. But the larger photo that usually sat on the top right-hand floating shelf was . . . on the middle shelf? And the funky rabbit sculpture—the steampunk creation composed entirely of old watch and clock parts—that Linc bought her for her twenty-sixth birthday, which he correctly knew she'd love, was now on the top shelf.

That was just wrong.

Had she done that?

Now you're being stupid. Who else would have?

She'd done a full cleaning last weekend, taking everything off the shelves, dusting and putting everything back up. She must have been on autopilot and put the photo back in the wrong place. And then not noticed all week?

She'd let the coffee filters run out. And then there was the twenty minutes she wasted yesterday looking for the tiger's-eye-and-citrine bracelet her mom got her for her last birthday, which she wanted to wear out to dinner with Hailey the night before. She'd looked through her jewelry box on her dresser, in the bathroom, and then through her top dresser drawers, and finally her purse. No trace of it.

It wasn't expensive or made of precious materials. It wasn't worth stealing if someone had broken into her apartment—which obviously no one had, because why take a tiger's-eye bracelet and leave behind the gold-and-diamond stud earrings Linc had bought her the Christmas before he died?

Suddenly insecure, she set down her mug, pushed off the couch, and strode back to her bedroom door, one hand resting on the jamb as her gaze found her dresser and the long silver chain stretched out just in front of the mirror, a diamond ring at one end of its length. Relief flowed through her, rapidly followed by a gentle scold. *If you're going to misplace a piece of jewelry, that's the last piece you'd lose. You only take it off at night. It goes two places—around your neck or on the dresser.*

The light streaming in the window glinted through the nearly square Asscher-cut diamond, bezel set into a platinum band. When Linc bought her the engagement ring, he intended it to be a ring she could continue to wear to work, one that wouldn't scratch clients in her hands-on profession, one that wouldn't get in her own way and also didn't sit too high so as to be an impediment. She'd happily worn it to work for the sixteen months they were engaged. And then, when he'd died, she'd continued to wear it for a full year. She'd only been able to slide the ring from her finger after the first anniversary of his death. But she couldn't completely stop wearing it, severing what remained of their connection forever, so she'd taken to wearing the ring on a chain around her neck. Most of the time, the ring didn't show under her athletic wear for work or her regular clothes, so there were no questions from curious strangers or new clients. For those who knew her best, there were still no questions, because they knew how much she missed Linc.

Reassured her ring was safe, she wandered back to the living room and straight to the shelves flanking the TV, studying the small metal sculpture and the framed photo, both in the wrong place.

This Twitch fiasco was apparently bothering her more than she realized, and was making her focus on all the wrong things.

She picked up the photo, smiling down into Linc's joyful face. "Sorry, babe. Things have been a bit weird this week." She swapped spots with the bunny statue, putting Linc on the correct shelf. "Back on top, where you belong. I promise to pay more attention." She kissed two fingers and pressed them to the glass over his face.

Her cell phone rang where it lay on the coffee table, and she turned to find the screen illuminated with her brother's name and his goofy, smiling face. She answered the call. "Hey, Zach."

"Morning. I thought I'd better check in when you went silent over the past few days. I thought you wanted to do dinner last night."

Something else forgotten. "Oh, no." Guilt sliced sharp. "I'm sorry. Let's see, what was I up to? I had to make an emergency trip to Reno? The president called and needed a one-on-one? No, no, I have it. France called. They want the Statue of Liberty back, and I'm leading the negotiations."

"Forgot, huh?"

She sighed, knowing the sound and its embedded apology carried straight to him. "Yes, I forgot. I'm sorry. As you can see, I have no excuse."

A grunt came over the airwaves as if Zach had been poleaxed. "Now that hurts. Look at me, so beneath your notice."

"I'm really sorry. How could I do this to you? You know you're my favorite brother."

"That's not actually saying anything. I'm your *only* brother."

"Details, details." A baseline level of banter was the norm for their relationship, but she let the frivolity drop so he knew she was sincere. "We made plans, but things have just been . . . so . . ." She sagged back down onto the couch. "Damn it."

"Hey, it's just dinner. I get it if you're busy. You're allowed to have a life. Were you on a date?" he asked, his voice taking on a sly tone.

"Only if the date was with Hailey."

"Definitely not a date, then." His tone was dry.

"Not even kind of. We've been having some trouble on the channel."

"Your apple orchard?"

"Ha ha. Yes." She pictured Zach as he would be right now, his whip-lean body clad in track pants, a sweatshirt, and gym shoes, just in from an hour-long run on the Lakefront Trail. His dead-straight, dirty-blond hair would be disarrayed from the jog, wet with sweat along his hairline, but his pale skin would be warm with color, his blue eyes bright from the exertion. Nothing her brother loved more than a long weekend run, instead of the usual predawn sprint he squeezed in each morning before heading into his office at a local civil engineering firm. "The channel's actually been slowly taking off since our first broadcast. We're really building our viewership. More than that, we're building a community."

"That actually sounds nice."

"It is."

"You've had problems? I admit I watched a bunch of the early streams, but it was almost all about gaming issues, and that's not my jam, so I haven't tuned in lately."

"You should try it again some time. We now have a broad spectrum of issues being discussed. Maybe you'd learn something."

"Funny girl. So, what's gone wrong?"

"Lately, what hasn't?"

"Sounds like we have some catching up to do." In the background came the sound of clanking dishes, then the fridge opening. "I got time. I got coffee. Lay it on me."

"Coffee." Krista looked glumly at her tea, something she'd normally be happy to drink. She was so far off her game this morning, it wasn't funny. "I remember coffee."

"You remember coffee?"

Krista could hear the question behind Zach's repeated statement. "I do. What I didn't remember was coffee filters. I'm out."

"No coffee for you, then. What about one of your ridiculous teas? Something like kung pao chicken with boysenberry tapenade and sausage-and-marshmallow stuffing?"

"How about plain old English Breakfast?"

"*Borrrrringgg.*" Zach stretched the word out, letting the last syllable linger for a few seconds at the back of his throat.

"At least it has caffeine."

"I'll drink to that."

Krista could imagine him raising a mug to her as he stood in his own kitchen about ten miles away. "Says the man who probably just ran eight miles to start his morning."

"Ten miles," Zach corrected. There was a pause as they both drank. "What's going on at the old Twitch homestead?"

"We have some nutjob who's coming in to spoil our fun."

"In what way? Being abusive?"

"Didn't start out that way. He came into the chat to ask a question about how to win some woman he was attracted to. Hailey and I gave him some basics of how to connect, without being a total creep, but then he came back in the next stream saying he knew better than us what she wanted. We moved on from him in that stream. Then he came back the next time, and at that point, he became abusive, calling us stupid bitches and the woman a whore who didn't get to make her own choices. Hailey put him in time-out."

"'Time–out'? Seriously? Like a toddler?"

"It basically takes them out for the rest of that broadcast."

"Why didn't she ban him?"

"That was a question I asked her. She said we needed to have defined chat rules in place that everyone had to sign off on before she would start banning."

Zach snorted derisively. "That sounds like BS to me. If you have someone abusive, you block them."

"In retrospect, that would have been the right call. But Hailey's the tech side of our partnership, so I depend on her to tell me how this platform works. And she said we needed an official code of conduct for the channel. So we went with that."

"And did he come back?"

"Did he ever. He popped in to say he'd murdered the woman and she hadn't deserved to live." Krista sucked in a shaking breath as her body flashed cold with the retelling. "*Then* he got banned."

"Holy shit. Kinda buried the lede there, Kris."

"I may be trying to forget it ever happened."

"Did you call the cops?"

"I did. And Hailey came over that night and we met with a Detective Miller. Who, after scaring the crap out of us by making us think he thought we were doing this to gain fame and fortune, made it clear he was on our side, but his hands were tied because we didn't have enough for him to go out and get a warrant. Everyone involved is unknown."

"And they might not even be local to Chicago. The internet is a big place."

"Raised that issue, too."

"Well, hell. No wonder dinner with me slipped your mind. Have you told the parox?" he asked, using the slang term for their parents from their childhood.

"*No.*" The word snapped out so quickly, she nearly cut Zach off. She hung her head and berated herself to get it together. "Sorry. Didn't mean to snap your head off there. I just don't want them worrying. This jerk might be on the other side of an ocean from me and is just trying to freak me out, so I don't want them to worry over nothing. And you know they will."

"At the very least, Mom will. Is there any indication this guy might be local?"

"None. And we're super careful not to give out any information that could lead to our real identities." Krista paused for a moment. "Though I may have made a mistake."

"How?" Zach's single word carried a note of caution.

"My screen name. Hailey's always called me Ziggy, so I went with ChiZiggy. It hints at Chicago."

"Maybe. It's also a letter in the Greek alphabet. So was that stream the end of this guy?"

"We should be so lucky. Hailey put up a whole bunch of security roadblocks, and he cleared them all. Also came back under a different ID. And yes, before you ask, we're sure it was him. And that's when he threatened us. Told us we wouldn't get rid of him and that we might be next."

"I don't like the sound of that." Any trace of banter was wiped from Zach's tone.

"It's big talk with nothing behind it. As Detective Miller rightly pointed out, he could just be doing the whole thing to watch us freak out in real time. He could be in Antarctica and his woman might not even exist. He could be all talk and no action."

"I might believe you really thought that if it wasn't for the forgotten coffee filters and dinner. He's shaken you. You're off your game."

You have no idea. "I'd be lying if I said I hadn't given him another thought. But if I let him get inside my head, he's won. No matter where he is on the planet."

"You're sure?"

"Yes," she snapped. Then she ran a hand through her loose hair and stared up at the ceiling as if asking for both peace and patience. "Sorry."

"It's okay. I get it." Several seconds of silence passed before Zach broke it. "I'm footloose and fancy-free tonight. Dinner, take two? You pick, I'll pay?"

"You don't have to pay."

"Don't argue. I'm offering. Take advantage of it."

Single Zach, with few financial responsibilities and a good income, was often generous with his money, and she knew it made him feel good to take care of people, so she didn't insult him by refusing. "What about that Thai place in Logan Square you took me to for my birthday last year? The one with the knockout crispy chicken pad Thai? That was really good."

"Oh, yeah, that *was* good. Meet you there at six?"

"That sounds great. See you then. And, Zach. . . ?"

"Yeah?"

"Thanks for checking in."

"Always. Later."

As the call ended, she found herself looking forward to dinner. A last oasis of peace at the end of the weekend as she prepared for the workweek. As she prepared for Tuesday's stream. A chance to recharge with one of her favorite people, to get perspective, to get clarity. To get leftovers for tomorrow's lunch.

It was the perfect springboard into a week she hoped could only be better than the last.

Chapter 14

"Hey, guys, we're live with another *A Word from the Wise*—real advice from real people." Hailey's tone was upbeat and cheerful, replacing the serious tone of just a few minutes ago.

They'd met in Discord fifteen minutes before the stream went live. They were now running with a few new security measures in place: three-months-or-longer follower-only mode, verified accounts only. They had decided not to make an announcement of the changes. Anyone who entered the chat who didn't fit the bill would be informed by Twitch's automatic system at that point. They wanted to appear normal, even if so much had changed in the last few weeks.

They were ready.

Krista, Hailey, Emily, and Rob knew the man behind Chase547 could come in with any number of IDs, but they were all hoping the restrictions would knock out at least some of his IDs, if not all of them. They just wanted to get back to normal, something Krista suspected might not be achievable with their increased numbers. Hailey might be happy about that, but she certainly wasn't.

But here she was, pasting on a bright smile, making sure she looked loose and relaxed in her chair, a host without a care in the world.

A host, who was internally tied in knots, waiting for the next shoe to drop.

"Hey, Mortie, how was your weekend?"

"Awesome. Yours?"

"Quiet. Peaceful. Refreshing."

"Love it! What do you have for us today?"

"Vetpet1997 has a sticky one for us. She wants to know how to handle wedding planning when her mother-in-law-to-be is being a total wet blanket. They were recently touring venues for booking next year and she found fault with everything, kept up a steady stream of criticism, and kept comparing all their ideas and plans to her own much smaller wedding. Vetpet wants to know how best to deal with this, when they're just in the beginning stages of planning and have yet to tackle food, the wedding party, the guest list, and so on."

Hailey winced dramatically. "That's going to make for an awkward Thanksgiving table next month."

"Possibly." Krista glanced at the chat to see a slower roll than the last broadcast filling the stream. The clenched ball of stress in her gut relaxed fractionally. *Off to the right start.* "Vetpet, my first question to you with this is where is your fiancé in this, because you didn't mention him. Your first line of defense should be him, because it's *his* mother. Now, that doesn't mean you won't have interactions with her, but he should be leading the charge for your joint plans to be just that—*joint*."

"We have some great suggestions coming in, Zig," Hailey said, her gaze fixed on the chat window. "Allegedead says that in their experience, money is the cause of a lot of wedding drama. Parents give money and then expect to control how it's spent." She looked up. "I've had friends say the same thing. Mom and Dad offer five thousand, but want these particular roses, or that venue, or these extra fifty people added to the guest list."

"It can definitely happen. That's one way to maintain control— plan the wedding you and your fiancé want and can afford if just the two of you are paying for it. Yes, that might mean your parents don't contribute, if you really want to keep things clean. But if they're upset about that, maybe ask them to put their contribution into your wedding present. A lot of couples now live together long before they get married and don't need a fancy china place setting or a blender, so cash gifts at the wedding can help offset the expense of a honeymoon."

"Or can contribute to the down payment of a house," Hailey interjected. "I know several couples who have gotten married lately who asked for cash, as they're saving for a house."

"Also, a good point. Cash gifts are fairly normal now, and with the housing market the way it is, people understand if that's a young couple's focus after the wedding. I'd also suggest not giving your mother-in-law-to-be the platform for criticism. If she's going to be a Negative Nancy, who constantly complains, but doesn't offer a solution to those complaints, and who just walks around with a dark cloud over her head, protect your own mental health and stay clear. Make your decisions, pay for what you can afford, invite the guests you want and can manage, present your plans as *fait accompli*, and then let your fiancé make it clear to her that's the way it's going to be, and there'll be no further discussion. Most importantly, have a wonderful day when you get there."

"And let us know how it went!" Hailey chimed in.

"For sure." A quick scan of the chat. "Also, we have lots of good suggestions coming in from the chat. Ways to save money, ways to keep the event exactly what you want it to be. We're moving pretty quickly, so hit the VOD later to make sure you don't miss any of chat's suggestions. Moving on to our next question . . ." Emily had the next question queued up so she could launch right into it. "XxHornetDiabloxX has a question about finances with her partner."

"Always a hot-button issue," Hailey agreed. "Whether you're single or partnered up, financial troubles can push anyone to the wall."

"They sure can. It's a hot-button issue we need to deal with before it could implode the relationship. XxHornetDiabloxX says that she and her partner both work full-time, but she makes considerably less than him. He wants to split all their expenses, fifty-fifty, which she agreed to because it's reasonable, but he spends like he makes the salary he does, and then she can't afford to pay the bills because he's not living within *her* means."

"That's not going to end well." Hailey sounded slightly detached, her gaze downcast, a furrow building between her eyebrows.

"Not if it continues. If it hasn't already, it's going to lead to stress, mismatched expectations, and a power struggle." Krista followed Hailey's gaze to the chat, and she realized why Hailey wasn't paying full attention.

> noebha: Have you guys discussed working out a bugdet? 🥴
>
> noebha: budget*
>
> blackcraigchocolate: Been there done that
>
> Slayer4923: You think changing the rules will get rid of me? 😵 👆
>
> o0slinkystorage0o: Start a joint account for household spending. Stick to it. 👍
>
> Slayer4923: I live here now 😈

He was back.

Somehow he'd gotten through. Again.

She couldn't prove it, and the ID wasn't familiar, but the tone certainly was. He'd taken on a new persona—no longer the hunter, but the victor. And he was letting his flag fly for all to see.

Krista could tell from Hailey's intent expression she was already on top of things. The Discord message only reinforced it.

⊘Slayer4923   now
Banned by Dumortiere

How many accounts could he have? She suspected they might never know, but he'd cleared their hurdles with at least that one.

> widemotley: fuck off @Slayer4923 👍 👍
> vecnadefiant: @Slayer4923 die die die 💀 ☠️ 💀
> 2lightsweeping2: Do you keep your finances separate? Do you really know what he has? 🙄
> beinnegaff: you dont run this place. we'll fuck you up first
> Butcher666: you can try 😼
> Butcher666: you cant stop me 🔪 💧 ⌛ 🗿
> RobBot_Tinker: @vecnadefiant Warning issued. Comply with community rules or you will be banned.
> emily_brontesaurus: @beinnegaff Warning issued. Comply with community rules or you will be banned.
> Butcher666: who to target next? 😼

Her Mod View window showed the inevitable bannings scrolling through the Mod Action panel as insults and taunts continued to fly.

> ⊘ **Butcher666**   now
>   **Banned** by RobBot_Tinker
> ⊘ **jO1ntcOh3r3nt**   now
>   **Banned** by emily_brontesaurus
> ⊘ **beinnegaff**   now
>   **Banned** by Dumortiere

There were multiple entries in the Mod Action panel as the chat took off. Snappy retorts morphed into violent threats as Chase547 returned time and again: Cutthroat265. Executioner1965. Hitman712. It was the worst-case scenario Krista had dreaded.

Either he'd planned ahead or had changed his username after his declaration of murder.

Krista knew she was still on camera, but she suspected no one was watching her. All eyes were on the chat, where others were on the same wavelength.

> silkypurr: nice try chase547
> silkypurr: you try to hide but we see you, you filthy casual 😒
> monmaterial: Hey chasey boy go home to yo mama 😜 🙃
> Exterminator228: you all can go on my list 🔪
> judeophobiastan: manbaby chase 👶 🍼

"Guys, I'm calling it."

Krista pulled her gaze from the chat to Hailey's face on-screen. Hailey wasn't looking up. Her gaze was locked down and to her left, on the broadcast software. But Krista knew Hailey was talking to herself and the mods because they just couldn't keep up.

Even with all the restrictions they'd put in place, it was a losing battle.

"Apples, see us on Friday." The broadcast ended and the channel window went blank. Krista turned to the Discord video chat, where Hailey appeared, head down, typing. In the chat came her instructions to Emily and Rob to join the conversation. Seconds later, two more windows opened for them. "What the fuck was that?" Hailey snapped.

Rob's only reaction was uplifted eyebrows, but Emily jumped in, her tone ratcheted with stress. "We were moving as fast as we could, but he kept coming back in. How did he have that many IDs that fit our restrictions?"

"I'd like to know that, too," Hailey muttered, head down.

"That had to be Chase547 under different screen names," Krista stated.

"Seems pretty clear-cut to me." Hailey's reply carried an edge of *Only an idiot would miss that.* Then she raised a hand in front of her face and took a deep breath. "Sorry. I'm taking it out on you guys, and you're the last people responsible for this. But honestly, if we can't figure out how to beat this guy, I don't see how we can go on. The chat function is the way this channel works to have real-time discussions with the viewers and to have the community respond, again in real time. We could move the whole thing to YouTube, take questions through the comments and let the community interact there, but it won't be the same."

"There'd be no immediacy," Krista agreed. "It's why you wanted to do the show on Twitch. You can't replicate that kind of community interaction anywhere else."

"Exactly." Hailey stared glumly off to the side at one of her monitors. "It's the follower count I never dreamed of on my own channel. But at what cost? The end of the channel?"

Krista flipped to the channel's main page, her gaze snapping to the follower count—95,372. For a moment she stared in shock, and then her gaze rose to take in Hailey's misery. "Almost one hundred thousand. You always wanted to reach one hundred thousand."

"Yeah. That was my goal. I'm not that big a gamer, and I knew I wouldn't make it with my own channel. I had hopes for this one. But not like this." Hailey's tone was flat, colorless, as if she was so exhausted, she was numb even to disappointment.

Taking in her friend's demeanor, Krista couldn't help but be concerned. She was invested in the channel herself, but Hailey seemed to be taking it to the nth degree. She started to speak, to offer words to share her disappointment, but Hailey was already talking.

"Not because we were a spectacle of violence and death. I'm too tired to deal with this anymore tonight. Let's meet up tomorrow or Thursday to come up with our next plan of attack. We need to make more changes or this isn't going to work and we're done." Hailey raised a hand in farewell, then disappeared before anyone else could say a word.

Krista said good night to both Emily and Rob, waiting as they each left the meeting, and then closed it down.

Hailey was right. They needed a plan or the channel was done. She wasn't sure such a plan was possible.

Chapter 15

"Hey, you."

Krista placed the last dumbbell on the rack and turned around to find Hailey standing at the far end of the gym area. Behind her, the doors of the exam rooms stood open, their lights off. The day was over, and Krista was doing the last of the cleanup. "Hey, didn't expect to see you here."

"It's Wednesday. I knew you'd be working late tonight." Hailey's gaze rose to the clock on the wall. "Don't you normally have a client now? Isn't that why you stay late?"

"Normally, I'd have a seven o'clock, but she called in about an hour ago. Family emergency, so I'll see her next week. It was too late to fit in someone else, so I get to go home a bit early. Did Melanie send you back?"

"Yes. I didn't actually expect the front desk to be staffed."

"Either she or one of the assistants always stays for the last client. It was her turn tonight." Krista rolled a yoga ball next to the wall, holding a hand on it until she was sure it wasn't going to roll. "What's up?"

"I wanted to stop by and see you. In person."

Krista slowly straightened, tension clutching her muscles tight. "What happened?"

Hailey held out both hands, palm out, a gesture of caution. "Don't worry, it's nothing bad. We . . . uh . . ." She shifted her weight from foot to foot as she hesitated as if swinging between joy and foreboding. Then settled on joy with a half smile. "We did it. *A Word from the Wise* has been awarded a Twitch Partnership."

Ice sluiced through Krista's veins as she remained frozen, staring across the recumbent bikes at Hailey. "You mean *you* did it."

Hailey's smile melted away at Krista's glacially detached tone. "Well, yeah, but for us. Remember last night, how we said we needed to make a plan so the channel is more secure? This is our way to do it. Now we'll have the option of locking down the chat in new ways, like subscriber-only chats. If we'd locked it down like that before, we'd have only had the mods able to talk. The necessity of the chat function has been tying our hands, so this gives us a tool in our toolbox."

Krista tried to tamp down her displeasure as she attempted to keep her tone light. "Lucky us."

"And I'm going to talk to support and ask for additional assistance. We can't be the first channel to have trouble like this."

"I'd like to hope not too many channels have someone stroll in and announce a murder." The snarky statement popped out before Krista could stop it. She closed her eyes for several breaths to calm herself, then opened them to find Hailey staring at her, her stance stiff, her expression guarded. "Sorry."

"I know you didn't want this, but I think it will give us some benefits we really need right now."

"It's also going to plaster us on Twitch's main page, isn't it?"

"Not permanently, but we'll be highlighted, yes."

"Which will bring in new followers. Isn't that the point of the Partner program? To build successful brands?"

"Of course."

Krista picked up a blue stretch band from a pile of colored bands on the counter and started to neatly fold it, simply to give her hands something to do. "Which would be great, except we're not winning new followers for our content; we're winning them for our outright chaos."

"I don't think that's necessarily true—"

"Oh, come on! How can you not see it for what it is?"

"If we can't get things nailed down," Hailey continued, "and get things back to normal, we'll likely lose the followers who just came for the spectacle. Hopefully, we'll keep some of them, because they like the content and want more of it."

Krista clutched the folded band tightly enough her nail beds shone white, but it kept her from gripping her hair and pulling. "They're not going to stay, Hailey. They're coming to rubberneck the car crash and when—*if*—the mess gets cleaned up, they'll be gone. And in the meantime, we'll have lost some of our regulars because the show they wanted to see doesn't exist anymore or because we've banned them after they came to our defense a little too enthusiastically. You're also going to lose your precious Partnership, I assume, if we fall out of compliance. But that's the direction it will go." She turned toward the counter and set the folded band down precisely, like her continuing employment depended on it.

"You're still mad."

Her hands now empty, Krista whirled to face her. "Yes, I'm still mad. You applied for this goddamn designation without discussing it, tried to sell it as all puppies and flowers, and then said our chance of getting the Partnership was practically nil. And here we are, four days later . . . Twitch Partners." She turned her back on Hailey and strode away, picking up one of the mats and carrying it over to where a small stack lay against the far wall. She knew one of the assistants would pull it out first thing tomorrow morning to put it in the same place, but she just needed to move, to do something, before the tension rocketing around her body erupted. She slapped the mat on the top of the pile, exultation sparking at the childish move. "Did it ever occur to you this could destroy what's left of the channel? Why are you so dug in on this?"

"You have it all backward. This could save our channel." Hailey's voice was hushed, as if all the fight had gone out of her. "I want to fight for it. Do you?"

After all the stress the channel was causing, Krista didn't have an answer for her. But she knew very well the channel wouldn't exist without her, at least not in its current form. This was the chance Hailey was taking with it.

Hailey gave her ten seconds, then shrugged. "I just wanted you to hear it from me. I'll talk to you later to get our plans in place for Friday. Have a good night." She turned and trudged down the corridor.

Krista watched her friend go, feeling the chasm between them stretch wider with each step.

Chapter 16

ANY HOPE KRISTA HAD THAT the next stream, with all its added security, would put them back where they needed and wanted to be was quickly extinguished under a landslide of chat comments. Their follower count was up again—Hailey's wish for one hundred thousand followers was finally granted—but the real problem was their viewer count, which was up easily twice their latest high. And even with verified accounts and follower-only mode, the chat was buzzing, comments streaming by too quickly for anyone to actually read.

The chat made Krista's head spin, forcing them to depend solely on questions Emily pulled out of the previous session, so while Krista was discussing how to handle making plans for Thanksgiving when the viewer and their family were on opposite sides of a political chasm, Hailey was working on slowing the chat down.

"Apples, we love you, but we can't keep up with your hype." Hailey let a sunny smile stretch wide. "You're awesome, but you're so darn chatty today."

"Really chatty," Krista agreed.

"So we're going into slow mode, guys. I'm not going to time you out all the way to two minutes, but we're going to go to thirty seconds, and we'll see how that works. You have five hundred characters per comment, so make it count. We want you to talk, but we need to be able to get your questions through or else Ziggy might as well just put her feet up and take a nap."

"Boring!" Krista chimed in. "Communication is key, so talk to me, Apples."

The chat abruptly slowed from an energetic stream to a roll where individual comments could be read.

"How's that?" Hailey asked.

"So much better." Krista scanned the comments rolling by. "And there's a great question just meandering by, so I'm going to jump on it. Dattebayomama wants some advice about her husband and his 'work wife,' a colleague at the same level as he is, who works with him closely. She's jealous about the relationship he has with his coworker, even though he says nothing is going on—it's just business—and his coworker is also married. I can kind of speak to that from my own experience. For those who don't know what it is, a 'work spouse' is someone you work with, often of the opposite sex, but not always, who you have a strong connection with. You help and look out for each other. It's a partnership that's not dissimilar to how married couples support each other. I have a work husband—someone I'm particularly attached to, but it's an entirely platonic relationship. For me, it actually borders on work brother. How about you, Mortie?"

"I've had a work wife in the past. She was an amazing partner—brought me homemade baking, made coffee, stood up for me in meetings, and we were always in sync on projects. In return, I kinda did the same for her—covering for her when she needed to slip out because one of her kids was sick, troubleshooting bits of code when she was ready to hurl her monitor out the nearest window." Hailey sighed. "I miss her. But she moved on to bigger and better things. Work spouses are the bomb."

"Unless your own spouse thinks there's something hinky going on, and then they're a problem. This is another moment when communication is key. You have his reassurance nothing untoward is

happening. Maybe it would make you feel better to see their interactions in person. Invite the work wife and her husband over for
dinner. Get to know her yourself. Your husband likes her; you may
find you do as well. Sometimes the unknown is a huge fear,
whereas the reality is really quite ordinary." A quick scan of the chat.
"That's a solid piece of advice—Brothumbsup says to remember
sometimes men have trouble seeing things from a woman's perspective. If you and your husband have a fight and he blows off steam
with the work wife, she may actually be an ally and could help him
see things from your perspective. Great stuff, Brothumbsup." Krista
looked up and grinned. "Hey, Mortie, I guess this makes you my
work wife."

Hailey toasted with her coffee mug. "Wouldn't have it any
other way!"

Krista was pleased with the restored connection between herself
and Hailey, feeling in step with her in a way she hadn't since the trouble began, and even more so since the Twitch Partnership issue had
reared its ugly head. Added to that, the stream had been going well
so far, with no sign of Chase anywhere in the chat. Krista was beginning to relax and enjoy herself like she hadn't for three full weeks.

Three weeks. How had it all fallen apart in such a short time?

Perhaps today was the turnaround. Everyone seemed to be on
their best behavior, knowing Hailey would shut the broadcast
down at the first sign of a loss of control. They'd be the ones calling
the shots, not Chase, and if he wanted to take over, he'd find the
rug pulled out from under him pretty quickly. Hailey began the
broadcast with the announcement that they expected everyone to
be on their best behavior, and if things got out of hand, viewers
would be banned on their first offense and the broadcast would
end. She finished with a request that if Chase547 returned under
any of his obvious guises, their viewers shouldn't pile on, but rather
leave it up to herself and the mods to take care of it. They appreciated the loyalty of their viewers, but they wanted to get back on

track and asked their viewers to keep their comments to the relevant discussion.

So far, so good. Even running the chat in slow-mo, they were getting good comments.

"Our next question comes from Kengeskahnn, who wants to know if he and his girlfriend are moving too fast. They've only been together for three months, but he's sure she's the one and would like to propose. Is it too soon?" Krista looked up from the message Emily had loaded into the Discord chat. "Kengeskahnn, you don't say how old you and your girlfriend are, but unless there are serious health issues at play, you're taking religious restrictions into account, or you're over seventy-five and you're worried the clock is ticking, yes, I think you're moving too fast. Three months isn't enough time to really know someone, especially if you aren't living together. What's the situation?" She paused to see if kengeskahnn was right there to give her an answer.

> kengeskahnn: Been living together for a month and we're both 20
> SonOfSam1976: you think you can go on like nothing happened? 😠😠😠

The bottom fell out of Krista's stomach. Between the username and the message, she had no doubt that Chase was back.

Time to meet this head on for once and remove all Chase547's oxygen. "Apples, we got this," she said, talking directly to the community on their attempts to silence their intruder. "If we ignore him, he'll eventually go away. Pretend he's not there. Don't make us lose you as a viewer by banning anyone who piles on." *If you can't beat 'em, join 'em.* "The way to beat Chase's ass is for him to be below our notice. He means nothing. Treat him as such." Her voice was deadly calm and ice cold.

This is our line in the sand.

⊘**SonOfSam1976**   now
Banned by RobBot_Tinker

"Kengeskahnn," she continued, her tone back to her usual friendly modulation. "Thanks for the extra information. You're in the early stages of living together, which is great. This is the best way to learn about each other. And you're young. I'd *highly* recommended giving the relationship time. I'd love it if you come back next year or the year after and tell me I was way too cautious and the wedding was last week. The take-home message is you have time. You're committed to living together. Give that some time. When you have, you'll be ready to take that next step."

"Best of luck to you both," Hailey added. "And be sure to pop back occasionally and let us know how it's going for you and your girlfriend."

As Hailey talked, Krista checked out the chat, where Chase continued to make himself known with a new ID. *On the bright side, he won't have long to be concerned about only being able to post once every thirty seconds because he'll be banned after his first statement.*

🍎**JeffreyDahmer1978**: you cant just ignore me

Oh, yeah? Watch me. "We have several viewers in the chat who are all giving similar advice. Diltɪazempɪtch, thanks for sharing your comparable experience. Dilt has been with her partner since they were both eighteen. They're now thirty-two. She says to not rush things, just to get used to the challenges of sharing your daily life with someone without the stress of a legal commitment. They did, and they were married at twenty-four, when it felt right for them, but they lived together for four years before that. Something to think about."

⊘ **JeffreyDahmer1978**   now
Banned by emily_brontesaurus

Behind the scenes, Emily and Rob were staying on top of things. Just the thought of Chase's frustration gave Krista a burst of pleasure. *See how you like it, jackass.*

"Here's a difficult one for you, Ziggy," Hailey said, staring at her screen. "QuoncernedQuokka says she's a married twenty-nine-year-old female. She and her husband always planned to have kids, and she wants to get started because she doesn't want to be in her mid- to late-thirties when they are just beginning their family. But now, her husband has changed his mind and is talking about getting a vasectomy. What should she do?"

Krista felt the emotional blow as if it were an arrow straight to the gut. She knew in her bones Hailey hadn't handed her that question to make her feel bad, but because she knew Krista would have empathy toward this viewer. From one devastated childless woman to another. She wasn't torturing her; she was giving her a chance to outshine Chase and his background rage.

It still hurt like hell.

You can do this.

Krista took a deep breath, stalling for time while she tried to decide how much of herself to put out there. She'd been so careful to not give away too much of herself, but if she was going to, it needed to not be a sympathy play, but an empathetic attempt at connection. "Quoncerned, first of all, I'm sorry you're in this position. Before I give you my opinion, I want to tell you why this hits me so hard. I haven't told you guys too much about myself, but I was engaged. I lost my fiancé a little under two years ago to a brain tumor. We'd planned on having kids." She let her gaze roam around the room, let her sadness and regret show on her face. "In fact, I'm sitting in what was supposed to be the nursery." She brought her gaze back to the webcam. "I understand a little of what you must be feeling. The devastation of being blindsided by circumstances beyond your control. But you have to live with the loss of those plans." Her tone grew thoughtful. "So many plans . . ."

drunkardcranium: 💜 ziggy 🫥
perkinscapreolella: My condolences ziggy
cardloremaster: I can't imagine what you've
gone through. So sad. Hugs... 🫂
Logjammer: That double loss must be so
hard. I'm sorry

Krista snapped back to the question at hand. "But this isn't about me. This is your life, and these are your plans. I've spent time thinking about this as well. If having kids is something we want and the partner we currently have doesn't fit that bill, or, if you're me, isn't here anymore, then you need to make a decision. What takes priority? For me, it's about the memory of a man and a few short years of a blissfully happy life together cut tragically short by cancer versus getting out there and finding a new partner, something I haven't been able to do so far.

"For you, it's going to be about what you see in your future. A childless life with this man, or maybe children with another man, or on your own. Don't ever discount going it alone, because you can do that, either through a sperm bank or through adoption. The one thing you can't do, though, is blame your husband for changing his mind. Maybe he was always on the fence and hid that uncertainty from you. Maybe he changed his mind because something happened to him. Either way, the first thing you need to do is have a full discussion with him about why he's made this decision. And if he's set in it, just as he can't force you to not have children, you can't do the same and force him to have them. Nor would you want to. A man who is forced into having a child he doesn't want won't be a good father. If you're going to do this, you're looking at making a break from your current husband and either finding the right man, if that's the path you want or need to take, or going it alone. If you have family you're close to, you won't be alone. It takes a village to raise a child, and that village can be made up of our own parents, our siblings, our friends. I truly believe you wouldn't be going it alone. But the weight of the decision is now on you. He's partially wrested the choice from you, forcing you to choose between him and a possible child. And while this is a decision you won't want to take years to make, you have a little time at your age. Think about it, listen to your gut, live with the decision to make sure it's the right one, and then set your feet on that path and don't look back. No regrets."

> 🐹💬QuoncernedQuokka: Thank you. So much to think about. Blessings. 🖤
> 🐹JohnWayneGacy1972: ill give you regrets. you fucked this up from the start. want to know how bad? go to rosehill, section 101, ferdinand siegel mawzoliam. i left you something 🪦 😈

Krista couldn't breathe, certainly couldn't speak. *Rosehill. Section 101. Could it be true?*

She grabbed her mouse and opened a browser, ignoring the fact she was still on camera. She opened the Find a Grave website and entered the name Ferdinand Siegel, with Chicago as the location and hit search. And got a single hit.

The lines shifting in the Mod Action panel distracted her for only an instant as JohnWayneGacy1972 was banned before her gaze snapped back to the search results: Rosehill Cemetery and Mausoleum, Chicago, Cook County, Illinois, USA.

It was the worst of her fears realized.

Chase was right there in Chicago.

Chapter 17

HAILEY ENDED THE BROADCAST IMMEDIATELY after Chase left his clue. She hadn't gone to the extent of searching for the grave site as Krista had, but had jumped to the conclusion Krista had arrived at, only after hoping to prove she was making an incorrect assumption.

No such luck.

Hailey shut it all down—Twitch, OBS broadcasting software, Discord—and called her cell seconds later in full panic mode, which was exactly how Krista felt, too. Hailey didn't even bother with a salutation. "What do we do? Do we go find it? Whatever *it* is?"

"In a cemetery at night? In the dark? No chance in hell."

"Do we call Miller, then, or would that be sending him on a wild-goose chase?"

"It might be." Krista lunged out of her chair and bulleted out of her studio, slamming the side of her fist on the light switch to darken the room, then pulling the door shut behind her, as if she could entomb everything that had happened behind a closed door forever. She strode to the couch and then collapsed down on it, drained, her nerves frayed. "I think we have to call him. It may be nothing, but he said to let him know about anything new. This qualifies. I mean, what else are we going to do? Go off half-cocked and look for ourselves in a nearly two-hundred-year-old cemetery in the dark? That's the kind of things dumb girls in horror movies do just before they get killed. No, thank you. I'll call him."

Silence hummed for a moment before Hailey broke it. "What are the chances Rosehill is a coincidence?" Her voice was a half whisper.

"In my opinion? Zero. Somehow this guy knows we're here in Chicago. And if he's really killed someone . . ." Krista let her voice trail off, not wanting to actually say the words out loud.

"He might try for us."

There it was. The real risk they were facing. Were their lives on the line?

"I don't know. Maybe. We have no idea what he knows. Maybe all he knows is we live in town. He'd have to find us in nearly three million people. There's safety in numbers. Or he knows more and we're truly in danger. At this point, I think we have to assume we might be targets."

"God, Zig, I'm so sorry." Hailey sounded beaten down. "When I suggested we do this, I never imagined anything like this would happen."

"I know. You'd never have knowingly put either of us at risk." Krista dragged herself up to a sitting position. "It is what it is. We just have to deal with it. I'm going to call him now."

"Let me know if you hear anything. I'm going to call Aiden and then find some tequila to help take the edge off."

"Just don't take so much edge off, you spend the night puking and then are nursing a massive hangover tomorrow."

"You take the fun out of everything." A little of Hailey's normal humor snuck back into her tone. "Night."

"Night." Krista ended the call, then pulled up her contacts and called Miller, drumming her fingers on the couch cushion beside her as it rang once. Twice.

"Detective Simon Miller, CPD."

"Detective Miller, it's Krista Evans. You asked us to call if there was anything new. I think we have something."

"You had a show tonight?"

"Yes."

"Chase547 was back?"

"Oh, yeah. Not under that name. He came instead as Son of Sam, Jeffrey Dahmer, and John Wayne Gacy, but it was definitely him."

"Subtle."

"Not even a little bit."

"What did he say?"

"It's not so much what he said, but what he apparently did. And where. He told us he left us a clue to prove he killed that woman. At Rosehill Cemetery and Mausoleum, section 101. At the Ferdinand Siegel mausoleum." She dropped her head, squeezing the tight muscles at the back of her neck with her free hand. "He's here."

"He said that on the stream?"

"In the chat."

"Just as bad. If there's anyone local, they may try for it. We don't know if it's real, but if it is, we could lose it."

"Isn't the cemetery closed?"

"That won't stop anyone who really wants in. I'm going to check it out. Thanks for letting me know." Then Miller was gone.

Krista dropped her phone into her lap, all movement seeming overwhelming right now.

She'd been holding on to hope that Chase was somewhere across the planet, but now it was clear he was much closer. It would need to be all precautions, at all times, from now on.

She wasn't sure how long she sat unmoving, but finally she forced herself to stand and move to the kitchen to put on the kettle. Back to the couch to turn on the TV, queue up the next episode of *Friends,* and crank the volume, just so she didn't feel so alone. She wandered into the bedroom, set her alarm for the next morning, then returned to the kitchen and made her tea. As it steeped, she fussed with the mail she hadn't opened yet and organized two bills that still needed paying.

Then she sat in front of the TV simply for company, staring blankly at the screen and not really following the episode.

She missed Linc desperately. If he were here, she'd be able to draw from his strength, his determination. She'd have someone standing behind her, no matter what. But Linc was gone, and she needed to stand on her own two feet. She could do it—she'd always been independent—but tonight she was feeling both his loss and her loneliness more intensely than usual.

She picked up her phone, idly scrolling her notifications as the episode played. She tapped a Twitch notification for a stream Hailey has suggested for her, and the Twitch app opened. Her gaze was drawn to the notification of an unread whisper, Twitch's version of the private message.

From Logjammer?

Logjammer. The guy Hailey went to college with. The one she trusted as a substitute mod, if needed. *Not a threat.*

She opened the notification.

Went to Rosehill. Found the item. Meet me?

Her heart hammered against her breastbone so loudly, she swore she could hear it outside her own body. Miller had called it—one of their viewers had gone to Rosehill Cemetery, found whatever Chase had left, and wanted to give it to her.

Think this through. You just learned tonight Chase is local. What if this *is Chase?*

She picked up her phone and sent a return whisper. **You understand meeting a stranger after someone on the channel threatened murder would be insane.**

He must have been waiting for her reply, because his answer came seconds later. **Not really a stranger. I've known Hailey for years. Since Northwestern**

She hadn't offered Hailey's real name, and their community knew her as Mortie. He was reinforcing what Hailey herself had said earlier, confirming a friendship with her partner.

You're her friend. Did you tell her about this? Krista queried.

I messaged her. No response. That's why I contacted you

Hailey had possibly been drinking for over an hour, which might explain why she was ignoring her phone.

Logjammer continued to text. **I assumed you'd want to know right away**

She certainly did. More than that, she was tired of being inactive. This was the time to be—safely—proactive. She checked the time in her system tray: 10:22. She'd get all the details and then let Miller know. He could meet them there, ensuring her safety. But she wasn't going to sit this one out. **I do. You're in town. Can we meet at the Bourgeois Pig Café? They're open until midnight.**

Yes

I'll be there at 11.

See you then. Red sweatshirt, navy UIC vest, Flames ball cap

Krista redialed Miller, but it rang four times and then switched to voicemail. "You've reached Detective Simon Miller of the Chicago Police Department. Please leave a message, including your full name, phone number, and the reason for your call." *Beep.*

He may still be at the cemetery with his phone on silent, in case the "item" is a trap and Chase is lying in wait.

"Detective Miller, it's Krista Evans again." She could hear that she was speaking so quickly, she was nearly tripping over her own words, and forced herself to slow down. "I just got a call from one of our channel followers. He went to Rosehill and got whatever the item is. We're going to meet at the Bourgeois Pig at eleven o'clock tonight. If you get this message in time, please meet with us. Otherwise, please give me a call and I'll update you. Thanks." She ended the call.

The fact Krista couldn't get Miller gave her pause. The coffee shop would have staff and patrons on a Friday night, but what if she was jumped on her way into the shop? What if Logjammer had been followed from the cemetery and Chase was outside watching him wait for her?

She skipped sending a text and called Hailey directly, but the phone rang four times, then flipped to voicemail. She was either deep into the tequila or she was ignoring her phone. Either way, she was going to be no help to Krista tonight.

But she knew someone who could be.

Krista placed a call to her brother, waiting as it rang twice before he picked up.

"Hey." A laugh sounded behind him, mixed with other male voices in the background.

She winced, knowing she was interrupting his evening. "Hey. What are you doing?"

"Shooting the shit with Chuck and the guys."

"The guys?"

"You know, the fantasy football guys. Neil, Harv, Barty, Doug, Tim, JC, and Steve. But you didn't call to catch up on my social life. What's up?"

She hated to ruin his evening, but there was no help for it. She cut to the chase. "I need your help. Now."

"With what?"

"I need you to go somewhere with me tonight. I have to meet someone, and it's not a good idea for me to do it alone."

"This all sounds extremely cryptic. Is he tall, dark, and mysterious?"

"I have no idea. Zach, this is no joke. Something happened on the stream tonight. Something bad. Will you come? I'll explain in the car."

"Where and when?" All trace of laughter was gone now.

"The Bourgeois Pig at eleven. Have you been drinking?"

"I've had a couple of beers. I wasn't planning on going home for hours."

"I'll pick you up. Where are you?" She pulled up her map app and typed in the address as he rattled it off to her. "I can be there in fifteen. We'll just make it. I'll text you when I'm in the driveway."

"See you then."

Fifteen minutes later, Krista pulled her SUV up across the bottom of the full driveway and texted Zach of her arrival. Even knowing he was coming, she still jumped when her passenger door opened.

Zach slid in and slammed the door behind him, then simply stared at her.

"What?"

"You're okay?"

"For now."

"What the hell is going on?"

She stared through the windshield for a moment before she shifted into drive and pulled away from the driveway. "Let me fill you in on what's been going on since the last time we talked about this." As they drove through the quiet suburban streets and then into the major arteries, still well-traveled roads despite the time of night, she laid out everything that had happened since she'd told him, nearly a week before, about Chase547's announcement of a murdered woman.

Zach stayed quiet, holding his questions until she'd talked herself out. "I'm glad you called me. With Miller out of touch, I wouldn't want you going out to meet this Logjammer guy on your own. Any idea what Chase left for you?"

"Logjammer didn't say. Obviously, it's something that can be brought into a coffee shop."

"So . . . not a body."

Krista didn't say anything, but she felt the heavy weight of Zach's stare.

"You thought of that yourself," he stated.

She made a right-hand turn onto Ashland Avenue. "No body has been identified, so . . . yeah. As soon as he said to go to a cemetery, it's what came to mind."

"What are you going to do with the clue?"

"Hopefully, nothing, because Detective Miller will meet us there." She glanced at her brother. A tall man, his head nearly brushing the roof of the SUV, Zach's face was cast in shadows as he stared out the windshield, his features strobed by each passing streetlight. "We've tied his hands on this up to now—"

"You didn't tie his hands. This son of a bitch did."

"You're angry."

"You're damned right I'm angry. This guy is putting you through hell. It pisses me off." He turned to face her. "And while I'm glad you knew you could come to me when you needed help, you know I'm annoyed you didn't loop me in sooner."

"I know." Her tone lacked defensiveness; she'd screwed up and she knew it. "I had myself convinced it was something none of us could deal with. The cops felt the same way, since Chase could have been from anywhere."

"Welcome to the internet," Zach mumbled.

"Totally."

"Must have been a hell of a shock tonight to find out he was local."

"That's putting it lightly. That's when we knew we were potentially in real trouble. And then the item—whatever it is—turned out to be real." She was silent for a few seconds, then put her deepest fear into words. "I think someone died. I think she died because I couldn't talk Chase out of killing her—"

"Bullshit."

"What?"

"You taking responsibility for this is bullshit. Just calling a spade a spade. Bull. Shit."

"But he came to me for advice."

"My clients come to me for advice. I design a bridge, make sure it's structurally sound. Then let's say the developer decides to add his own flair to the design so it looks prettier, but now it's not as sound. Is that my fault?"

"Of course not. You didn't specify those changes. Certainly didn't approve them."

"You didn't tell him to kill an innocent woman." His hand came down lightly on her shoulder. "Think about it. You did what you could to protect a woman you didn't know actually existed. You even went to the police, and they told you there was nothing to be done with what you had, and the guy could have just been yanking your chain. You are *not* responsible."

She flashed him a sideways smile that only tipped one side of her lips. "Thanks. Hailey said the same thing. You want to keep reminding me if I forget?"

"No problem. Because you're stuck with me at this point. Think of me as glue."

"You can't stick with me for every minute of every day while we're figuring this out."

"Maybe not, but I can be around a lot more than I have been." He sat quietly for a moment, watching the lights of Chicago stream by, then said, "You should tell the parox."

"Oh, yeah, I'll call them and say, 'Hey, Mom. Hey, Dad. I have a stalker who found me on the internet, killed a woman, and might be coming for me next. Anyhoo, how did your pickleball tournament go?' That's not going to set off anyone's alarm bells. Not a chance."

"Of course, it's going to. But do you know how hurt they'd be if you didn't at least let them know what's going on? At the same time, you're going to let them know I'm all over this, so there's no need for them to run out here."

"Like that's going to work on Dad."

"It might not, but I can talk to them, too. And I'll tell them, if you're at risk, more loved ones in the area could be a target for this guy."

Krista's hands jerked momentarily on the wheel, but she quickly corrected before they hit the curb. "Jesus, Zach. What was I thinking? If you're right, I should never have called you."

"Yes, you should have. My eyes are wide open. Besides, pretty sure I could outrun the fucker."

"We should start a swear jar for you. Normally, you never swear like this. I could make millions."

"As I said, I'm pissed off."

"Clearly. We're going to be arriving just in time."

"How are we going to know we have the right guy?"

"He's going to know me from all those Twitch broadcasts, so us knowing him isn't as important. He told me he was wearing a red sweatshirt, a navy University of Illinois Chicago vest, and a Flames ball cap."

"Hometown boy showing hometown pride."

"Does that make you feel better?"

"Better than if he was wearing a Redbirds cap."

"Goes without saying."

"Does Miller know what he's wearing?"

"No, but he knows me. It'll be fine."

They were quiet for the rest of the ride. Krista found street parking, just a half block away, on the far side of West Fullerton Parkway, pulled in, and cut the engine. "Ready?"

"You bet." Zach opened the door, but stopped and looked back when Krista laid her hand on his arm. "Are you?"

"Yeah. I just wanted to say thanks. For giving up your evening, for letting me unload all of this on you, for coming with me tonight."

"Like I said . . . glue." He gave her a reassuring smile. "Let's do this."

They walked back to the coffee shop. Located in a refurbished nineteenth-century brick house, they walked past both a verdigris pig and a raised metal model of the Eiffel Tower at the sidewalk, then up the front walkway and steps. Zach moved ahead, held open the door, and let Krista precede him, but then he followed so closely when she paused just inside the door, he only barely managed to stop himself from crashing into her.

The café was all warm cream walls, mellow taupe brick, and vintage tin signage, set off by dark wood counters and shelving. Three massive framed blackboards high on the wall behind the counter displayed the extensive menu. Even at eleven o'clock at night, there was a line waiting to order. They both scanned the wooden tables at the front of the café, instantly spotting a man facing into the shop. He was wearing a red sweatshirt, navy vest, and matching navy baseball cap.

"I got him," Zach murmured.

"Me too. And he has us. Or rather, me. No Miller yet, though."

"Give him time. He's not going to ignore your call."

When Krista took one step toward the front of the café, Zach grabbed her arm. "We're not splitting up. Let's blend in. We'll place an order, grab our stuff, and then go over. He already has a coffee. It will just look like friends meeting for a late-night drink."

"You think we're being watched?"

"I have no idea. Let's not take chances. If we don't stand out, no one will even notice we're here."

They were fourth in line, and they slowly shuffled forward. When they got to the front, Krista ordered a decaf cocomocha and Zach a caffe miel.

When Zach pulled out his wallet, she swatted his hand away. "You come out here for me, I pay."

He acknowledged the offer with a tilt of his head and slid his wallet into his pocket.

When their drinks were ready, they picked them up and made their way to the front of the shop, Krista leading the way. She pulled out the chair across from the man, while Zach took the chair to her left.

"Krista." The man held out his hand. "Dan Cumberland, better known as Logjammer."

"You know my real name."

"As I said, I've known Hailey since Northwestern. I knew you were her roommate, but we never met back then. Hailey and I graduated in the same class, then stayed in touch over the years. When she started her gaming channel, I was one of her first followers, and then I came over to *A Word from the Wise*." His gaze shot sideways to Zach, then back to Krista. "I thought you might bring Hailey."

"Just like you, I couldn't get in touch with her, and didn't have time to drive over there to pound on her door."

"She brought me, instead." Zach stuck out a hand. "I'm Zach, her brother."

The men shook. "Good to meet you," said Dan. "Good idea, you coming along. Considering..."

"Krista has brought me up to date. You went to Rosehill tonight?"

"Yes. I didn't know if you'd be doing the same thing, so I actually left you a note on the mausoleum steps saying I had the item and would contact you, in case you came."

Krista looked at her brother. "Miller will find the note."

"Could still be checking the place out, though," Zach said. "Chase could still be there, waiting for you, not someone else from your channel."

Logjammer's brows drew together. "You think it was a trap for you?"

Krista shrugged. "I have to consider it. But he had to know putting it out on the stream, publicly like that, anyone could have gone for it. How did you get in? Wasn't it closed for the night?"

"Parked about two blocks away so my truck wasn't right there, walked to a spot on North Ravenswood, where the perimeter was hidden behind a bunch of trees and bushes, and climbed the fence. The grounds were dark, but there was enough moonlight to get by. I'd looked the grave up on Find a Grave, which gave me a map link to where I needed to go. I found the mausoleum." He took a sip of his coffee as his eyes scanned the café around them, and then he dug into the front pocket of his jeans. He pulled out something wrapped in a tissue. "This was attached to one of the wrought-iron bars of the front gates of the mausoleum." He extended his fist, waiting until Krista extended her hand, palm up, and then he placed the tissue in her palm. "I couldn't be totally hands-off with it, but I tried to be as much as possible. In case there are fingerprints."

The tissue and its contents were warm from being in Dan's pocket. Krista balanced the tissue flat in her palm and carefully pulled back the corners to reveal what lay inside—a piece of silver jewelry. She shook her hand gently to spread it out, then pulled it closer, holding her hand toward Zach so he could also see it.

The bracelet was comprised of an oval medallion on a silver Figaro chain, with a run of small rings followed by a larger oval in series. The medallion had an embossed caduceus—the universal symbol of medicine, with a snake coiling around a staff—flanked by the words "Medic" and "Alert." Slipping her index finger under the tissue, she flipped it over to find the words "TYPE 1 DIABETIC, INSULIN DEPENDENT," a hotline phone number, and a long string of numbers engraved on the back.

Zach whistled. "That's not just a bracelet. That's a bracelet with a registered ID." He met Krista's eyes. "It could identify the owner. Not only who they are, but full contact information."

"That's what I thought," said Dan. "It's why I didn't want to sit on this until even tomorrow. When it was hanging on the bars, I could see from the light of my cell phone flashlight it was a Medic-Alert bracelet. I had to use my fingers to open the clasp, but that's all I touched. I had a clean tissue in my pocket, so I let it fall into that. Haven't touched it since." He met Krista's eyes. "Maybe he left fingerprints."

"Definitely worth a shot, but we'd have to be pretty lucky for that to pan out."

"In this day and age, everyone knows how to wipe down an object for prints," Zach said. "Or to wear gloves so there aren't any in the first place. After all, he'd just admitted to murder. But why didn't you call the cops? You possibly have evidence to a murder."

"At first, it was straight-up curiosity that drove me. Here was this guy, causing chaos, being disruptive, claiming he'd committed a murder. I thought he was just shit disturbing, for the shock factor." His gaze dropped to the bracelet, his lips going tight. "Now I'm not so sure." His gaze rose again. "I didn't want to be connected to it. You know what cops are like—they'll be suspicious of anyone involving themselves in a case. And I'd just involved myself."

"I have a cop on his way here," Krista said. "There's no escaping your involvement."

"Yeah, I know. I needed to calm down enough to think. It was too late, the moment I went to the cemetery. And now my fingerprints are on the clasp."

Krista scanned the café once more—still, no Miller. "Before we go tonight, I need you to give me your full contact information," Krista said. "I can pass it on to Detective Miller, and he'll be able to get your prints to discount them when they analyze any fingerprints on the bracelet." She wrapped the corners of the tissue over the bracelet and slipped it into a side pocket in her bag, securely zipping it shut. "Obviously, you were in the chat tonight?"

"Yes. I've been in the chat every night since Chase547 appeared. He's the bringer of chaos. Or at least he was until tonight, when you froze him out." His eyes sparkled and he grinned his approval. "It was magnificent." His smile faded. "Well, until he lost it and taunted you with the bracelet."

"Yeah, that." She patted her purse, over the small lump of the wrapped bracelet.

As soon as she and Zach left the café, she'd call Detective Miller again. If he was amenable, she'd wait up for him to come and retrieve the evidence. Maybe they could match the number on the bracelet with an actual person.

Then, finally, they'd be able to find out if the murder was real.

Chapter 18

KRISTA'S CELL PHONE RANG QUIETLY from inside the side pocket of her yoga pants just as she was saying goodbye to her last client before her lunch break. "Great session today, Mr. Steahern. Just keep working on those exercises I gave you to continue to strengthen your left side. Before you know it, we're going to have you back to where you were pre-stroke!"

She watched him make his way down the hall, using a cane to compensate for his left-side weakness, as he cheerily greeted Melanie. Such a nice man, so determined to use every tool available to him to regain as much of his normal life as possible. She wasn't going to get him trained for a marathon, but her aim was to actually get him in better muscular strength than he'd been in before the stroke, to avoid issues around falls and for improved general independence in his own home. Their progress pleased her. His determination to succeed certainly did a lot of the heavy lifting for both of them.

She pulled out her phone to check her missed call. And froze when she saw it was Detective Miller.

Had he identified the owner of the bracelet?

On the way home after dropping Zach off at his car on Friday night, she'd made contact with Miller from her car and he'd arrived at her apartment only about ten minutes after she returned.

Miller had sat with her while she told him about the last few broadcasts of *A Word from the Wise*, her private message from Logjammer, meeting him at the café, and getting the tissue-wrapped bracelet. He'd donned a pair of nitrile gloves he pulled from a pocket and examined the bracelet before slipping it into an evidence bag and taking pictures of the details on the back of the medallion. He left with Dan's information and a promise to let her know just as soon as he had any new details. He hoped it wouldn't be long, as MedicAlert often worked with 911 operators to identify individuals. The only difference in this case was the individual was possibly already deceased.

Her hands trembled slightly as she returned Miller's call, waiting as the phone rang several times before it was picked up.

"Detective Miller."

"Detective, it's Krista Evans. I'm sorry I missed your call. I was finishing with a client. Did you find out anything about the identity of the person who owned the bracelet?"

"I did. I'd like to meet with you and your partner about this. What time are you done work?"

"I'm off at five tonight. Same for Hailey."

"Can I meet you at your place at five-thirty? Does that give you enough time to get home?"

"Yes. I can call Hailey and ask her to meet us there."

"That would be great. See you then." Then he was gone.

The call was short and ended a little abruptly, but Krista could only imagine in a city with a not-insignificant murder rate, the man must always have multiple cases on the go. She was grateful he'd cleared some time for her tonight.

She texted Hailey to tell her about the meet. Hailey texted back immediately, saying she'd be there.

Krista hesitated for a moment, torn, then decided to shoot a text to Zach, just to keep him in the loop. He had, after all, dropped everything for her on Friday night. Cutting him out now wouldn't be fair.

When his immediate answer was he'd be there before five-thirty himself, she really shouldn't have been surprised. He, too, wanted to know if she was legitimately threatened.

Chase's words as Hunter68 rang in her head . . .

youll never get rid of me.

you can try.

youll fail.

maybe youll be next.

She jammed her phone into her pocket and strode out of the treatment room and toward their staff room, tucked behind the records room. She needed her jacket and she needed some air. She'd take a walk in a well-trafficked area for safety while she tried to clear her head during her break.

The idea of lunch was a thing of the past, her appetite wiped clean by the thought of what could be waiting for her tonight.

Chapter 19

Krista jumped at the knock on the door.

"You seem a bit twitchy. Want me to get that?" Zach asked from where he leaned against the kitchen counter, nursing a mug of coffee.

"Of course, *he's* not twitchy," Krista muttered to Hailey from where they sat, side by side, on the couch.

"He hasn't been directly involved with the situation from the start, like you and I. Though it was nice of him to come."

"Yeah, it was." Krista looked over her shoulder at Zach. "Yes, please."

Zach put his mug down on the counter and strode down the short foyer to the front door, where his voice carried back to the living room. "Come in. Zach Evans, Krista's brother."

"Detective Simon Miller, CPD Homicide."

"Krista and Hailey are eager to talk to you."

Eager. Krista wasn't sure she'd put that kind of positive spin on it. She stood as Miller stepped into the living room. "Detective, thank you for coming to see us. Can I get you a cup of coffee?"

"No, thanks." Miller took the chair as Zach swung around behind him, grabbed his mug, and came to perch on the arm of the couch beside Krista. Miller glanced up at him, then continued, his gaze shifting between the women. "First of all, I want to thank

you for being so proactive about this case. You brought your original concerns to me, so we knew someone might be in trouble, but
it just wasn't enough at the time. And we didn't know if it was a
local crime. But this bracelet . . . It's helped a stalled investigation."

"You identified her?"

"Yes."

"She's dead? Murdered?"

"Yes."

Hailey dropped her face into her hands and murmured, "Jesus
Christ."

Krista couldn't find any words. Even though she'd felt all along
this was coming, being confronted with the reality of it still managed to take her breath away.

Zach filled the void. "Can you tell us who she was and the circumstances of her death?"

"Next of kin was identified, so yes, I can. Her name was Shanna
Garner. She was twenty-eight and worked as a bartender at the
Crooked Barman on North Clark. Her body was found in the
North Branch of the Chicago River, two weeks ago. She'd been in
the river for a few hours at that point."

"She drowned?" Krista finally had her voice back.

"No. She was stabbed, and her throat was cut." Miller's tone was
matter-of-fact, a cop reciting case details as information, not as
nightmare fuel.

It occurred to Krista this could be a strategy he used to distance
himself from the horrors he must face daily. For her, there was no
way to leave the horror out of the image he sketched with so few
words, and she physically drew away from Miller in response.

"I heard about that death," Zach said. "It was in the *Tribune.*"

Krista turned to look up at him.

"I didn't say anything about it," he explained. "Murders aren't
uncommon, and I certainly had no idea that one story would have
any significance. Also, at the time, there wasn't even a confirmed
victim."

"She went into the water with no purse and no valuables. The initial assumption was she was killed for whatever she carried on her at the time. It took a full day for her to be reported missing and for the dots to be connected."

"That's a pretty violent death just for someone's purse."

"That crossed my mind as well, but at the time, we didn't have anything more to go on, and no one seemed to have any animus toward her. But now . . ."

"Now there's every indication she was stalked," Hailey said. "And all that knife work makes sense."

Krista laid her hand over Hailey's forearm and squeezed as she stared into her friend's face. She'd gone pale with undertones of both gray and green. "You don't look good." She laid the back of her fingers against Hailey's forehead. "You're clammy." *A little shocky. Can't really blame her.*

Hailey's distress helped center Krista, allowing some of the impact of Miller's announcement to fall away as she focused her attention on her friend. It gave her the space to take a breath and think logically, to push some of the horror into the background. It would roar back as soon as she let her guard down, but for now, it split her attention and kept her balanced.

"I'll get her some water." Zach stood and headed for the kitchen, and returned shortly with a glass of cold water. He circled the couch from the other end, crouched down in front of Hailey, and held the glass until she wrapped both hands around it and he was sure she wasn't going to fumble it.

She took several sips of water, then gave them a wan smile. "Sorry. Not used to all this talk of death and violence."

Krista reached across Hailey, grabbed Balto from where he lay tucked against the far arm, and placed him in Hailey's lap. "Don't laugh. Balto's helped me through some bleak times." As Hailey's hands grasped the stuffed dog, Krista rubbed a hand up and down her back. "I guess I have an unfair advantage there over you." Krista turned to Miller. "My fiancé died two years ago of a glioma. Brain cancer. Unfortunately, I'm a little more familiar with death."

"I'm very sorry for your loss. Not something you want to get used to. And you don't really get used to it; you might just have a better coping mechanism in place at this point. Let me tell you, even after all these years in Homicide, no death is commonplace. The day you don't feel anything when you're standing over a body is the day you leave the force."

"Scary thought," said Zach.

"Tell me about it."

"So, where are we?" Krista appreciated Miller's attempt to gentle this blow, but the need for information beat like a tattoo inside her head, demolishing her patience.

"We have a body inside our jurisdiction connected via the bracelet found at Rosehill Cemetery to an individual contacting you through your channel's Twitch chat," said Miller. "The homicide case was originally Detective Jansen's, but once we connected the cases, it was clear I'd been working the case almost as long as he had, but I had more promising information, so I became primary. Everything you previously told me has been entered into the records for this case. The bracelet was enough to get a warrant, so that was sent to Twitch first thing this morning, along with the list of usernames you provided."

"Unless he's an idiot," Hailey said, now looking a little more alert, "and I don't think he is, it's not going to be simple to track him. He's going to be using a VPN, more likely multiple VPNs to VPN chain, funneling his signal through different servers in different locations, possibly in different countries. He'll use the Tor Browser to ensure the signal is end-to-end encrypted. And he's probably using disposable email addresses to get all those usernames, too."

"A disposable email address? Like he gets a free email address and then deletes the account afterward?" Zach asked.

"No, it's an actual service that makes up email addresses and provides a server for it so you can use it to make any number of kinds of accounts—free trials of Netflix or Amazon Prime, for instance. Keep making up free, temp email addresses, keep enrolling in new free trials, and you can get away with never paying for these products. In this case, he's not using this service to scam streaming platforms—he's using it to make as many Twitch IDs as he wants. The address is live for the initial onboarding email from Twitch to verify the person making the account is the legit owner of it, and then after that email is verified, the entire account is shredded, leaving no trace. Then all that's needed is the typed email address and the password you used for it, and Twitch is never the wiser. From our perspective, there's no way to trace it, because the hosting server no longer has a record of it. It's anonymous and clean. That's why people use it. It's called a throwaway email service for a reason."

"So, then, this guy basically has a table of all the fake emails and their associated passwords to use on Twitch?" Zach asked. "Then as you block him on one user ID, he just logs out, logs in with the next, and keeps going."

Hailey nodded. "That would be my guess."

"That whole process would take seconds. No wonder you never managed to lose him."

All this talk about tech left Krista feeling itchy. A woman had died and they were focusing on the man who killed her, almost as if they were in awe of his skills or how he was ingeniously outsmarting them. Time to steer the conversation back to the person who really mattered—the woman whose future he'd stolen. "We know from what Chase said he'd been trying to get this woman's attention and had been unsuccessful. Did anyone in her life give you a lead on that?"

"When her body was initially identified, Detective Jansen interviewed her family, friends, and coworkers," said Miller. "But the information that came from you put an entirely different spin on things. I went to the Crooked Barman and talked to the owner, one of the other bartenders, and the waitstaff they had on hand. I'm going to talk to everyone else tomorrow. What I heard was, there wasn't any one guy who was bothering her. The other bartender is also a woman, and she said guys being a little pushy happens all the time. They try to strike up a conversation and take up their time. She's had guys bring her gifts and try to get her to go out on dates, and she knows Shanna faced the same pressures. Shanna occasionally commented about one particular guy, an older guy, who liked to hang out at one end of the bar, nursing a drink and always watching her, but he was never pushy, never in her face. More like he just pined after her. I got his name from the owner and I'll be talking to him. The owner, by the way, thinks he's just shy and kind of weird, maybe a little lonely, but not a threat."

"Not a threat to the owner, maybe, but don't they always say it's the quiet ones?" Hailey murmured.

"It can be. I'm going to follow up with the rest of the staff tomorrow, but so far, nothing jumps out."

"What about security cameras?" asked Zach. "A lot of those places have cameras to prevent theft, either from employees or patrons."

"I asked about that. They have security cameras with footage going back four weeks, but anything older than that is lost. They don't review it on a regular basis—only if something happens. It's not been looked at, as they haven't had any incidents, but I'm going to go over everything they have." Miller slapped his hands on his thighs and looked ready to rise. "Thanks for your time tonight. I just wanted to make sure you heard about this from me."

"Is there anything we can do for the family?" Krista asked. "I know it's stupid, but I feel responsible. Maybe if we'd moved faster or dealt with him differently, we could have stopped him."

"There was nothing you could have done to change this outcome." Miller ducked his head a bit to get down to her level as she slumped on the couch. He leaned in toward her, making eye contact. "You brought us all the information when you could. You held nothing back. He purposely didn't give you anything substantial to work with."

"What happens if he comes back? Our next stream is tomorrow. He left the bracelet, so he knows he's tied himself to the murdered woman. Is this when he disappears?"

"Possibly. You'll need to be prepared for anything." Miller's gaze shifted to Hailey and back again. "I'll be joining you tomorrow night."

Hailey perked up at that, her eyes brightening. "You will?"

"Yes. I made an account earlier today and have already followed your channel. If you see me, I'm BowStreetPeel."

"Bow Street? Like the Bow Street Runners in London?"

"Exactly like that. Robert Peel is the guy who turned the Bow Street Runners into the Metropolitan Police. That's why London cops are called 'bobbies,' after Robert Peel. I'll be there, watching, though it's unlikely I'll join in. Specialty sites have their own rhythm and lingo. If I tried to chime in, I'd likely give myself away as a newbie."

"A noob," Hailey muttered automatically.

"What?"

Hailey colored slightly. "Sorry. Knee-jerk reaction. Beginner gamers are called noobs."

"You're illustrating my point for me. I'd give myself away as a noob, so unless there's a real need for me, I'll stay in the background. Eight o'clock?"

"Yes."

"Do you want access to the chat?" Hailey asked. "I'm going to have it locked down even more tomorrow. If there's a real need for you, you won't be able to talk with your current restrictions." She turned to Krista. "What about if we make Detective Miller a mod? That way, he'll have full access." She met Miller's eyes. "If we make you a moderator, you have to promise not to mess with the channel."

Miller held up both hands defensively. "I wouldn't know how to. Is that going to be the only way to get me in?"

"I've restricted the chat to people who have followed the chan-nel for more than three months and who also have a subscription to the channel already. No new subscriptions to get around the restriction. We're trying to limit Chase from coming back, but that will also limit you. If I make you a mod, you get around those restrictions. As long as you don't go into Mod View, you'll be fine."

"Since I don't know what that is, or how to do that, you'll be fine. Can I ask a question about the restrictions?"

"Sure."

"Are subscriptions something you pay for? Or are they free if you've watched for a certain period of time?"

"They're paid for. By someone."

"Meaning?"

"Meaning you can gift subscriptions so the recipient doesn't pay for it."

"But someone does."

"Yes."

Miller rubbed his chin, his gaze fixed unseeingly on the slats of the hardwood floor. "Can you limit the restriction so that new subscriptions are allowed, but gift subscriptions are not? That way, whoever buys the subscription uses it to gain access to your broadcast?"

Hailey blinked at him twice, her confusion evident. "Yes. Why would I do that?"

"So the purchases can be traced," said Zach. "This is all online, right? They have to use credit or debit cards? Something that can be traced?"

Hailey's back shot straight as it all came together in her head. "That's right. If someone gets blocked and can't have access, but really wants to, they can buy their way in."

Miller leveled an index finger at her. "That's it. And then there's something for us to trace from those interactions."

"I can set that up. I'm not sure it will lead anywhere, but I can do it."

"Every opportunity, no matter how small, still counts." Miller pushed to his feet. "I'll see you tomorrow, not the other way around. If anything comes up or if you have any concerns, I want you to contact me." He reached into his jacket pocket and pulled out a business card, which he handed to Zach. "Since you don't have one. Reach out anytime." His gaze touched on each of them. "I want you two to be careful, to take extra precautions. We don't know if he lives in Chicago, but it appears he's relatively local. If he has any idea of your real identities, he may be following you in person or online. If he watched the mausoleum at Rosehill, he might have followed Logjammer to the café and saw the two of you in person." He met Zach's eyes. "That means you could also be in jeopardy now. Be aware of your surroundings at all times. Try not to be alone and unprotected while you're moving from place to place. Once you're home, make sure all your doors and windows are locked. If you have any concerns, call me, day or night. I can have a patrol car come to you in minutes, wherever you are in the city. This guy, he's . . ." Miller paused, as if searching for the correct word.

That even the seasoned cop was having trouble putting his concerns into words scared the hell out of Krista.

"Brutal," Miller finished. "Don't let yourself be caught by him." He picked up his coat. "Now lock the door behind me."

When Krista returned to the living room after seeing Miller out, both Zach and Hailey were standing.

"I'm going to head home." Hailey stood stiffly, her shoulders hunched, her lips pinched, subtly telegraphing her distress through her miserable body language.

"You okay?"

"No. I think I need some time to process all this." She rubbed fingers over her forehead as if trying to exorcise the pain that pounded there. "She's actually dead."

"You were holding out hope she wasn't?"

Hailey flushed, blood rushing some needed color into her un-naturally pale complexion. "Yeah. I was hoping he was full of shit and trying to crank us." Her laugh was ragged. "No such luck." She drew in a shaky breath. "At this point, I just want to go home, lock all my doors and windows, and try not to think about it. Tomorrow is soon enough for that." She gave Krista a tight hug, unknowingly revealing the tremor running through her. "You're doing the stiff upper lip thing, but this has to be bothering you as well."

"It is. I'm like you—still processing. Zach, will you walk Hailey out to her car? I don't want her doing that alone."

"Are you okay being alone?"

"Pretty used to it at this point." She gave him a sad half smile. "I'll be fine. Give me a call or shoot me a text later tonight if you want to check in. But not too late. I think I'm with Hailey and I'll want to turn in early." She matched her frown with a shrug. "All this tragedy is exhausting."

He stared at her for a moment, as if torn by his responsibilities. "If you're sure."

"I'm sure."

"I want to hear the dead bolt lock behind us when we go." He moved to the balcony door, made sure it was locked, and pulled the long oyster-colored curtains closed, shutting out the courtyard lights. "You're set. Hailey, let me walk you out to your car."

Krista walked them to the front door, then held the door for Hailey. As Zach went past, she gripped his forearm. "You be careful, too."

"I'm always careful."

He started to pull away, but she held on. "No, I mean *careful*. Not 'look at me, I'm a man, I'm invincible.' Be aware, be watchful, be cautious. Detective Miller is right—you might also be in the crosshairs now. It would end me if something happened to you."

"I'll be careful, I promise." His serious eyes told her he wasn't kidding around anymore. "And put some thought into this—we need to give Mom and Dad a call tomorrow and loop them in."

"They'll just worry—" She cut herself off at the look in his eye, then shrank slightly under the weight of his gaze. "Fine. We'll call."

"Great, I'll be here tomorrow at seven-fifteen. We'll call together, then I'll be here for your broadcast." He pointed an index
finger at her to stop her protest. "Miller's going to be watching,
and so am I. I'll be off to the side, staying off camera, or in the
next room on my laptop and headphones, but I'm going to be here.
We do this together." He turned to speak directly to Hailey. "Even
if together is across town. We'll be connected." Back to Krista.
"Okay?"

"Okay." Krista's ragged laugh was quiet and breathy. "You're
pretty good at this big-brother stuff."

"I'm a rock star. Now, I'm not leaving until I hear you lock up
after us."

"Yeah, yeah, I got it." She closed the door behind them, then
locked the dead bolt.

"Thank you!" Zach's parting words filtered through the solid
wood door.

"You're welcome!" she called back. A peek through the spy hole
showed them quickly disappearing down the hall.

Krista wandered into her now quiet and deserted living room.
She grabbed her tablet off the shelf by the TV, then flopped onto
the sofa. She woke the tablet and brought up the browser, then
stared at the empty search bar for a moment. She took a breath,
then typed "**Shanna Garner stabbing**" into the search box.

The first link was the *Chicago Tribune*. It told the story of the
body being discovered, caught in some brush at the bank, by a man
walking his dog along the North Branch of the Chicago River in
the Lincoln Yards area. He tied up his dog, then waded into the
river to pull her out, but didn't get any further than turning her
over when he realized he was interfering with a crime scene. He
called 911, and then he and his dog stayed to watch over the scene
until CPD arrived. He described being deeply shaken by the experience and would only say the victim had been stabbed
repeatedly. An article the next day identified the victim as Shanna

Garner, and described her devastated family, who would never be the same again.

No, you won't be. For a long time, you'll move through a fog, just trying to survive the day. Then one day, you'll realize you gradually left the fog, but there's still a gaping hole in your life. The jagged edges of that hole will slowly soften, not ripping at you daily, but you'll never truly be free of it. And you won't want to be, because it's your last connection to that person.

She clicked back to the *Tribune*'s home page, then over to the tab for the obituary listings, where she entered Shanna Garner's name in the search bar. Then she sat back, staring at the photo in the search results.

Shanna had been beautiful and full of life. In the photo, she was half-looking over her shoulder, as if someone had just called her name. Her pale skin had a charming scatter of freckles, her blue eyes shone bright, and a smile curved her full lips. Her long, wavy red hair tumbled loose over her shoulders to partially cover a V-neck mint-green blouse. She looked happy and ready to take on life's next big adventure.

Now she was dead.

Krista tried to push away the thought of how she must have looked when she was pulled from the Chicago River, her red hair matted and filthy, her pale skin gray, and her eyes filmed with the translucent white of death, the gaping wound at her throat revealing bloody strands of—

"Stop it!" She said the words out loud, sharp, the sound reverberating off the brick wall opposite her. She pushed the mental image away, focusing on Shanna as she looked in life. "I'm so sorry." The words were a whisper of sound in the quiet. "I didn't know how to help. I did everything I could."

Somehow, in those bright, shining eyes, she thought she saw forgiveness.

She snagged Balto from where he lay on the couch after Hailey had discarded him earlier. Pulling him into the crook of her arm to bolster her, she took a deep breath and opened the obituary.

Obituaries were rarely light or amusing—though they could be infused with the joie de vivre of the deceased—but since Linc's passing, she tried to avoid reading them. She still felt his loss so keenly; obituaries, even about strangers, always impacted her deeply, and she didn't want to drown in those feelings. But this time, she wanted to read, needed to feel that impact. She'd tried with everything she had to help Shanna. She hadn't been able to, and while that hadn't been a personal failure, it still left her with frustrated regrets and a burning fury at Chase, who'd given them just enough to realize what was happening, but not enough to actually save her. Now she wanted to know who it was they hadn't been able to help:

Taken far too soon, Shanna Lorraine Garner passed away at twenty-seven years of age on October 4. Born in Chicago on November 18, 1997, to Mitchell and Meredith Garner, Shanna soon became the beloved older sister of Tracy (Dean) and Vicki (Leslie). Shanna was loved by her family and all who knew her, including her friends at the Chicago Coalition to End Homelessness for all her volunteer work, especially with vulnerable young people. Shanna had the ability to reach out and touch fragile hearts, strengthening them and teaching them how to face the world around them.

Shanna's passion for life shone through in everything she did. From her community service in high school, to her work at the Lake Shore Animal Shelter, to time spent aiding the homeless, she was dependable and depended on. In her role at the Crooked Barman, she touched many and was always there with a ready shoulder or an uplifting joke.

Shanna was passionate about her causes, often putting in long days before her shifts at the Crooked Barman, generously giving of her time and talents.

A celebration of Shanna's extraordinary life will take place on October 11 at four o'clock at McMurray and Sons (3438 West Armitage Avenue). In lieu of flowers, the family asks you to please consider a contribution in her name to one of Shanna's beloved organizations.

Krista didn't realize she was weeping until a single teardrop splattered onto the tablet's surface. So much loss, so young. The same age as Linc. So much yet to live for, cut tragically short.

A man was free to walk the streets of her city, the man responsible for cutting that life short. Nameless, faceless, free to find a new target.

Hopelessness, helplessness, rose in a wave.

She buried her face in the soft fur of Balto's body and wept for all that was gone, and for all that could still be lost.

Chapter 20

KRISTA PUSHED HER UNEASE DOWN and forced out the words. "I think this is a mistake."

"What's a mistake?" On-screen in a Discord window, Hailey's crumpled brow spoke to her confusion. "The restrictions? You think we need to ease off on some of them?"

"Not at all." When the words stuck in her throat, Krista forced them past frozen lips. "I think they're not enough. I think we need to consider shutting down the channel."

"What?" Hailey leaned into her monitor, not staring into the camera, but directly at Krista's face, so on-screen her gaze seemed disconnected.

This discussion was why Krista had asked her to meet for coffee right after work, but Hailey had been slammed and knew she'd be coming home late. She'd offered to meet up on Discord an hour before the stream, instead, so they could talk without Rob and Emily. The concession didn't thrill Krista, but if it was all she could get, she'd take it.

She'd spent a lot of time thinking about Shanna in the twenty-four hours since Miller had told them about her. Not about what they could have done for Shanna specifically, but Krista had found herself coming back, again and again, to the woman herself. The volunteer work she'd done, the loss felt by her family, friends, and

coworkers. She'd found the Facebook page for the Crooked Barman, had read the comments left by patrons of the establishment
on the post about her passing. From there she had found Shanna's
different volunteer groups, read those tributes, each one tugging
at her heart.

She needed to stop, but didn't know how.

Shanna Garner had been a part of the Chicago community.
Krista knew at a time like this, people only focused on the positive
impact of a person's life and didn't talk about wet towels left on
the bathroom floor, power struggles at work, or snide comments
snapped during a fight. Shanna hadn't been a perfect woman;
Krista didn't know what Shanna's faults were, but she had them.
But she'd been living an active, meaningful life when it had been
cut short.

All because a man who thought she should be his was rebuffed.

Maybe it wasn't even that overt. Miller had talked to her coworkers and hadn't found anyone who particularly stood out as a
predator. Of course, people didn't need to *actually* know someone
in order to become obsessed with them. Strangers became obsessed
with famous personalities, simply through their on-screen personas.
After watching a character in a series, following them through their
lives, episode after episode, they felt they knew that person inti-
mately. But those actors were playing a part, their own personalities
obfuscated while they embodied someone else. Or they believed
a performer's music was speaking to them personally.

People had lost their lives—John Lennon, Selena, Rebecca
Schaeffer, Christina Grimmie, just to name a few. And many never
knew their killer.

Maybe Chase had never met Shanna in person. Or maybe he'd
been to the bar, but had blended in like any other patron, never
giving away his obsession, hidden behind a mask of friendliness
or detachment, acting as one of those who saw the waitstaff as
below their notice, as long as they provided a needed service without difficulty.

What she kept coming back to was whether their channel and the discussion she'd had with Chase had focused his attention on Shanna. Had he not come to get advice about how to win her over, had Emily not picked his particular question, had Krista and Hailey not tried to persuade him to back off, causing him to resist and to focus more strongly on success . . . would Shanna still be alive today?

Their original idea for the channel was to give light advice in a fun way that no one took too seriously. The show was on a gaming platform, for God's sake. It was never intended to be a forum for serious therapy. But the community itself had changed their initial vision. People had been brutally honest about their deepest feelings and fears, and the community had risen to the occasion, treating those concerns fairly, without mockery or derision. In the end, the platform hadn't set the tone; the platform had provided a haven for like-minded individuals to share ideas and care for one another.

She'd been skeptical at the beginning that the channel could be a success. Once she saw how much better reality could be, she'd had such hope of creating a safe space for all.

Shanna was part of the community by connection. Shanna had paid the ultimate price for that connection.

"We have one bad actor creating chaos," Hailey stated. "We need to figure out how to deal with him and then we can go back to the channel, as it was before."

"You honestly think that's a possibility? I don't. It's been permanently changed. More than that, do we want to go back? Look what happened because of this channel. If we hadn't pushed back at Chase, maybe he wouldn't have needed to prove he could win her attention. And that attention turned into an obsession we couldn't control."

"That's crap. We didn't cause this. If he was obsessed, we were just a brief stop on his way to the final conclusion. We couldn't have talked him out of it. We tried; it didn't work."

"Maybe he felt we challenged him by disagreeing with him about how he was handling it. Maybe he would have left her alone if we hadn't pushed back at him."

"Or maybe he was looking for an endorsement of what he was doing, and our disapproval of his methods slowed him down for a day or two. Or more. Honestly, Zig, I think his feet were already on that path. Whether he talked to us or not didn't change the end result. The timing? Maybe. But not the end result. The channel had no effect on him, so shutting it down would mean he wins."

"That's not what it would mean. It would mean we're looking at what happened and taking responsible action."

"We're going in circles here. Look, I met up with you early because you wanted to talk. We talked. I'm not shutting down this channel. We finally have traction. We can use it for good."

"You need to stop chasing follower counts as a metric of your success in life."

Hot color flooded Hailey's cheeks, and she opened her mouth to shoot back a response, then seemed to catch herself, folding her lips together so tightly they went white. "See you at stream time," she ground out, then disappeared.

Krista hung her head, embarrassment twining through her like molten steel. She'd let a thought slip out without a filter and had possibly just alienated her best friend in the whole world. They were both too emotional about the channel now, and likely neither was seeing it or the situation as actual truth.

Her head snapped up at the triple rap on her front door, and she checked the time: *Seven-fifteen. Zach.* She checked the spy hole at the front door, confirming it was her brother before opening it.

"Hey." Zach stepped in, wearing a light jacket over jeans and a Henley, his laptop bag over his shoulder. He shut the door behind him, locked it, then turned to face Krista. He stopped, his attention squarely focused now on her face. "What happened?"

"Nothing."

"Well, that's garbage. It's like you think I can't read you after all these years." He met her eyes. "What happened?"

Krista rolled her eyes and turned her back on him to walk toward the kitchen. "Hailey and I just had a fight."

"About?"

"The channel."

Zach set his laptop bag on the counter, letting the strap swing free. "This is like pulling teeth. Care to elaborate?"

"I suggested we shut it down."

Zach's eyebrows shot skyward, but his continued silence said, *Go on . . .*

"Hailey didn't like that idea," Krista finished.

"Teeth, I tell you," Zach muttered. "Why did you want to shut it down? Because of Shanna Garner's death?"

"Indirectly, yes." She walked Zach through her logic. "Hailey doesn't agree."

"Hailey has a lot more invested in this than you do." Zach's voice was calm, logical, a cooling balm to Krista's rioting emotions.

"I know that."

"I know you do, but I'm not sure you give it the credence she does. This is a sideline for you; it's not for her. She wanted her gaming channel to take off, but it didn't, not like this. Especially not now." He pulled out one of the tall stools that made up her breakfast bar, perched a hip on it. "Have I told you about Darla, one of our new interns?"

"At the firm? No. Why?"

"As always, we have a couple of students interning with us as part of their degree at Northwestern. And don't get me wrong, Darla is great—smart, efficient, knows her stuff, is totally focused when she's working. When she's not working, when she's on lunch, or after work, she's all about gaming. Watching Twitch, talking about Twitch personalities and streams. This is a big deal for the Gen Z crowd, which is her demographic. From what she says, it's a big deal for the late Millennial crowd, too, and that's where Hailey slots in. You would too, but you're not a gamer so your knowledge about the platform is probably as limited as mine. I didn't pay a whole lot of attention, but some of the other staffers talked to her about it a lot. I caught her in the break room yesterday, so I asked her about her experience with the platform." He laughed and rolled his eyes. "We'd still be there if I hadn't ripped myself out of the conversation. That girl is passionate about Twitch. It's her tribe. She found a group of people she really fits with. She apparently moderates for a couple of channels, and I suspect she spends more money than she actually admitted buying subscriptions, gifting subscriptions, donating bits—which I gather is a way to donate money to a specific streamer as a way of support."

"Gift subscriptions, buying bits . . . spending so much money when you could watch it for free—I used to think that was weird, but now I see it happening all the time through our channel and our followers. It's all part of the community aspect of the platform."

"As Darla explained it to me, it's her entertainment. You go to the movies and drop thirty bucks on popcorn, a drink, and a ticket, and it's all over in three hours. For her, that same amount of money could be a month-long subscription to get special perks on two, three, or maybe four channels, depending on the . . . what did she call it . . . right, the subscription tier. When she watches a stream, they can be easily as long as your movie, and she still has the rest of the month to enjoy. Money aside, she's invested as a viewer. Now imagine Hailey's perspective. Probably started as a viewer, but then wanted to make a go of it as a streamer, the person who gets all the attention. But never quite found her feet there. Then you and she create something new, something different from anything on the platform, and it takes off, blowing her gaming channel out of the water."

"You're pretty astute. She basically told me the same thing. But somehow when you say it, I hear it differently."

"It's everything Hailey wanted, but you have to think it's not quite as shiny as she would have liked, because it's not just hers, and it's not gaming. But she keeps going, and maybe the fame and attention make up for the lack of some of that shine." He met her eyes. "Now you want to pull the plug."

Krista leaned on the countertop across from him. "I wasn't doing it to blow up her dream."

"I know that. And if she wasn't so invested, she might be able to see that herself. It's all wrapped up for her. Maybe if she thinks about it a bit more, she'll begin to see it from your perspective."

"Maybe." Krista's tone was glum.

"And on that note, if we don't get moving, you'll be late for the stream you don't want to be on."

"Get moving on what?"

"Did you block out that I came this early so we can call the parox?"

Krista dropped her forehead into the heels of her hands. "Oh, God. It totally slipped my mind."

"Good thing I'm here, then."

"You know, maybe we can leave it until tomorrow."

Zach pulled his cell phone out of his back pocket. "Putting it off isn't going to make it easier. You can explain not calling last night because it was too late, but if you keep pushing it back in time, it's not going to go over well. I'm here, too. We'll lay it all out for them."

"They're going to want to get on a plane."

"They're *not* doing that. If both of their children might"—he held up an index finger—"*might* be in the crosshairs, having them here could add targets. I can make Dad see that, even if Mom won't, and he'll keep her clear of it all."

"What a mess." Krista groaned and threw a sour look at the phone in his hand. "Fine. Do it."

Zach speed-dialed their mother's number and put it on speaker, the phone lying between them on the counter.

The call picked up after two rings. "Hi, Zach." A smile radiated through Leila Evans's tone.

"Hey, Mom. Krista's here with me, too."

"That's lovely. Hi, honey. You two hanging out tonight?"

"Sort of," Krista said. "Is Dad there?"

Her mother paused for a moment. "He is. Do I need to get him?" Her voice carried a note of caution now.

"Yes, please."

"Just a second. Keith!" The final word was muffled, as if Leila had covered the microphone with her hand, or set the phone down and walked away from it. "Krista and Zach want to talk to us." A pause. "He's coming." Her words were clear once again. "Should I be worrying about something?"

"Let's wait for Dad."

"That's a yes. Keith, hurry up!"

Krista recognized the certainty in her mother's voice. Leila's understanding of her children went bone-deep. It was one of the things Krista was most afraid of.

"I'm coming." Their father's voice sounded in the background. "I'm here." Closer now. "What's up?"

"They'll tell us." Leila's voice sounded a little farther away, her phone clearly on speaker.

Krista could picture them: Leila, tall, willowy, and athletic; her dark hair typically pulled back and out of her way in a ponytail or low bun, because Krista's efficient mother hated her hair falling into her eyes; dressed in yoga gear simply because it was comfortable and practical. Keith, his short, sandy hair starting to show tendrils of gray; wearing his typical at-home outfit of jeans and a T-shirt emblazoned with a humorous or irreverent picture or slogan. They were probably sitting on the living-room couch, with Meatball, their perpetually overweight white-and-tan corgi, sprawled on the rug nearby.

It made her miss home and the security of her parents. Yes, she was an adult who'd been living on her own or with her fiancé for years, but sometimes the need to sit on the couch with her mom and let it all spill out, like she had when she was a teenager, rose up to swamp her. These were the people who'd shared their love of eighties pop music, had given both her and Zach their sense of humor, and who would be there at a moment's notice if either of their children needed them. Or, in this case, if both of them did.

"Tell us what's going on," Leila stated when Krista remained silent.

Zach arched his eyebrows and pointed at the phone on the counter. *Go ahead.*

She nodded. As much as she didn't want to drag her parents into this, it was her explanation. "Zach and I want to share something with you. I want to preface it by saying we know your gut instinct will be to get on a plane and be here by tomorrow morning, but I'm going to ask for your promise not to do that before I say anything more."

"We don't know what's going on," said Keith. "We can't make that promise."

"I need you to do it anyway. Zach and I love you too much for you to be anywhere near this."

"Krista, you're scaring me." Leila's voice held a slight quaver.

"In some ways, that's good. Promise me."

Long seconds ticked by, then Leila asked, "Zach? Do you agree with this request?"

"Yes." A single-word response, backed by absolute surety.

Leila's sigh rolled through the air between them. "Fine, then. But I want to know *everything.*"

"Deal." Krista laid it all out for them. They knew about the Twitch channel, and had watched some of the early streams Krista had sent them after Hailey uploaded them to YouTube. Explaining how the show worked, why chat was a crucial part of the show, went easily. What wasn't so easy was explaining the implied violence, and then the actual violence, the clue left at the mausoleum, meeting with one of their viewers, and calling in Detective Miller, which led to the victim being identified and the horrific realization the killer was right here with them in Chicago. That he could be a threat to any or all of them.

After Krista wound down, there were ten full seconds of silence as her parents processed her news.

Her mother finally spoke. "Where do you go from here?"

Krista flicked a glance at the time displayed in white on her stove. "We have our next broadcast in about twenty minutes."

"You're going to keep going?" When Krista paused, her mother jumped back in. "You don't want to."

"No, I don't. Hailey and I had a fight about it a half hour ago. She wants to keep going. I think we should shut it all down. Detective Miller wanted to watch the stream tonight, so we're going to run it, but after that . . ."

"You'll quit?" Keith asked.

"Maybe. I'm not sure what Hailey would do. She could keep running it herself. The advice isn't so much her wheelhouse, but she's watched me do it for months now. And we've always been honest that we're not therapists. We're regular people telling things like we see them, giving our opinions." She shrugged. "She could do it without me."

"You'd rather see it stop than go on without you," said Leila. When Krista started to protest, her mother spoke over her. "I've seen quite a few of your streams. Though I'm sorry to say, I've been so busy lately, I've missed your most recent ones, so I haven't seen any of this. It may not be evident to everyone, but I can see you're pleased when the stream goes well. You love it when you find the right answer, your viewers give kind and compassionate comments, and you make a difference to someone who is hurting, lost, or confused. If that was me, I'd like to think I wasn't so insignificant that when I needed to step out, I wasn't easily replaced by just whoever happened to be around to pitch in. Am I right?"

"You're always right."

"This Logjammer," Keith said. "Could he be the killer getting an extra thrill out of getting that close to you without you knowing it was him? I know it happens on TV more than in real life, but there are people who commit crimes who then return to the

scene to watch the police scramble, or who report a crime to have
some role in the investigation. Could this guy be the same?"

"We don't think so. He's someone who knows Hailey from
Northwestern and who followed her from her gaming channel
over to this one. I mean, he could be involved, but Hailey says
no way."

"That's not the vibe I got, either," Zach said. "More than that,
he's now put himself in Detective Miller's path. But it doesn't look
like he had any connection to the dead woman, besides finding
her bracelet."

"I'm glad to hear that, because this is someone who could have
your address, Krista," Keith said.

"I know. Anyway, we wanted to let you know what's going on,
but also wanted to let you know that we're taking every precaution.
Traveling in a group, if possible, keeping the doors and windows
locked at all times, not walking streets in the dark. All of us staying
in communication with each other."

"We want to be in those communication circles, too," Leila said.
"I want to see messages coming into the family WhatsApp chat.
When you leave work, when you're home and locked in. *Both of
you,*" she stressed. "Zach, don't play the I'm-a-man card; I want to
hear from you, too."

"Yes, Mom."

"Us holding true to the promise you dragged out of us depends on it. It's null and void if you don't keep us in the loop.
And then we'll be standing on your doorstep when you least expect it. Got it?"

"Yes, Mom," Zach and Krista chorused together.

"Now you probably have to go."

"I do," Krista said. "I'll keep in touch. We love you, and we
promise to be careful."

"We love you, too," Leila said. "You stay safe."

"Promise," said Krista.

"Promise," Zach echoed.

Krista ended the call. "That went better than I thought it might."

"For now. If we don't stay in touch, she'll be standing in front of you that same day."

"I'd expect nothing less." Another check of the time and Krista's spirits sank a little lower. "Now it's nearly time to get online, pretend I didn't just have a blowup with my streaming partner, and that everything is hunky-dory. And wait for a killer to stop in to say 'Hi.'"

Chapter 21

"WELCOME TO *A Word from the Wise*—real advice from real people."

Krista had to hand it to Hailey—listening to her voice, she'd have never guessed they'd been sniping at each other an hour earlier. Hailey, as Mortie, managed to sound chipper, even upbeat, like she didn't have a care in the world.

Like they weren't terrified someone watching right now, possibly even in their chat, was a killer, keeping them on a razor's edge of frazzled nerves and short tempers.

"For those of you watching, and specifically those of you having trouble getting into the chat, we've added a few more temporary restrictions. Because we've had some bad apples making trouble in the chat, we've restricted the chat to those who are subscribers only, with gifted subscriptions not allowed. For those who want to be actively involved in the chat, it's time to put your money where your mouth is, as the saying goes. At least for now."

Krista tried hard not to be irritated by Hailey's impersonal tone. She understood the need to get the message across, but it made them sound like they had no trouble discounting their newest viewers or those who couldn't pay for access. "We just want you to know," she interjected, cutting Hailey off as she paused to draw breath, "this isn't a moneymaking scheme. It's simply a way to calm things down. For those asking questions tonight, you're either left over from the last stream or you're a paid subscriber. We don't want to limit our other viewers. Please remember this stream will be uploaded to YouTube, and the comments associated with the video will be open. Please share your words of advice or your comments there. Anyone who has a question discussed tonight, be sure to review the comments for community involvement, because you know what my Wise Apples are like—they want to help and be involved. Don't let that opportunity slip by."

She glanced at Hailey, weighing her words. On-screen, Hailey sat quietly, her face calm and serene; most people would think she was listening with interest. Which she was, but Krista could see from the way Hailey's lips were set, she was fighting back a comment or comeback. Further, the glint in her eye said she was displeased Krista had wrested the conversation away from her. She continued before Hailey took it back, even while she had to push her own misgivings aside. "And if you have questions you want us to discuss next stream, please put that into a comment as well. The mods will be sure to read every comment, and we'll get to it next stream. Thanks so much for your understanding, Apples. Mortie, you ready to dive in?"

Hailey only paused for a fraction of a second, enough that Krista heard her dissatisfaction loud and clear, but no one else did. "For sure!"

"Great. Emily has set us up with our first question. Meredunhealthy needs some advice. She and her husband have a three-month-old baby, their first, and things are hard at home. Lack of sleep and the workload of a newborn, on top of both of them working full-time, has them snapping and making digs at each other, so their homelife is very combative currently. They could only afford for her to take four weeks off after the baby was born, so she's been back at work for a few months now. She's found she's become attracted to a coworker. He helps her at work and always has an ear for her when she's down. She knows it's wrong and wants someone to talk her out of her attraction to him."

Krista looked up from where she'd been reading the question to find Hailey looking down, distracted. Temper flashed. "Mortie, what do you think?"

Hailey's head snapped up, her eyes flaring wide just for an instant before her face settled into neutral lines. "I don't have experience myself, but having a newborn is hard."

At least she listened to the first three seconds of this question. Krista could have let her spin, was almost tempted to, but opted instead to keep the stream moving as it should. If they expected the chat to behave, they should as well. Their disagreement could wait. "You have that right. I'm with you and haven't had a newborn, but I've heard from friends and clients who have, and those can be hard days. Meredunhealthy, the first thing I want you to do is to make an appointment with your primary care physician for both you and your husband. I'm wondering if there may be an insidious background depression issue at work here. Being a new parent is hard, and you aren't that far away from bringing this new life into the world. Lots of women struggle with postpartum depression, so I think it would be wise to be checked out to make sure that's not a part of the issue. Same thing for your husband. Men can suffer from depression as well. The fact that you're both short on sleep might only accentuate a clinical depression. First, make sure there isn't a physiological issue playing in the background exacerbating your conflict.

"Once you know that, you can move forward. Now, there isn't a switch anyone can throw to negate your attraction for this man, but I think you need to look closer at *why* you feel attracted to him. You were attracted to your husband at some point. That's how most relationships begin—an attraction that grows into something deeper once you actually get to know your partner. Currently that attraction with your husband is strained by practical realism. You're tired. You're constantly attending to your baby's demands, because at this age, that's good parenting. Your baby isn't old enough yet to be playing you for attention. And it's your first child, and no one knows instinctively how to do everything correctly with a new baby. You're still figuring out what works best for you, which isn't necessarily a comfortable feeling."

Krista quickly took in the chat, everything in her relaxing at the normal stream of comments from familiar names. They were up at 18,982 viewers, but she was happy to see that number was actually falling from when they'd started. People had tuned in to see chaos, and instead, they were getting a calm, quiet advice show with no fireworks.

Maybe they'd solved it. Maybe they could continue, after all.

She needed to let Hailey know they weren't on opposite sides of this issue, that they were still a team.

"Mortie, anything you want to add?"

This time, Hailey was prepared. "I think the guy at work is easy and familiar. He's a known commodity when there's all this strangeness at home, which can be uncomfortable. Add to that a stressed, exhausted spouse who may also feel like he's in over his head. The competent, confident guy at work, who looks put together and can ride in on his white charger to help carry your load at work, would look pretty yummy by comparison. My advice is to take a good look at him. He's not perfect—none of us are. While he might look damn fine, you're only seeing the surface. He has an apparent glow to him that might rub off under deeper examination. You don't see the dirty socks he dropped on the floor or the tendency to put off cutting the grass because there's a game on. Or the habit he has of hitting happy hour every night on his way home from work. You have a crush on an image, not the real man. And right now, your best partner may be at home struggling the same way you are. You could continue to poke at each other, or you could help support each other and together make it to the finish line."

A warm glow of pride filled Krista. Her best friend had hit it out of the park. "And that's such a perfect answer, I'm not even going to try to improve on it. And clearly the chat thinks so, too, from their positive comments. Let's have the next question."

A quick peek out the door and into her living room showed Zach still perched at the breakfast bar, his laptop open in front of him. He looked into the studio when it was clear she was looking right at him, and gave her a wide grin and a thumbs-up. *So far, so good.*

She smiled back, then settled in for the next question.

She'd expected the worst. But maybe they'd finally made it to the other side.

Chapter 22

KRISTA RAN A HAND THROUGH her hair, a low growl emitting from the back of her throat. *Where is it?*

It hadn't been a bad day at work, just exhausting. It had been a physical kind of day, with her roster of clients needing a lot more help from her. She flexed her tired hands, curling them into fists, then releasing them, easing the slight ache in the muscles. She had very strong hands and arms because so much of her job was hands-on—searching for stiffness in joints, releasing tension from tight muscles, or providing physical support for weight-bearing exercises. Mobilization techniques required a lot of effort from her as she helped her clients regain lost movement; she never resented the effort, because it was so gratifying to see those same clients need her help less and less as they recovered. Today had just happened to be a stream of early injury clients who needed a much more hands-on approach.

Now all she wanted to do was sit in front of her TV with her rechargeable heated hand massager. Linc had bought it for her in the months leading up to his death. He used to do it for her, holding her exhausted hand and gently rubbing and massaging out the tightness and aches. But as his strength waned, he bought her the heated massager to ease her hands when he could no longer do the job. It normally sat on her dresser when she didn't need it—a compact oval with one open end to insert your hand. Heat and three different massage intensities meant relief for her, but she always missed his touch, even back in the day when he was still sitting beside her while she used it.

Now she just missed him, period.

Where had she put it?

It had been known to float around the apartment, and it had been a few weeks since she'd last used it, or even noticed it, but there were only so many places it could be—her bedroom, the living room, or maybe even the studio, as she had been known to use it out of sight during a stream if she was really suffering. It would only treat one hand at a time, so she always had one hand free, if needed.

She checked the studio, but couldn't find it, then wandered into the living room, her gaze roaming over every surface. The coffee table, couch, shelves . . . not there.

Her heart started to pound. What the hell was going on? Had someone been in her apartment? Had she been robbed?

She swung toward the studio where her computer equipment was still dark, just where she'd left it. Back into the living room, with her tablet on the shelf, and a quick trip into the bedroom proved her jewelry was intact. She laid her hand over her breastbone, the lump of her engagement ring dangling from the chain firm under her palm. All her valuables were here.

She gave herself a mental slap. *Someone broke into my apartment and ran off with nothing more than a hand massager? Be serious, Krista. Stop being paranoid over nothing. It's here somewhere. You probably weren't thinking and stuck it in a drawer or closet without paying attention.*

She walked back into the living room, still scanning the space. A sensation ran up her spine, like the skittering of centipede legs, sending a chill through her body. Her head swiveling from side to side, questioning her unease, her gaze finally came to rest on her balcony door, the curtains pulled back to reveal the lit courtyard and the darkened windows of the opposite-facing apartment beyond.

Was she being watched? Was someone standing on the far side of the dark glass, staring at her spotlit in the copious light of her fully illuminated apartment? She strode across the living room and yanked the curtains closed with considerably more force than necessary. She stood there for a moment, staring into the fabric of her curtains, expecting some relief to come with her privacy, but finding none.

With a muttered curse, she turned to face back into her living room, still looking for her massager. Maybe it somehow got kicked under the couch?

She took one step toward the couch, then froze.

Balto wasn't where she'd left him on the cushion.

The knife of panic sliced deep. To the outside world, she was the happy physical therapist, blasting her music and dancing around the treatment room, using the chipper tunes to distract her clients, as well as to encourage their exercise. But here at home, all the walls fell away, and she sometimes leaned on a silly stuffed toy to bolster her and to link her back to her past love. Current love, if she were honest, because that kind of love didn't turn off like flipping a switch.

And now Balto was gone?

The thought of the stuffed dog missing cut deeper than any electronics. Deeper than any jewelry. Because of his association with Linc's death, she was bonded to the toy far beyond its actual worth.

"Balto?" Part of her knew it was ridiculous to call out to an inanimate object that couldn't respond, knew she was treating it more like a real dog who would come when called than polyester and cotton.

She hurried over to the couch, pushing at the couch cushions to see if he'd slipped behind. Then she did the same with the chair. Nothing but a few crumbs and a discarded tissue from the last time she'd been sick and spent hours on the couch with the TV for company.

She took a step toward her bedroom, knowing very well she'd had Balto beside her on the couch—so, how could he be in the bedroom?—when her gaze landed on the coffee table. There was a lower shelf that sat about five inches off the floor that held a selection of board games. She dropped to her hands and knees and pressed her cheek to the hardwood.

And there he was, lying on his side, almost in the center of the table, hidden from view except from this angle. He must have fallen off the couch at some point and she accidentally kicked him under the table, not realizing he was there.

Reaching underneath, she pulled him out, then levered herself off the floor to sit on the edge of the couch, the stuffed toy in her arms.

This was bad. She was forgetting ordinary things at home, being careless, not taking care of her belongings. The stress of the past few weeks must be hitting her harder than she'd realized, and she was starting to lose her grip on reality. And if it was happening here, it would overflow into her work life, where a mistake could injure one of her clients, interfering with their recovery or possibly freezing it forever in place. That would be unforgivable.

She had to find a way to pull it together, but how?

Holding the toy tightly, she closed her eyes, bowed her head, and rocked.

Chapter 23

KRISTA HAD SPENT THE DAY trying to decide what to do. Losing track of Balto last night was the final straw that made up her mind—she wanted out.

She'd thought she was stronger than this. She'd thought the channel had made her stronger than this. Maybe it once had, but now just the thought of the channel and what had happened—and might still happen—on the stream chipped away at her. She'd felt better after the last stream, felt the warmth and camaraderie of the community, but even after that, she'd made a mess of things at home.

The channel had been a pleasant distraction for months, but now it was ruined for her. She would always be waiting for the other shoe to drop, for Chase to come back with someone new to torture, to kill.

She refused to be a part of it anymore. If Hailey wanted to keep running the channel, keep hosting streams, she had Krista's blessing. She didn't want to hold Hailey back. If she had the stomach for it, had the fortitude, more power to her. But if Krista had any doubts about her ability to hold it together, last night had been enough to convince her otherwise. Her mental health was suffering, and she had to take care of herself before she could take care of anyone else. Maybe then she'd be clearer, more meticulous, more careful.

Stop the world. I want to get off.

She never had figured out what she'd done with the hand massager. In the end, she chalked it up to one of those things she'd find two weeks from now when she went into the linen closet to look for fresh towels and tripped over it in a place that didn't make any sense. In the meantime, she'd have to live with her aching hands.

Fifteen minutes until stream time—time to pull the trigger. She wouldn't cut Hailey off without any warning; she'd give her time to make plans. Then she was out—her own mental health had to come first.

Maybe it had been stupid to take this on in the first place. Maybe she'd been floundering after Linc's death, and she'd been grasping at anything to help her make the transition to life alone. And the stream had helped at the beginning, so maybe that was a job well done. But not anymore.

She grabbed her phone and texted Hailey. **I need to talk to you. Are you free for me to call you?**

Her phone rang ten seconds later. *Hailey.*

Krista answered. "Thanks for calling me."

"We don't have a lot of time here." Hailey's words were clipped, her tone carrying the edge of ice.

Still mad that I want to shut it all down.

"What is it?" Hailey asked.

"I just wanted to talk to you before we began." Krista paused for a moment, then decided in the name of the friendship she was about to blow up in self-preservation, she owed Hailey nothing other than the unvarnished truth. "I'm quitting the channel."

Several beats of silence passed before Hailey hit back. "So that's it. You didn't get your way shutting down the channel, so you're going to bail on me. Tonight? With fifteen minutes to go?"

"That'd be pretty crappy if I did that. Not tonight. I want you to be able to do whatever you need to do to keep going. Would two weeks do for you?"

Hailey's laugh was harsh. "Two weeks' notice?"

"Four broadcasts seems fair to me. I don't want to leave you high and dry."

"Seems to me you're doing exactly that."

"I'm trying to give you time to figure out how to handle this. Look, Hailey, I'm sorry—"

"Don't give me that bullshit."

"It's not bullshit," Krista snapped. Anger was rising like a hot flood, and Krista was trying to keep it tamped down, but it was starting to overflow the banks. "Stop making me the bad guy in this. I can't take it anymore. I thought I could keep it together, but after the last few years, I'm not as strong as I used to be, I guess. The stress is affecting me in too many ways, and if it keeps up, I'm going to make a decision at work that could have some serious effects. I could hurt someone, or cause a new injury. I'm not going to let that happen."

"That's it, then? All these years of friendship and you're going to throw it all away."

"I'd like to think after you gave it some thought, you'd realize I'm actually doing it to protect myself and it has nothing to do with you. I'd like to think our decade-long friendship would survive it. But I guess that depends on you. I don't feel any ill will toward you—I understand why you want to keep it going, and don't resent you doing it without me—so the ball's in your court." Sudden exhaustion rode heavy and Krista didn't want to talk about it any longer. "I'll see you in ten." She ended the call, tossed her phone onto the couch, and walked away from it and into the kitchen.

She spent the next seven minutes doing busy work—making tea, putting together a lunch for the next day, general puttering—and went into the studio at the last possible minute. She signed on with less than a minute to go and found private Discord messages from both Emily and Rob, asking if she was going to join them. She ignored them, instead just jumping into the video call, with seconds to spare. Hailey's stiff posture and pinched lips telegraphed her fury.

So be it.

There was no preamble this time, only a short announcement of the channel's name and tagline, then Hailey fell silent. The implied punt of the conversation to Krista caught her off guard. She'd held off coming in until the last minute because she didn't want any time for Hailey to take a swipe at her. In doing so, she'd put herself at a disadvantage, leaving herself twisting in the wind. She had no doubt Hailey would tell her it served her right.

She wouldn't let it trip her up. "Hey, Apples, good to see so many of you here tonight." A quick look told her that while their follower count hadn't changed, their viewership was down, something she knew would bother Hailey. Something Hailey would be watching closely over the next weeks as the channel experienced significant changes. Something that could lose her beloved position as a Twitch Partner.

The Discord chat showed her Emily had a few questions loaded and ready to go for her. Normally, she would have come on early enough to review them, pick the one she wanted to start with, and jot down some notes on it, angles she wanted to cover. This time she just jumped into the first issue without questioning it. "Definitelybooz wants some advice about how to deal with his wife. They have disagreements and the arguments get extremely heated. He wants some advice on how to turn down the temperature. First of all, Definitelybooz, I want to stress that disagreements aren't the issue. Partners disagree. It happens. It's how you disagree that matters. Needless to say, if there's physical violence involved, that's not acceptable, and the most important aspect is safety. Not that I'm implying this is your scenario, but it's a good time to remind people about the National Domestic Violence Hotline number: 1-800-799-SAFE. Now let's look at tools you can use. If you're the one losing control, the first thing is to step back for a minute. Anger isn't inherently wrong—it's just an emotion. It's what you do with it that matters. And if that means forcing yourself to take a breath before responding, then do so. Apples, if you have some advice for Definitelybooz, make sure you talk to him in the chat."

In the chat, the comments started to roll.

> saithaghruagaich: Sometimes it's better to walk away and come back when you're not mad.
> SigmarsRavenna: Count to 10 🕐
> Huntsman452: its nothin a knife wont solve 🗡

Krista only barely managed to swallow the gasp that pulled at her lungs. Huntsman452. Huntsman.

Chase was back.

⊘**Hunstman452**   now
Banned by RobBot_Tinker

Rob obviously understood, too, and had acted quickly. The last time Chase got in, banning him hadn't been enough, and he'd been back, again and again, using different IDs.

But to get those IDs, to be able to take part in the chat, would now require a paid subscription. And that meant Detective Miller now has a way to track him.

Maybe it wasn't so bad, after all, if it was a means to an end.

Krista knew her job here was to keep things rolling, so she kept talking, ignoring the fact Chase had just suggested killing a partner rather than talking to her. "It helps if you can keep the argument civil," she suggested. "That will help keep the temperature down. Yes, you have to discuss things, but this is your partner, the person you're committed to. So no name calling, and try to keep the profanity down, if not out. All that stuff ratchets up the emotions. If you have an issue you're disagreeing on, you want to deal with that, not the tone of the argument. That will just get you off track."

> ☕🖼️fl00dlaunch: If it's a constant issue, maybe couples' therapy?🧑‍🤝‍🧑
> ☕Huntsman452: who needs women anyway 🖕
> ☕Huntsman452: better to just get rid of her... permanently 💧🔪🪦

Krista nearly gaped at the messages. Huntsman452 was back. *How is he back?*

She found the Mod Action panel in the Mod View window, and then all she could do was stare.

> ↩️**Huntsman452**   now
> **Unbanned** by ChiZiggy

She'd unbanned Chase?

She absolutely hadn't unbanned him. She didn't even know the command.

But from her furious Discord message, Hailey clearly thought she did. **WTF are you doing, Krista?**

Krista was aware the stream was just dead air, but took the time to message back. **Not me!**

What is happening?

> ⊘**Huntsman452**   now
> **Banned** by Dumortiere

Krista took advantage of the time she'd spent looking at the chat to throw out some other answers. Which was good, because she felt like her brain was short-circuiting. "Kiritosgirl says that she and her partner have a safe word to table an argument for a minimum of twenty minutes if things get too hot. That could be another strategy to try."

🚫**Huntsman452**   now
    Unbanned by ChiZiggy
⊘**Huntsman452**   now
    Banned by Dumortiere

It was like playing Whac-a-Mole, except not nearly as fun. As soon as they banned Chase, he was right back again. Because of her?

Krista gave up the pretense and looked directly into the camera. "Mortie, it's not me. I don't know what's happening, but it's not me."

🚫**Huntsman452**   now
    Unbanned by ChiZiggy

A message from Rob in the Discord chat caught her attention.
You've been hacked. You need to change your Twitch password
    Wouldn't I have to leave the stream? Krista messaged back.
    Yes

If that's what was needed, she'd do it. "Hey, guys, I'm having some technical difficulties. I'll be right back. Mortie, hold down the fort for me." She left the stream and quickly set about navigating to her Twitch account details and changing her password, having her password manager set it to a twenty-four-character keyboard smash, and saving it.

"—a really good question, MomOfBoy, and one that's right up my alley. As a female in the tech community, I've had to put up with some of the same issues you're talking about. Oh, hey, Ziggy, welcome back."

Krista gave her webcam a sunny smile. "Sorry to drop out like that." She shrugged comically with upraised hands. "Technology . . .

whatcha gonna do? But I'm back now and I'm good to go." She knew Hailey would deduce her password was changed to something complicated—it was Hailey, after all, who'd set her up with her password manager in the first place—and they should be clear. If Hailey was still talking to her after today, she'd like to pick her brain about how her Twitch password was hacked in the first place. If she wasn't talking to her, Krista would go straight to Rob. He'd be willing to help her, even once he found out she was leaving. Rob was a good guy. "Don't let me stop you. This sounds like a question you'll be much better at answering."

"Thanks, pal." Even over a webcam connection, Krista could see Hailey's smile didn't quite reach her eyes. "MomOfBoy was just asking about how to manage sexism in her tech workplace. Let me give you some tips that worked for me."

As Hailey launched into details about lack of female representation and mentorship in the tech sphere, with the lack of numbers creating a negative feedback loop, Krista studied the chat. All quiet, all normal.

For now. Just because they'd blocked Chase from coming back as Huntsman452 didn't mean he didn't have more IDs up his sleeve. And they had help in the background, because Detective Miller had texted both her and Hailey late this afternoon to confirm the stream time and to let them know he'd be watching. Zach wasn't physically with her tonight, but she knew he'd be with them on the stream as well. She was willing to bet her parents were also watching, and had been since she and Zach had called them just before the previous stream.

Knowing her parents were watching, and following along, added an extra layer of stress. They'd know she was having some kind of issue and they'd recognize the killing aspect of the Huntsman452 screen name. They'd identify Chase.

How long until a new ID popped up using the name of a serial killer or a killer by nature? What would his new word choice be? Assassin? Executioner? Exterminator?

Stop it. He's not here now. Value every second of that.

"The 'brogrammers' can be a real issue," Hailey was saying. "You know the type—the programming bros who lock arms together and intentionally cut women out of opportunities for collaboration. Or who coast if forced into collaboration with you. Seriously, no love for the 'brogrammers.'"

> 🐢Ethelinda1998: 💬💬💬Don't forget work/life balance! Women do most emotional labor, so when you're exhausted from home life, you don't have as much energy to fight the BS at work
> 🐢☑️dannatunes: Sorry your strugglign with this
> 🐺Huntsman542: women dont belong in tech
> 🐺Huntsman542: women belong at home workin for there man

He was back. *How could he be back?*

On-screen, Hailey was frozen, her gaze locked on her broadcasting monitor, her horror reflected in her slack-jawed expression.

Krista's own realization came as a physical blow hard enough to rattle her entire frame: *We're never going to be rid of him.*

⊘Hunstman452   now
Banned by emily_brontesaurus

Then Hailey's gaze dropped down to her keyboard, followed a second later by a Discord message. **He's in your password manager**

Krista jerked back in her chair, reacting as if Hailey had reached out and slapped her, the shock turning her extremities to ice. But her brain immediately locked on the real risks involved. Not just the infiltration of a virtual gaming platform, but of every corner of her life— Chase had access to her bank and credit cards; her online photos, including those spanning her life with Linc; her email . . . every facet of her online life. And in today's world, that was everything.

Another message came in from Hailey. **Change your master password**

Krista flipped to her password manager. Funny, it had been active only moments ago, but now it said she was signed out. She quickly typed in the one complex password she needed to remember, but it refused her. She clicked on the eye to show the password. Terror bolted through her when she saw she'd typed it correctly.

Chase had beaten her to it and changed her master password to something she didn't know. She was locked out of her own life.

Her one thought was to protect her finances. If he ruined her in any other way, she'd survive, but how would she live if he took everything she had?

She didn't even bother to sign off the stream, just exited and ran for where she'd left her bag in the chair in her bedroom. Every card had an emergency number on the back to call if you suspected fraud or if a card was lost or stolen. She had to freeze every asset she had. *Now.*

If she'd had any doubts before the stream, she didn't now. They were no longer in control, and she wouldn't be a part of it anymore. She'd come back one last time, the next stream to say goodbye to the Apples—she owed them that much—and then Hailey was on her own.

She was done.

Chapter 24

"CAN I GET YOU A coffee? Water?" Detective Miller looked over his shoulder toward the watercooler in the far corner of the bullpen.

"Water would be great, thanks." Krista gave him a wan smile of gratitude.

"Be right back."

Krista's gaze passed over the detectives' bullpen. She'd never been in a police station before—never had cause to be—but it was exactly as utilitarian and busy as she thought it would be. Some detectives sat at their desks pecking away at reports, others ran in and out, and there was the low buzz of voices and typical background noise you'd find in any office. Except this wasn't a typical office. This was Homicide.

Krista had endured a hell of a night. She'd spent it contacting her bank and each credit card company. A half hour into it, she'd paused long enough to respond to the pounding on her door, letting in her brother. Zach had been alarmed at Krista's disappearance from the stream. He'd tried calling, only to find the call going right to voicemail, as she was already talking to her bank. He'd left her a message to call him ASAP, then jumped in his car, heading for her apartment. Along the way, he'd fielded a call from his parents, who'd also tried to call Krista and found her line busy. He'd assured them he was on his way over and would keep them apprised.

Zach had stayed for hours, helping her use her backup password export to compile a list of all the stolen information. Then he'd sat beside her and helped her freeze her accounts, cancel her cards, use her email security questions to regain control of her email, confirm which log-ins needed some form of two-factor authentication by text or app authenticator and were therefore still safe, as well as keep their parents in the loop via text. They'd worked for hours, then he'd stayed for another half hour, talking through it all with her and their parents when they'd finally had time to call them. He'd offered to sack out on the couch for the night, but she'd sent him home. She was physically safe, and they'd done all they could do for the night.

Shortly after Zach had arrived, Detective Miller called following a conversation he'd had with Hailey, giving him a heads-up as to what was likely happening with Krista. When Krista had reassured him she and Zach were doing everything they could to block Chase's access to any part of her life, Miller had asked her to come to the station, at nine the next morning. Zach had argued he should go with her, but she'd told him to stay home, as he'd already given up his Friday evening for her. She'd be with Miller, so she'd be as safe as it was possible to be.

Detective Miller returned with a plastic cup of cold water. Grateful for something to soothe her parched throat, Krista took a long sip as Miller settled himself behind his desk.

He gave her a long look, up and down. "How are you?"

Krista's laugh carried a harsh edge. "Hanging in, considering. Last night wasn't the best night of my life. Did you see the stream?"

"I did. Was Hailey correct? Chase got into your password manager?"

"Yes. And changed the master password, so I lost access to my bank of passwords. He had access to it, and that meant he had access to every facet of my online life. Finances, photos, communication, stores . . . everything."

"We live our lives online now. I talked to one of the guys in computer forensics this morning for his insight. He had some questions for me to pass on to you. First off, did you have two-factor authentication turned on for your password manager? He said that's an option, so the first time you sign in from a new device, it needs some kind of double check."

"It's been a while since I set it up, but I'm pretty sure I did that. I hardly ever need to use it, because I have the password manager already installed on my PC, tablet, and phone. Let me check." She pulled out her phone, opened her authenticator app, and scrolled down the list. "It's here, so yes to two-factor authentication."

"That's important to know. Because that's on, anyone who got ahold of your master password and tried to log on remotely should have been stopped at that point. What devices are connected to your password manager? You said your PC, tablet, and phone. Anything else?"

"No."

"You have your phone right here. Where are the tablet and PC?"

"At home in my apartment."

"I saw your PC setup the last time I was there. It's not going anywhere easily. Do you take the tablet out and about with you?"

"No. I have my phone when I go out. I don't need that, too."

"Is your phone ever out of your possession? Do you leave it lying around at work? Have you ever lost it for a short period of time, then found it again?"

"No to all of that. I carry my phone in a side pocket in my yoga pants at work. We always have people coming in and out of the clinic, so no one leaves valuables lying about. I have a locker at work for my bag, and sometimes I forget and leave it in there, but never just lying around in the open. I haven't misplaced it, either. I mean, sure, I've used my fitness tracker to find it when it's slipped out of sight behind a couch cushion, but it's been with me the whole time. I've never lost it outside the apartment." Krista studied Miller's hard eyes and furrowed brow, and her gut curled with stress. "What?"

"We have a bigger problem. Next question. Has anything seemed off at home?"

"Off? Can you be more specific?"

"Anything missing? Anything moved?"

Jaw sagging, Krista simply stared at him.

"Christ." Miller swiveled to face his computer and the file open on his monitor. "That's my answer. When did it happen?"

Krista grabbed his forearm. "Wait. Are you saying what I think you're saying?"

"That considering the two-factor authentication, the limited devices, and the fact that no one had access to your phone when you were outside your apartment, the only way for someone to break into your password manager would be to do it from inside your apartment. You're gone all day at work, giving someone a long time to get in there and do whatever they needed to do. What's missing?"

Krista's mind was racing ahead, trying to put pieces together. If Miller's theory was correct, that someone had broken into her apartment to get access to her account for Twitch and her password manager, then it wasn't just a missing bracelet and hand massager. If that was true, if this was Chase, he knew who she was and where she lived. He'd stood in her bedroom, the place where she was helpless when asleep at night. A shudder of terror rippled through her. "Hold on, back up. You're saying Chase not only broke into the six-flat building, but he broke into my apartment itself?"

"That's my theory."

"There's been no actual trace of that. He would've had to come in through the front door because he'd have had to scale the wall of the apartment or climb the tree and jump the last twenty feet to get to my balcony. He'd have been heard or seen doing that, and then he'd still have faced a locked door he'd have to open in sight of the neighbors."

"You have a basic dead bolt on your front door. That's likely how he got in, by picking the lock. You live in a six-flat, and there's only one other unit on your floor. Do you know the other residents?"

"Yes."

"Do the occupants have jobs that take them out of the building every day?"

Defeat rolled over Krista, leaving her spent. "Yes."

"So your lock may have been picked without leaving any external evidence, but the internal mechanism may show signs. I'll get a crime scene team to meet us over there to check out the lock and go through your apartment together. Take me through it now. What's missing?"

"It's all weird stuff, and I don't know if it's related."

"Better too much info we can then eliminate rather than leaving something off the list. Give it all to me."

Krista massaged the headache pounding behind her temples with the fingers of both hands. "First thing I noticed missing was a silver tiger's-eye bracelet. Big, multi-stone link bracelet, tiger's eye interspersed with pale citrine. I went to put it on one night when I was meeting Hailey for dinner and it was just . . . gone. I still can't guarantee it didn't fall behind my dresser or anything, so I may be blowing this out of proportion."

Miller typed the information into the file. "Or you may not be. What else is missing?"

"A hand massager. It's an oval-ish box you stick your hand into that gives it a heated massage." She flexed both hands. "It's not expensive, but it's useful to me after a long day working with patients. Sometimes my hands cramp or get really tired."

"The bracelet is small, and yes, it could fall behind your dresser. This sounds bigger."

"It's about . . ." Krista used both hands to indicate the three dimensions of the massager. "It's maybe eight or nine inches by five inches by five?"

He added details to the file. "Not something to lose behind the dresser, then."

"No. Honestly, I've been so off my game lately, I chalked it up to me cluelessly sticking it somewhere it didn't belong and I'd find it later."

"What else?"

"That's all that's gone missing. But . . ." She paused, looking away to stare at the far wall, cataloging.

"But. . . ?" Miller pressed.

"There have been a few odd things."

"Odd things count, too. Give them to me."

Here goes. "I ran out of coffee filters."

Miller paused with his hands over the keyboard. "You ran out?"

"Yes. But that's the thing. I never run out of filters. I love my coffee in the morning, so when I get down in number, I add filters to my shopping list. I can't swear to it, but I think I went from about a third of a box to nothing. I went to make coffee one morning and couldn't because I had no filters and had never added them to the list."

Miller added the filters to his notes. "What else?"

"A photo and a little sculpture weren't where they were supposed to be on the shelves beside my TV. They were in flipped position. And then Balto, my stuffed toy, disappeared, and I found him under the middle of the bottom shelf of my coffee table. I assumed I'd just kicked it there."

"I find it hard to believe you'd kick that toy under the table. I've seen you with it. It's a touchstone for you; you handle it like it's a cherished object."

"Because he is. Early on, my fiancé won him for me on a date. Through the end of his struggle, Balto was with him in the hospital. He was there . . . at the end."

"You wouldn't carelessly boot him under a table without noticing. And to coincidentally land under the middle of the shelf? How hard was it to see?"

"Impossible from any direction, unless you had your cheek pressed to the floor."

Miller made a noise in the back of his throat that clearly expressed his opinion that Balto had been helped into that spot.

Krista met Miller's eyes, and the surety she saw there gave her permission to open up a bit. "I thought I was losing it. That the stress from Chase on the stream was making me careless and forgetful. Making me crack. That I was so fragile after losing my fiancé, I was shattering under the slightest stress."

Miller patted her knee awkwardly, like he was trying to comfort, but was uneasy making physical contact. "In my opinion, that's not what's been happening. I think someone's been in your apartment, moving things, taking things, purposely trying to make you feel small, feel unbalanced, so you'll be more susceptible to what he was doing to you online. He's been playing with you. Gaslighting you."

Krista surged out of the chair, paced a half-dozen steps away, turned, and paced back. "Why? Why is he doing this?"

"I don't know yet. But I'm going to find out."

"Is he stalking me?"

"I'd classify it as that."

Cold stole through her and her head started to swim.

Her unsteadiness must have shown on her face, because Miller shot to his feet, gently grabbed her wrists, and steered her back to sit in her chair. He picked up her glass and handed it to her. "You've gone pale. Drink some water and take a minute to breathe. Put your head between your knees if you think you're going to pass out."

Krista did as directed and sipped her water, trying to focus on anything else, but continually coming back to what happened to the last woman this man stalked. *Dead in a river, stabbed, with her throat sliced.* "Does that mean I'm not your problem anymore? Who covers stalkings?"

Miller gave her a sharp look. "It began with me; it ends with me. I'm not going anywhere. If that's a concern, you can put that one to bed." He turned back to his computer. "Let's nail down details. Did everything move at once?"

"No." It took a few seconds for Krista's overwhelmed brain to catch up, and she groaned and hung her head. "Oh, God, he's been in my apartment more than once."

"That's my take on it." Miller's voice was matter-of-fact.

Krista appreciated that he didn't sugarcoat it for her. This man would give her the straight goods; she'd know exactly how much trouble she was in, besides a lot. She already knew that much.

"When was the first time you noticed something?"

"I noticed the bracelet missing the night I went out to dinner with Hailey, which was the day after we first had Chase show up as multiple accounts during a stream. That was a few days after you introduced yourself."

Miller scrolled up his file. "The first day I met you in person was Tuesday, October seventh."

"Then the Friday stream on the tenth was when things started to spiral. Which means Hailey and I met for dinner on the eleventh. That was when I first missed the bracelet, though I admit it could have been missing weeks before and I just hadn't noticed. I hadn't worn it for at least that long. I noticed the coffee filters and the switched photo and steampunk rabbit the next morning."

"Steampunk rabbit?"

"It's a rabbit sculpture made entirely out of watch and clock parts."

"Right. I remember seeing that on your shelf. That was Sunday, October twelfth."

"Yes."

"Then everything stayed in place until when?"

"Two days ago."

"What happened then?"

"I came home from work and my hands were aching, so I went looking for the massager, and couldn't find it." She held up a hand when Miller started to speak. "No, I don't know if it went missing then or at the same time as the bracelet and the coffee filters. That day was also when I noticed Balto was missing."

He finished typing and sat back in his chair, meeting her gaze. "You understand what he was doing, right? Trying to get into your head, to shake you, to make you think you were losing it. You didn't remember using the coffee filters because you didn't, but it's such a commonplace thing, it was totally believable that you'd dropped the ball there. The picture and rabbit being swapped—surely, you questioned yourself there, too."

Krista nodded.

"Losing a bracelet, it happens. And it may indeed be behind your dresser. Or he may have taken it as a trophy. A little token to remember you by, something you might not even miss. Was it worth anything?"

"Nothing significant. He didn't take the expensive stuff. Had my diamond earrings gone missing, or my engagement ring"—she laid her fingers over the lump under her sweater—"that would have raised alarm bells. But a piece of jewelry with semiprecious stones? It means more to me because of who it's from than its worth. I love it for it, not because it's valuable."

"Do you have a picture of it?"

"I'm sure there are pictures of me wearing it. I'll send one to you."

"Thanks. Let's circle back to the master password, because that's something else he took you didn't notice. Is there a way to find that out from any of your hardware?"

"No. That information isn't stored on the machine. That's the point of a password manager—it creates an unlimited number of super-complex and long passwords that you don't have to remember. You just have to remember the one master password, so make it complex, but find a way to remember it."

"It's not something that includes any information that could be found somewhere else? Not your birthday, or your late fiancé's? Not your childhood street or the first pet you owned?"

"No. It isn't anything that someone, even someone who knows me, would be able to come up with."

"And it's not written down on a Post-it somewhere? Stuck to your monitor or tucked in a drawer? Or . . ." Miller trailed off, staring at Krista's face. "It's written down somewhere?"

"Yes. Only Zach knows where it is."

"Why Zach?"

"Because if something happens to me—I get hit by a car or have a heart attack and die suddenly—my family needs to have access to all my things. My financials, my accounts. It's recommended you write down your master password and put it somewhere your family knows where to find it. It's written down on a piece of paper with no indication as to what it was, and the piece of paper is wrapped around a USB key with an encrypted download of all my passwords."

"Where is it? Do you know you still have it?"

"Yes. I needed the USB key Friday night for the backup of all my passwords to get into my accounts before he changed them. It's in the top drawer of my bedside table. I saw it again last night, so it's not missing."

"If Chase went through your apartment, searching through all your things, he could have found it. Could have taken a picture of your master password and then put it back exactly as it was. All he needed was the information—he didn't need the actual piece of paper."

The thought of someone pawing through her things shook Krista to her core. Her privacy had been violated to an extreme degree, and everything she owned was now tainted.

"That would explain how he could lock you out of your account. He could log onto the password manager from one of your devices in your apartment and turn off two-factor authentication. You wouldn't notice unless you tried to sign into your password manager from a new device, which you didn't, so you were none the wiser. And then he could go home, log into your account, and from there have access to every online aspect of your life, including your Twitch account, so he could pull that BS from last night, unbanning himself every time someone banned him. Which reminds me, the subscription restriction of no gifting led us to how he bought his subscription."

Hope flared as a tiny white-hot light, burning bright. *Finally some good news.* "You know who he is?"

"We do not."

The light flickered out under a sudden hurricane wind.

"Twitch has been extremely helpful," Miller continued, "and they provided us with all the information they had. The subscription was paid by a Visa cash card. We tracked it down to a mom-and-pop shop here in Chicago. He came in wearing a ball cap and a hoodie with the hood up a few days ago and bought the card with cash. They don't remember his face—he kept his head down—and none of the cameras got him. Dead end." He nearly growled the last two words in frustration.

"He's really winning, isn't he?"

"He's not going to continue to win. We're not done here. First thing we're going to do is get crime scene techs over to your place to go through it. You and I will be there, too, and you'll work with us to let us know if anything else is missing or out of place, as we can't do that without you. Then I want you to pack a bag and stay with your brother. This guy knows where you live, so I don't want you there, at least for now. Give me Zach's address, and I'll get it on the patrol list for extra protection." He pushed back from his desk and stood. "Give me a couple of minutes to get this all set up, and then we'll head to your place."

Krista watched Miller stride out of the bullpen. Then, her hand shaking, she dialed Zach's number. He must have been holding his phone, because he answered before the first ring had even completed. "Hey, it's me. Can I come and stay with you for a few days? Or maybe more?" She paused, thought about crime scene techs and strangers invading her safe space, her last sacred space shared with Linc. It made her want to weep. "Yeah, I think it'll be more."

Chapter 25

"WHERE IS SHE?" KRISTA MUTTERED as she glanced nervously at the time again. Five minutes until the stream was supposed to start and she was alone in the Discord video chat, as Hailey had yet to come online.

She couldn't help but feel something was wrong. She'd received a text from Hailey in the late afternoon that had left her uneasy.

Can I call you tonight before the stream? I've screwed up bad and I need to explain

What had she done? They'd agreed Hailey would call her cell at six-thirty, then Hailey said she had to get back to work and she'd talk to her in a few hours.

She never called, and now she was late for the stream. Had something happened?

She turned to look out the studio door to where Zach was perched on one of her stools at the breakfast bar, his laptop open, ready to jump into the stream with her. He was head down over his keyboard, probably catching up on all the work he'd missed while he was distracted by her crisis. And by the time taken up with a phone call, when he got home, to catch the parox to wish them a happy anniversary before they went out for a fancy dinner to celebrate.

207

She owed Zach so much. He hadn't questioned when she'd called him, simply opened his home up to her for as long as she needed, and then offered a shoulder she could lean on.

She'd spent the previous night at Zach's, sleeping in his spare room, but had come back to her apartment to do the broadcast because it wasn't worth it to her to cart all her equipment over to set up at Zach's when this was going to be her last stream as part of the *A Word from the Wise* channel.

She'd already made the decision to move. The sanctity of the apartment as the last place she lived with Linc was ruined. Someone else had come into the space, spoiling it forever as a place of peace, and she'd never feel safe or comfortable there again. She'd spent her lunch break that day searching for a new place to live. She'd gone back for this stream, and would return to pack up, but she didn't live there anymore.

Even with everything that had happened—the abuse on the stream, Shanna's death, all the stress associated with it—losing this last connection to Linc was what hurt the most. She'd lost her security, her privacy, her in-place memories of Linc, and for what? The money didn't matter; she'd been doing fine, thanks to the money Linc left her. And the fame was entirely unimportant.

She'd upended her life for nothing.

Four minutes until the stream began and still no Hailey. She typed a message into the chat, where Emily and Rob had previously signed in.

Has anyone heard from Hailey?

I haven't

Nothing here

Krista took a sip of tea to wet her suddenly dry mouth. What if she'd had a medical emergency? Or been involved in a car accident on the way home? Or, God forbid, Chase had gotten to her?

She suspected they were all considering that possibility, but no one had put words to it.

Can one of you start this if she's not here by 8?

Rob answered quickly. **You can as the Editor. I can talk you through it. Did Hailey set you up with OBS?**

Don't think so

Then Hailey was there in the chat. **Hey guys, sorry I'm late. Disaster at work, crap traffic, nearly home now. I can start the broadcast on time remotely from my phone. Krista, can you carry the stream until I get there? I'll join in as soon as I'm home. Ten minutes late at most. Hoping for better**

Relief washed through Krista. Hailey was okay, just suffering from the mundane complexities of life. She'd make time to talk after the stream. **Yes. If you start it, I can do the intro and launch into the first question. Emily has me queued up and ready to go.**

Awesome! You'll see me soon. Hop in. I'll just have my camera off until I'm settled in the studio

As promised, two minutes later, the broadcast began, this time with only Krista's single window floating over their neon title. *She'll be here soon. You know what to do.* "Hey, gang, welcome to *A Word from the Wise*—real advice from real people. I'm flying solo to start things off here today, but Mortie will join us shortly." She took in the chat, where words of support and greeting were already flying. "Look at you all. It's great to see you. Why, yes, Daughterofmorningstar, that is a new plant." She turned toward the new succulent in a diminutive teal pot sitting over her left shoulder. "No, I didn't kill the other one," she said with a laugh. "It got too big for this little space. It's currently enjoying a larger spot at my kitchen window. So I treated myself to a new plant." She pushed down the thought that she and her plants were going to have to find a new place to live, smiled widely, and smoothly switched gears.

"Let's get going. Labonnepoupee posted this question last stream. He wants some advice on how to handle his teenaged son. He has real concerns that his seventeen-year-old son is addicted to social media—TikTok, Twitch, and Instagram, mostly—and thinks he needs to cut back. It's not doing great things for his mental health, and he's been really focusing lately on what others can do that he can't." She looked up from the chat message she'd been reading to look directly into the camera. "Apples, this is where the hive mind can do some real good. I know it's a stereotype to say you're all tech geeks, but this isn't your grandmother's Facebook. This is Twitch. Let's get those ideas coming. Labonne can always come back and review the chat in the VOD, if there are too many comments. Let me go first, Labonne, while the others pitch in their ideas. First of all, you need to recognize that this is the time in a young person's life when he starts pulling away from his parents. Sometimes it's gradual. Sometimes that separation comes in leaps and bounds. Sometimes it's a two-steps-forward, one-step-back kind of process, where they see themselves as independent for some things and will still come and sit on your bed after a night out to tell you how things went." She chuckled. "That was me. I wanted my parents to give me space, and by seventeen, they were, with reservations. Still, I used to come home at eleven-thirty or midnight and poke my head into their room to see if they were still awake. And let's be honest, there were times when they weren't, but one of them would turn on the light, they'd both force themselves awake, and I'd sit on the bed by my mother's hip and I'd tell them about my evening. Looking back, for them, that I could share my feelings and experiences with them made them more comfortable with letting me go. On my part, that was definitely one step back when it came to pulling away, but it worked for all of us." Krista smiled at the memory.

"Social media is part of modern-day pulling away. Part of growing up is finding your tribe. In the days of our parents' generation, your local tribe was people you went to school with, your extended family, and maybe people at the church youth group. Now the world is so much larger. And for those people who say internet friendships aren't real, I think we know in this group they are. Whether it's a fellow gamer who sees the world through the same lens as you, from five hundred miles away, a moms' group that forms when everyone has similar due dates and is still together decades later, or people who meet in a forum because they love a certain fandom and then find they have much more in common . . . those are true friendships. Letting him find his tribe on social media isn't strictly a bad thing. But we've all heard about how hard social media can be on young people. And, let's face it, very few people post their failures on social media, because some individuals depend on their own anonymity to mock and denigrate the original poster for their efforts. Most post their best lives on social media, a falsity that makes it look like it's their only life. Meanwhile, some people look at those successes and wonder why they can't do the same, or at least can't do it consistently. And that brings them down." Krista paused to take a sip of her tea, then lowered her mug.

"I have a few suggestions right off the bat, then let's see what chat has to offer," she continued. "First off, as always, open communication. Talk to your son about what he's seeing on social media, and help him evaluate what's being presented to him. If he'll let you, watch some of it together. Is he simply seeing a *best-life* persona? Is everything on a channel a story of successive wins, or does the influencer explore their failures as well? Help him see the truth behind what he's watching. Next you may want to enforce a 'no internet devices in the bedroom' rule, or at least in the last hour or two before bedtime. Lots of teens drag their butts to school the next day because they're exhausted after being on their phones until the wee hours. Also, that blue light isn't good for their sleep, something they desperately need. Being short of sleep can lead anyone, adults included, to becoming more vulnerable to depression, which then makes sleep more difficult, and that can contribute to a downward spiral. Now, what ideas are there in chat?"

A surreptitious glance showed her Emily had loaded some of the better ideas as well as who had suggested it into the Discord chat. "Treasuringdina has a great idea—they suggest parents can be great models of good behavior. Whatever you decide for your teen should actually be a family-wide adoption. It's harder for you to argue with him about no phones in the bedroom if you have yours with you, and he sees you doomscrolling at midnight. Lead by example—great idea, Treasuring. Now, I totally understand that most families don't have landlines anymore, and your phone may be your only method of communication, so maybe have an agreement that when you and/or your partner go to bed, the phone can be in the bedroom, in case anyone needs to contact you if there's an emergency, but is to remain hands-off. And here's TheLord-Racer with some solid advice—if you want him to still have access to social media because that's where his tribe is, but you don't want him to overdo it, maybe set time limits on social media use. There are apps that can track the usage of other apps or limit overall time spent on certain apps. Maybe put one of those on his phone and review it together on a regular basis."

It was now 8:10 P.M. and Krista wondered how much longer Hailey would be than her estimated ten minutes. Krista had always suspected she could handle a stream solo, but liked the conversation aspect of Hailey pitching in occasionally, rather than Krista feeling like she was giving a lecture. Looping in the chat comments certainly helped, but somehow it wasn't the same.

She was just about to return to the chat to move on to another question, when Hailey's window popped up, resizing hers in Mod View down to her normal half of the screen with their banner centered under the gap between them. She was about to greet Hailey, but then froze for a moment in confusion at the dark screen.

Then the lights burst on, and a horrific sight appeared, one Krista instantly knew would live in grisly Technicolor in her brain for the rest of her life. Krista screamed and pushed off her desk, ramming her chair into the wall, hardly feeling the new potted plant fall off to strike her shoulder and then shatter on the hardwood floor below. She only barely registered Zach's startled curse from the kitchen.

Because nothing mattered but the nightmare on-screen.

The webcam wasn't pointed at its usual view, but instead focused on a rug Krista recognized as the one behind Hailey's desk in her studio. But she had no eyes for the rug, not with Hailey's body sprawled awkwardly across it, in a twisted position that instantly spoke of death. Blood soaked the neckline of her sky-blue top and ran into the puddle soaked into the light-charcoal rug. Her head was tipped far back, her wide eyes staring sightlessly at the opposite wall. But it was the ragged, brutally vicious wound at her neck that Krista stared at in horror, her mouth dry, and her breath frozen in her lungs. Something had shredded Hailey's throat, slicing it wide, exposing muscle, severed blood vessels, and the pale-pink rings of cartilage that had once made up her trachea to carry air down her lungs.

Now forever stilled.

The overall effect was as if Hailey was a marionette and someone had cruelly cut all her strings, leaving her to fall to the carpet, with no power to rise.

Hailey would never rise again. Never smile, laugh, dance, code, run the stream, or have a family. Have a life. Because hers had been brutally cut short.

Krista abruptly snapped back to life as a series of dings finally registered. She looked down at the chat to find a number of messages from Rob. Up to the Mod View panel to see herself, deathly pale, raggedly panting in shock, pressed back into her chair as if to distance herself from the gruesome violence on-screen.

Turn it off, turn it off, turn it off!

She grasped for her mouse with a shaking hand, missed, tried again, and held on tightly, then steered the jittering arrow to the red circle with the white telephone handset marked with an X to end the call. She clicked it and her window disappeared from the stream, Hailey's expanding to fill the empty space.

Not what she'd meant to do, but she couldn't let herself be seen freaking out like she was. Her gaze shot over to her phone to find the viewer count for the stream, and she watched in horror as it rolled higher in real time. Word was spreading and they needed to cut Hailey's feed.

She clenched her hands into fists to still the trembling she could see, but not feel—her entire body had gone numb—and typed a message in response to the stream of chat messages from Rob and Emily. **Turn it off!**

Rob was the first to respond. **Can't. Only the streamer can, once it's started, because only that software has the direct link to the encoder broadcasting to Twitch. I've reported to Twitch. They can pull it down, but someone has to see the request first**

It can be turned off at Hailey's end? On her software?

Yes

Every second Hailey lay there alone, her body ripped apart and on full display, was one second too long.

I'm going

Krista didn't even wait for a response. She simply rose from her desk and ran from the room.

Zach was already on his feet, staring at her in shock as she grabbed her bag out of her bedroom. "What are you doing?"

Her lungs were having trouble functioning. She was trying to draw in air, but her muscles were frozen, only capable of dragging in a trickle of oxygen. "I'm going to Hailey's."

He grabbed at her arm, holding tight when she tried to yank it back. "Are you insane? You can't just barge in. It's a crime scene. And what if he's still there?"

Fury rose in Krista like a wave of lava. Maybe she'd like that. Without actually thinking about what she was doing, she yanked her arm free, strode to the kitchen, and pulled her largest butcher knife from the knife block, for the first time regretting she didn't have a deadlier weapon on hand. "I think I'd like that."

"This is crazy."

"Maybe, but I'm going."

"Then you're not going alone." He thrust a palm in front of her face, forestalling her protest. "No arguments. I'll drive, you call Miller. Tell him to send officers."

"I can direct you, but I don't know her building's street address. I can't tell him that until we get there."

"He'll have it. Or he'll be able to get it. Loop him in. We may still beat him there, but we can wait for him if we do."

Krista looked back at her studio setup, the brilliant key and fill lighting still flooding the space. "I'm not waiting. I'm not leaving that feed open." A sob caught in her throat, and she battled back a moan of agony. "It's all I can do for her now."

She turned and ran for the door, knowing Zach would grab his keys and follow.

Chapter 26

She called Miller just as soon as she was buckled in and considered it a miracle she held it together through the short conversation. He was behind in joining the stream because a suspect interview ran long, so he didn't know what was going on. He told her he'd dig out Hailey's address and would send patrol cars, then be on his way himself.

She didn't tell him they were en route. She knew what he'd say, and she simply didn't want to hear it. This was the last loving, respectful thing she could do for Hailey. All Krista could see in her mind was the vision of her friend, displayed for the world to see in her final moment. Chase wanted to expose Hailey at her weakest, wanted to terrorize Krista and her team, wanted to show he had all the power.

Fuck him.

She didn't know the address, but she'd been there so many times, she knew her way there on autopilot and could direct Zach. Under normal circumstances, she was about ten minutes away, but at their current speed, on a quiet Tuesday evening after dark, it wasn't going to take nearly that long. Except for her short directions, silence rode heavy inside Zach's sedan.

What was there to say?

Zach found street parking close to the building and pulled in next to the curb, jerking to a stop.

Part of Krista knew that going into Hailey's apartment could be deadly if Chase was still there. She simply didn't care about her own safety, and while she didn't want Zach to set foot in the building, she knew her brother well enough to know that if she tried to get him to stay outside while she went in, he'd either ignore her and go anyway, or would try to stop her from entering. Better to leave it alone. Besides, she honestly didn't think Chase would still be there—she didn't think the big-talking man who terrorized people online, while hiding behind a screen name, had the balls to face incoming cops—but beyond that, it was a risk she was willing to take. It would crush her if Zach was hurt—or worse, killed—but she wouldn't let that happen. She'd put herself in harm's way first. Besides, apparently, it was *her* he wanted, *her* he was focused on. That would allow Zach time to escape.

If Chase killed her, she'd be reunited with Linc that much sooner.

The combined loss of Linc and now Hailey battered her, stealing her breath. Would it really be that bad to leave this world? There was so little left for her now, with two of her closest connections gone. She loved her parents and her brother, but the continual emotional battering was slowly grinding her down.

She would roll the dice and do this for Hailey. And maybe, just maybe, take a killer down with her as she went.

She gripped the hilt of the butcher knife. "Let's go." She was surprised to hear how steady her voice was. She opened her car door and climbed out, jamming her phone into the back pocket of her jeans. Holding the knife flat against her right leg to avoid attracting attention, she ran for Hailey's apartment building, Zach right on her heels.

Constructed of pale-tan brick, the building boasted two large bays on either end of the front face, each surrounded on three sides by windows. As she bolted through the gap in the wrought-iron fence that flanked the front walk, she looked up and to her left to the second floor, where Hailey's apartment was located. The front of the apartment was illuminated, nothing looking out of the ordinary.

They ran up the short front walk and pushed into the small vestibule to find a door leading into the larger foyer housing the elevators and stairs to the upper floors. She tried the door—locked, as it should be—turned to the intercom with its button pad, and pushed both apartments on the top floor.

Flat 6 answered first. "Hello?"

"Delivery for you."

The occupant didn't even question the statement, just buzzed the door open. As they entered the foyer, Krista found a rubber doorstop on the inside—likely to help residents prop open the door when they were moving or bringing in large deliveries—and jammed it into the gap, blocking the door from fully closing so the police wouldn't have to navigate opening a locked door.

She sprinted for the staircase she and Hailey usually used, as the elevators moved like they were installed in 1929 when the building was constructed, and it was always faster to run the stairs. Up the stairs, through the heavy steel door, and into the hallway on the second floor, Zach never more than a foot or two behind her. She cut left to head for Hailey's apartment and then stopped dead, breathing hard.

The door was cracked open.

This was it. Chase had either not latched the door closed behind him as he left, or he was making it easier for her to join him.

She knew she had to do this, but her heart was pounding so hard, it almost made her hesitate. Then she thought of Linc, of the strength he'd had right up to the end, and tried to channel that strength.

She gripped the handle of the knife harder, raising it to hold it in front of her, straightened her spine, and pushed the door slightly open with her left hand. Through the gap, she could see into the deserted living room, so she cautiously pushed the door open farther.

The smell hit her immediately, a mix of the copper tang of blood and the sharp scent of urine. She'd known her friend was gone, but the odor was a brutal kick to the gut. She turned her face away, took a deep breath of hallway air, and stepped into the small foyer that opened into the living room, scanning for any movement.

Nothing.

The entry to Hailey's darkened bedroom lay to Krista's right, followed by the door to the bathroom, and then the long stretch of galley kitchen. On the far side of the living room was what was supposed to be the dining room, but Hailey had turned that space into her studio, using the one long, uninterrupted wall shared with the next unit as her backdrop. From across the combined space, Krista took in the electric-blue illumination highlighting the shelves of action figures and lighting the framed gaming poster.

It was the backdrop she'd seen every time they streamed together, now gruesomely sprayed with what had to be an arterial arc of Hailey's blood.

Turn it off. Do it for Hailey.

The apartment felt empty, making her even more sure Chase was no longer here. But she had to force herself to move, to do what needed doing.

Do it for Hailey.

Hailey's couch blocked the floor of what was behind it, but as Krista circled the armchair and came parallel with the back of the couch, an even more grisly scene came into view.

Hailey lay on the floor behind her desk, her ripped faded jeans and classic red high-top Chucks visible where she sprawled on the carpet. Krista slapped her left hand over her mouth, her chest heaving with silenced sobs. She closed her eyes, dug deep, and made herself cross over to the far side of the desk from Hailey.

Get it done. Don't look at her yet. Just get it done.

She wasn't familiar with the software Hailey used to broadcast, so she had to hope it was obvious what to do, or else she'd have to text Rob for assistance. Her hands were shaking so badly, she'd have to ask Zach to do it if it came down to that.

Keeping her eyes locked on the monitors on the desktop, Krista circled the desk, able to unwillingly see enough in her peripheral vision to keep her feet back and lean into the desktop. Concentrating on Hailey's two monitors—one with the familiar Mod View of Twitch and the other with the unfamiliar OBS broadcasting software, both still broadcasting the gruesome image—she scanned the OBS window. Relief shot through her when the controls window in the lower right corner of the panel showed a white-on-blue button with the words "Stop Streaming" to guide her path. She tried to simply focus on the broadcast controls, but it was impossible to not see the live video of Hailey still being streamed, as it took up three-quarters of the monitor.

She passed the knife to her left hand, then grasped the mouse. With a single click, she cut the broadcast, and both video windows went dark.

Krista let out a shaky breath. She'd done all she could do for her friend. One last act of love.

Time to face what had happened tonight.

Straightening, she found Hailey's 4K webcam, normally attached to the top of her Mod View monitor, now clipped to the edge of her desk, pointing down. Krista followed its line of sight down to the carpet.

She knew what she was going to find, had seen it a ten-minute drive away at her apartment, but seeing it in real life was a physical blow that weakened her knees, driving her down to the carpet, barely missing the creeping puddle of blood. The knife struck the carpet, fallen from her lax fingers, just before Krista landed on her knees, a mere foot from Hailey's grotesquely angled head.

Krista's moan broke the silence, followed by her harsh breathing. For a moment, she was frozen in horror, then she extended one hand. There was nothing she could do here—she was far too late—but she still needed one last point of contact. She ran her fingertips over the crown of Hailey's bright-blue hair, the strands soft and shiny, the personification of her joy in life, her happiness, and her individuality. Now the ends were crusted and darkened with blood, snuffing out all joy, color, and life.

"I'm sorry." Krista's words were a barely audible, ragged whisper. "This was never supposed to happen." She pulled in a jagged breath. "I love you." The tears started to flow, choking her, drowning her broken words, even as the weight of her brother's hand settled on her shoulder, the squeeze of his fingers telling her she wasn't alone. "I'm so sorry."

She dropped her face into her hands, weeping inconsolably, as Zach stood behind her, one hand still on her shoulder, keeping watch as Miller's pounding footsteps echoed in the hallway as he came in at a sprint.

Chapter 27

MILLER HAD LEFT KRISTA AND Zach motionless by Hailey's body as he quickly cleared the apartment of any potential intruder. Krista figured at that point they'd already grossly contaminated the crime scene and Chase was the more important threat.

Once he was assured of their safety, he'd returned, holstered his weapon, and, with surprising gentleness, coaxed her to rise. He'd handed brother and sister off to one of the officers, who'd taken them downstairs, put them in the back of a patrol car, and then stood outside, facing away from them.

Somehow she didn't think it was for her protection, but to keep her from rabbiting.

Which was exactly what she wanted to do. To run as far away as possible from what had happened only fifty or sixty feet from where she now sat. But she was trapped—trapped in this life, trapped in this hellish situation, trapped in this cruiser. And she'd trapped her brother now, too. She should never have let him come.

She took the time to text the Discord chat, to let Emily and Rob know the police had arrived and had taken over. She didn't need to confirm Hailey's death with them; that was all too clear. Neither had pressed her for details, both knowing that experiencing the nightmare of Hailey's murder wasn't a topic for discussion right now. Nor was the fate of the channel. No one was thinking with a clear head.

Next came their parents. She didn't really think word of a single murdered woman would make it out West this quickly, but you never knew how fast news could travel, and she didn't want them to misconstrue any story that came their way. But she couldn't talk to them, not when she was riding the ragged edge of breaking down again. Talking to them, having to put the monstrosity into words, would drive her over the edge. She could ask Zach to contact them, but they'd want to talk to her in this moment of crisis, as she was the more directly involved. Better to keep the conversation in her control and in a method she could manage. Not that texting the family group chat would be that much better, but it would have to do.

Are you back from dinner? Have time to talk?

Beside her, Zach's phone whistled, making them both jump. He pulled it out of his pocket and muted all notifications.

When a full four minutes went by, she thought their time difference—two hours behind her current time—might play in her favor. Her parents might have their phones off while they were still at dinner, and she might get off easy for the night. She could just let them know both she and Zach were okay and she'd catch them the next morning.

Then her phone beeped with an incoming text—**We're here. Everything okay?**—and she knew she was going to have to work through it all with them so they understood the full impact of what had happened. The full impact of the danger she was clearly in.

She stared at her phone for a long moment. She should have known that with her parents currently on high alert, not even a romantic dinner would keep them from being parents if their kids needed them. How to break this news? She hadn't had to with Emily and Rob. They'd experienced the horror with her. Zach had been with her every step of the way. But her parents were a different matter.

She didn't want to text calmly about it. She wanted to push her way out of the car, to stand in the middle of the street and scream out her anguish and pain to the night sky, before running the streets of Chicago.

As if she could outrun the storm of emotions raging through her.

But that wasn't what calm, responsible women did. They took a breath, settled themselves down, and made sure everyone else was taken care of. Only after she'd taken care of everything, informed those who needed to know, and reported what she knew to Miller, would she be able to retreat to the quiet isolation of her apartment to grieve alone.

No. Wait. She didn't even have that kind of solitude, because her apartment was essentially a crime scene. All she had was a little borrowed space in her brother's life.

She remained frozen too long, because Zach tapped his index finger on her forearm. "Just get it over with. Stalling isn't going to help. Pull the Band-Aid off quickly."

She nodded and typed a reply. **Hailey died tonight.**

Leila didn't even bother texting back, just moved right to a phone call. Krista's phone lit up with the incoming call, her mother's smiling face displayed on-screen. She simply couldn't talk to her parents with the roar building in her head. She was afraid if she opened her mouth, she might not be able to stop screaming.

She rejected the call and brought her text app up again. **Can't talk on the phone. In police car waiting for Det. Miller.**

Are you okay?

How to answer that? Anything she said had to be a lie, because there was no way to put what she was feeling into words.

Zach read her frozen stance and jumped in. **Neither of us is injured**

Are you under arrest? That one came from their father.

Krista forced herself to answer, to not leave the conversation and explanations to her brother, who was only here to support her. It was her mess; she needed to take the lead. **No. I was on camera in my apartment when it happened. Zach was with me.**

Back up. When it happened... It was an accident? Her father again, latching on to the tiny but important details. She knew how this would work. Leila would be focused on their health and well-being, both physical and emotional. Keith would look to their protection from any kind of legal action because of their involvement.

No. Krista stared at her screen for a long stretch of seconds, then decided they'd find out about it in a Web search in about an hour's time, so she should be straight with them. **She was murdered in her apartment. Throat cut.**

Her phone rang again, and she put her head down and rocked back and forth, waiting until it stopped. Until they got the message, she just couldn't talk to them that way. Not right now.

Her father clearly got the message, because he kept texting. **You're at the scene?**

Yes. It happened on the stream. Whoever killed her started the stream from her computer and pointed her webcam at her dead body. Only way to stop the stream without Twitch taking it down was for me to get here to do it manually. Zach drove me. He's been with me all along.

You went into that apartment? Her father again.

Yes.

He could have been there.

I know. He wasn't. I had to do it. I couldn't leave her like that for everyone to see.

A tear fell to her phone screen, and she scrubbed a hand over her wet cheeks. She was starting to crack and didn't know how much more of this she could take.

This time, Zach didn't reach out to touch her. Her brother knew her well enough to know she was hanging by a thread, and that a single act of kindness, or connection, could be enough to break her. And she couldn't afford to fall apart yet.

Keith was texting again. **You saw her?**

Yes.

Are you okay?

Her father had seen Zach's response about neither of them being physically injured, so she knew what he was really asking. She took a long time responding, then opted for honesty. **No.**

The sound of voices outside the patrol car attracted her attention. Miller stood on the sidewalk, directing two techs dressed in full-body, white Tyvek suits up the front walk.

Crime scene techs would document the scene. Only after they were done would someone from the medical examiner's office arrive to take Hailey away forever. After that, it would be up to the family to manage arrangements. Considering what had happened, they might not even want to see Krista at a visitation or funeral. She might have just said her one and only goodbye to her friend.

Her heart simply ached.

Miller was walking toward the car. Krista sent off one more text to the group chat—**Detective Miller's coming. We have to go.**

Miller opened the door and slid in next to her, forcing her to squeeze in closer to Zach. It was a tight fit, even in a larger cruiser, but Miller clearly wanted to talk to them both now, and doing it through the divider between the front and back seats wasn't going to cut it.

He studied her face in the dim light of the overhead dome light. Even in the dimness, she knew she had to look terrible—blotchy skin, red eyes, tear-streaked cheeks.

"I won't ask if you're okay," he stated.

"Thanks." Her voice came out as a hoarse croak.

"I need you to take me through what happened tonight. I'd assumed you called me from home, and you didn't indicate differently, but you must have called from the car on the way here. Is that correct?"

"Yes." Krista closed her eyes for a moment, gathering herself. She opened them and haltingly began, her voice shaky at first, then gaining strength in the face of Miller's calm responses, mostly letting her speak, only asking a few questions until she talked herself out.

"The stream will be evidence you weren't present at the time of her death, that you were across town. Have you talked to Twitch about having the on-demand video taken down?"

Her breath caught in shock that the thought hadn't occurred to her. The idea of that video, of Hailey's death, spread all over the Web made her battle down vomit that wanted to rise into her gorge. "I never thought about that. I don't know how to do that, but one of my moderators might. Can I ask him?"

"We definitely don't want that content up on the internet. Once it's out there, it could be exploited. But I need to see it."

"Hailey always recorded each stream so she could post it later on YouTube, so there should be a local recording on her equipment. Let me talk to Rob about the Twitch copy." She pulled out her phone and brought the Discord chat back up again. **We need to purge the Twitch copy of the broadcast. We can't let it go up for everyone to see.**

A few seconds ticked by before Rob replied. **Already done. I reported to Twitch Safety immediately. VOD is about 20 mins behind our stream. They took it down right away. While you were still dealing with the first question**

Miller was reading over Krista's shoulder. "Good. That gets rid of part of the problem."

"Part?" A *ding* brought Krista's gaze back to her phone and Rob's next text.

Heads up. Screen cap images and video clips are up online already

Krista slapped a hand over her mouth, muffling but not silencing the escaping moan. To have Hailey's life reduced to a single image for which everyone would remember her was excruciating. And what if Hailey's parents saw it? Or Aiden? It was bad enough she'd seen it on-screen and then in real life. For the rest of her life, she'd carry that image as her final memory of her friend. But imagine that being the final image you'd ever see of the child you carried for nine months and bore in childbirth. Who you raised together as parents. Who you now had a relationship with as equal adults. Or, in Aiden's case, who was now your romantic partner.

This was a nightmare.

The phone slipped from her lax fingers, and Miller caught it before it hit the floor. He set down his pen, then without asking permission, but angled so she could see, he started to type. **Detective Simon Miller from the CPD here. I need my tech team to talk to you. Can I get your contact information?**

Rob immediately added his email address and cell number to the chat.

Miller thanked him, forwarded the message to his own phone, and laid Krista's phone back in her lap. Then he spent a long moment considering her. "You touched the mouse to turn off the feed, didn't you?"

"Yes. I'm sorry." Krista's voice trembled. "I didn't think about ruining evidence. I just needed to get that feed off."

"Anything else?"

"The door was ajar when we got there and I pushed it open, so I touched the panel. Nothing else."

"I need to get reference fingerprints from both of you. We need to be able to exclude your prints, as well as Hailey's, to see if we get a hit from anyone else. I'll get that set up, and then it's time to get you out of here. I still need an official signed statement from you, but we'll have you come to the station tomorrow for that. I'm not going to make you do that now." His gaze shifted to Zach. "She's living with you still?"

"Yes."

"Good. Keep it that way for now. How are you getting back there?"

"I drove here tonight. As long as I can move my car, I can take her to my place." He pointed back toward his car. "I'm the silver Civic over there."

"I'll make sure you can get out, and I'll have a patrol car escort you, to make sure you're not being followed. If this guy is still here, he might try to follow you if he knows you're living somewhere else. That's not going to happen with an escort, because he won't risk being seen. Give me a minute to set it all up."

Krista nodded, not trusting her voice.

Miller slipped out of the car, leaving them in silence, the muffled sounds of the police response—more vehicles arriving and taking their places to block off the street, more officers entering the building, others moving back the gathering crowd—filtering into the passenger compartment.

Krista didn't move, a blessed numbness finally setting in, quieting the flurry of anguish coursing through her. Numb was good. Numb was manageable. She'd happily stay like this for a while in the quiet dimness of the patrol car as controlled chaos swirled around her.

Turn off the world, make it go away. Stay inside where it's quiet and safe.

Safety was all that mattered now.

She raised dull eyes to Miller when he returned a few minutes later, holding the door open for them to exit the vehicle. He took them over to one of the crime scene techs, who used a LiveScan laser scanner to take a full set of their finger and palm prints. Miller then walked them over to Zach's car, told them to stay safe, and that he'd be in contact the next morning to set up their official statements.

They drove to Zach's apartment in silence, a police cruiser following behind. Krista sat in the passenger seat, staring straight ahead, not seeing the cars and buildings as they streaked by, but occasionally feeling the weight of Zach's gaze resting on her before returning to the road.

He parked in his designated spot. By the time he got out and circled around to her door, the officer had joined them.

She was conscious of Zach being there, but it took him calling her name for her to turn to look at him, then to focus on the hand he extended to help her out of the car. She put her hand in his, let him haul her out, then hold her steady until she was sure she could stand on her own.

He slammed the passenger door and locked the car, and then he and the officer escorted her into the building, up to his apartment, and finally into the dim quiet inside. The officer checked out the apartment, confirmed it was empty, then took his leave. Zach locked the door behind him.

Krista knew he was studying her, looking for some sort of response, concern gilding his features at her blankness.

"Krista?"

Her eyes stayed locked on the floor at her feet.

"Krista."

As her gaze rose to his, the wetness of a single tear streaked down her cheek as she was buffeted by emotion, by memories. All those years of friendship, all the good times, all the hard times around Linc's illness and death, the camaraderie and fun of launching the channel. The crippling guilt that their final weeks of friendship had been tangled in a morass of anger, hostility, and suspicion. That crushed her the most.

He crossed to her, wrapped her in a hug.

Her protective shell of numbness finally cracked, and pain flooded her. Giving in, she wept out her agony on Zach's shoulder.

Chapter 28

KRISTA CALLED IN SICK TO work the next day. She was a master at putting on a chipper front to mask the staggering pain beneath, but today she simply couldn't do it. No one at work knew what had been going on in what they jokingly called her "moonlighting gig," something they just considered a fun and light hobby. Serious health care was the practice's bread and butter; however, they supported outside activities to help balance the stresses, and sometimes the sadness, of working with clients who gave their all, but simply couldn't come back to the life they'd previously lived after a serious stroke or injury.

Kyle used athletics—specifically, an indoor soccer league he'd been a part of for years—to run off his frustrations, while Melanie was all in on crafting and ran an Etsy shop sideline making pretty much anything that could come out of a Cricut. Krista had her life with Linc before, but after his loss and floating rudderless for more than a year, she'd focused in on the Twitch channel to fill some of the gaping hole.

Now she could only think she'd have done better staying rudderless. At least Hailey would still be alive, running her smaller gaming channel, attracting no madman to her streams.

Stop it. You can't keep running what-if scenarios through your head. None of it is your fault, or was Hailey's fault. It's only his fault.

Only after asking about twelve times if she'd be okay on her own did Zach finally leave for work, telling her he could be back in twenty minutes if she needed him. And to lock the door. And to make sure Miller knew he was still available for whenever he needed Zach's statement.

Krista practically had to push him out the door. She appreciated his attentiveness, but she needed some time to think, without anyone hanging over her. She'd also hardly slept the night before, likely because after waking from a nightmare about finding Hailey's body—which had somehow managed to be worse than the horrific reality—she'd been too terrified to go back to sleep. She'd try to take a nap and regroup over the day.

But it wasn't the same as being at home. She found it hard to relax in someone else's space, even Zach's familiar space. For all her brother's graciousness, she still felt like a guest.

Chase had not only taken Hailey from her; he'd taken the comfort and security of home from her as well.

It all hurt so much.

After Zach had left for work, she'd spent too long curled on the couch, while the coffee he'd made her went cold, and the talking heads on TV discussed the latest political scandal, which she heard none of. She was too locked in her own head.

She flipped off the TV, picked up her phone, opened her contacts, and scrolled to the *S* listings. Then stared at the entry for Eileen Swanson for long seconds.

She'd known Hailey's mom almost as long as she'd known Hailey. Visits to campus with bags of groceries, care packages in the mail with gifts for Hailey, but always an item or two for Krista, and car trips to the Swanson homestead in Cortland on long weekends. From the moment Krista had entered Hailey's life, the Swansons had opened their arms to Krista, taking her in almost as an adopted daughter.

She wanted to reach out to Hailey's mother to express her condolences, to see how she and the rest of the family were doing. But she had absolutely no idea what to say.

I'm so sorry your daughter was brutally murdered. Please accept my condolences. I hope I didn't contribute to it.

With a groan, she dropped her phone into her lap and tipped her head back to stare up at Zach's ceiling. What do you say to a woman whose world has just been irreparably shattered? She'd been through a similar situation herself and still couldn't begin to put it into words.

Eileen Swanson doesn't need your words. She just needs to know you're there.

She sat up, blew out a breath, squared her shoulders to steel herself, opened the contact card, and placed the call.

One ring. Two. Three. Half of her was hoping it would go to voicemail. She'd think of something to say and her duty would be done and she—

"Hello?" The woman's voice was quiet and a little unsure.

"Mrs. Swanson?"

"Yes."

"It's Krista Evans."

There was silence for a few seconds, then, "Oh, Krista, how are you?" The voice was stronger now, more secure with a known caller.

The sob bubbled up so quickly, it caught Krista off guard. She pressed her fingers to her lips for a moment as she fought to get her emotions under control. Succeeded. "That's what I should be asking you."

"I'm getting through. But, honey, are you okay?"

"Not really. I'm kind of a mess. Hailey's been such a huge part of my life for so long, I don't know how I'll manage without her."

"She loved you, Krista. Loved being with you. She was lost when she first went to Northwestern, then she met you. You were her guide."

"We were each other's guide. Mrs. Swanson, I . . . don't know what to say. Being sorry doesn't seem nearly enough to cover losing Hailey. Giving my condolences seems empty."

"I understand," Eileen said simply. "Our light's gone out, and we'll never be the same."

Her eyes filling, Krista nodded, then realized Hailey's mother couldn't see her. "That's it. Is there anything I can do for you? Can I help you plan the funeral? Help you go through her things?"

"You don't need to—"

"I'd like to. She was the sister I never had by birth. I want to help. We . . ." She stopped, blew out a shaky breath.

"You what?"

You can't burden this woman with your guilt about your last days with her daughter. "I just miss her so much already. All the things we did together."

"You two were inseparable for so many years. And then to pair up again for your advice show? She absolutely loved working with you over the past months and said it brought you closer together."

Guilt crawled through Krista. *Until I tried to bail on her.*

"And she was so appreciative that you were always enthusiastic about helping her when she needed it most," Mrs. Swanson continued.

Krista froze, her gaze fixed sightlessly on the bookshelf across the room. "Needed it most?"

"You know how she was struggling with her condo payments, on top of her student loan repayment. She was fine when she first bought the condo a few years ago, but variable rates have skyrocketed and she's had trouble making her new payments. We didn't have anything extra to help out, and she was so thankful for the extra money coming in from your channel. She said it was a double blessing, getting to work with you and the income saving her from the stress of not making ends meet. The stress of possibly losing her home."

She hadn't known. Krista could barely breathe as scenes with Hailey replayed in her head. Clues to her having financial difficulties, never fully revealed. They were so well hidden, Krista had missed them entirely.

"We all have financial responsibilities, but that doesn't mean we'd fake someone's death to rake in the cash."

"Whether you're single or partnered up, financial troubles can push anyone to the wall."

Asking Hailey over dinner if she was okay, seeing her about to speak, about to confess, then pulling back. "No, it's all good."

The text Hailey sent the day she died. Can I call you tonight before the stream? I've screwed up bad and I need to explain

Hailey had wanted to come clean, wanted to confide in Krista, wanted to tell her why she'd pushed for so long to keep the channel going, to keep bringing on new followers, even as the stream spiraled out of control, and a predator stalked the chat. She'd wanted to explain why she'd pushed for Partner, when she knew it wouldn't be something Krista would want.

Because she was desperate. Desperate to support herself, though the burden was unimaginably heavy. Desperate to maintain her proud independence.

So proud, she hadn't asked her closest friend for advice, for help.

Why didn't you tell me? You knew Linc had life insurance. I could have helped. I would *have helped. You were my sister.*

She realized Mrs. Swanson was still speaking.

"That's why instead of a single eulogy, we'd like to have a number of people speak. Would you do that for us? For Hailey? Just a few words, nothing too long. Just some remembrances of my girl." For the first time, Eileen's voice broke, the first sign of the grief lying in wait for her. She was numb to it currently, but it was coming, and when it arrived, it would be staggering.

"I would be honored to speak at the funeral. What are your plans for it?"

Mrs. Swanson outlined her thoughts for the funeral, how she imagined her last day with her daughter would go.

But Krista only barely heard her. Her mind kept going over and over what she'd learned about Hailey.

She'd pushed so hard to keep going because she was drowning and needed the income.

All Krista knew is, she would have paid anything to keep Hailey safe. Would pay anything now to get her back.

But it was too late.

Chapter 29

AFTER THE CALL, AS THE morning progressed, even Krista got sick of her wallowing. By lunchtime, she'd forced herself into the shower, to get dressed, and to start figuring things out. She messaged Emily and Rob to ask if they had any time to meet later today. They both were free from work and family obligations in the evening and agreed to meet online at seven-thirty, Chicago time.

Miller sent a patrol vehicle to pick her up and bring her in to make her statement, then drive her back to Zach's again afterward. Zach had apparently come in on his lunch hour to complete his statement, so Miller had everything he needed from them for the case.

Zach kept checking in on her, nearly hourly, until she told him that she loved him, but to buzz off and that she'd see him when he was home. That gave her a kick in the ass to dive into looking at apartments in her price range around the city. If she could find something fast, she'd take it right away, even if it meant paying for two places for a month until her notice on her current place was up.

Two hours behind Chicago, her parents had called and texted later in the morning, and she'd texted back saying she was safe and she'd touch base when her father was home from work, only to find that Keith had told his office he had a family emergency and would be working from home that day, to stay available to his kids.

She knew she could only hold them off for so long; so after she'd raided Zach's fridge and made herself eat something small for lunch, she called and soon had them both on the line.

As she had with Zach, she let herself be honest, let her emotions well and overflow, knowing she was in a safe space. She stressed again she didn't want them coming and neither did Zach. It wasn't safe here in Chicago. When they suggested she come out to them, even if only to stay for a week or two, she told them as long as Miller okayed her leaving town, she'd consider their offer, because it was something she'd already been thinking about. Chicago was home to her—her friends and her business were here—but a break from it, from the stresses she now associated with it, was an option. She could take the time off work—Kyle would cover her without a second thought—and fresh scenery would do her good.

But it wasn't something she'd consider until after Hailey's funeral.

By the time she ended the call, she felt a little bit better, with some direction to guide her over the next few weeks. She'd find a new apartment, give notice on her current one, and then take some time off to get herself together before making the move.

Hopefully, in that time, Miller would have found the man responsible for this chaos. If not, the new place would hopefully give her the safety of anonymity once again. She'd be happy to lie low for a while, putting off meeting neighbors, just working on establishing a new place of solace.

Zach came home and talked his way through dinner prep and dinner itself. Krista knew what he was doing—trying to distract her and keep her spirits up—and loved him for it, even as it grated on her tattered nerves. After dinner, she excused herself to retreat to his guest room, where she sat with her back against the headboard, braced her tablet on her raised knees, and entered their Discord video chat. She was a bit early, but Emily and Rob soon joined her.

Emily looked like she hadn't slept at all last night, either. She raised a hand in greeting and gave them a wan smile. "Hey, guys."

"Hey." Krista was sure her return smile was equally strained. "You hanging in?"

"I guess."

"How are *you*?" Rob asked. For the first time, he appeared as more than a pale face floating in a black background. He was in a fully lit room, sitting on a couch. *Maybe he, too, didn't want to be where he'd experienced the tragedy.*

"Not going to lie, I've been better. I took today off to regroup, and it might have been a tactical error. Too much time just sitting and thinking when that's pretty much the last thing I want to do. I talked to Hailey's mother, though."

The sound that came from Emily was between a sob and a groan. "I can't imagine the pain her family must be in."

"At least for her mother, that's coming. I think right now she's numb. She was more concerned about how I was doing, and didn't break down once, not even while talking about funeral plans, which should be finalized by tomorrow, at the latest."

"You'll share the details when you know what's going on?"

"Of course. Are you going to try to come?"

"I'd like to. I know a lot of the community won't attend simply because of geography."

"Baltimore is still a lot of geography."

"If I can manage the time off work and can score a flight, I'm going to try. Rob, what about you?"

"I want to, but I can't leave Carly here with a toddler and an eight-week-old infant. She'd tell me to go, and she'd suffer through it, but it would be too much to ask. I'm sorry. I'd be there if I had the freedom to be."

"I totally understand, and so will Hailey's parents. I'll let them know some in the community can't make it." She thought of Log-jammer, certain there would be some locals who would attend. "I'll get their permission to share the details of the funeral with the greater community. Considering how Hailey died, though, they may want to clear that with Detective Miller."

"Or they may not want anyone from the community at all," Rob stated. "Considering."

"Yeah, maybe. Totally their call. They won't object to you being there, Emily, so I'll let you know the details as soon as I hear them."

"I'll put out feelers about time off and potential flight options."

"Thanks. Speaking of Detective Miller . . . Rob, did he get in touch with you?"

"Yes. He connected me to a Detective Serenski, one of their computer guys. Miller said I'd just lose him, and he wanted me to be able to talk to someone at my level. I gave Serenski access to everything I had. All the Mod Action logs from every stream, copies of those streams. He's not a Twitch guy himself, but I could walk him through our stepwise restrictions and how each one went."

"Thanks for doing that. I couldn't have done the same."

"No thanks required. It was literally the least I could do."

"There's not much any of us can do," Krista said. She took a deep breath and then dove in. "I want you guys to know I'm shutting down the channel." From the expressions on their faces, it was clear it wasn't a surprise to them. "I guess you guys saw that coming."

"Pretty much," Emily said. "Things have been kind of careening downhill ever since Chase appeared. We had a lot more people watching, but the latest increases were just because of the spectacle."

"Something I've been unhappy with. But considering what's happened . . ."

"Yeah," Rob said. "We get it."

"Thanks. I thought you would. I'd actually already told Hailey I was going to bow out. Last night was going to be when I said goodbye to the Apples, but then Hailey didn't show up, and it all went to hell."

"Yeah . . ." Rob hunched down farther on the couch, his shoulders riding high. "You know to shut this all down, you're going to need to get consent from Hailey's family, right?"

"I was going to ask you guys about how the process goes from here. But I'm not going to talk to them about this until after the funeral."

"If it was my kid," Emily said, "I wouldn't want to talk about the hobby that got her killed. Not now, likely not for a long time."

"Channel stays up until we can discuss it, then, but there won't be any new streams."

"Hailey made you an Editor, which gives you almost as much control as she had. You can't request the channel gets deleted, but you can make changes." Rob paused, gnawing on a thumbnail. "Are you going to ask Hailey's family to delete the channel? Not just no new content, but delete all traces of it? The full VODS will only stay up for sixty days, but the channel could stay up with clips and highlights."

"That's going to be their decision in the end if they're the executors of her will, something I know she has, because of what happened to my fiancé. A lot of people our age don't have wills, especially if they're not married, don't have kids, or don't own property, but she watched my fiancé pass away young and decided she needed one. I know one exists, but I'm not sure who the executor is. If whoever that is asks my opinion, I'm going to say they should delete it. They'll have to decide on her gaming channel, too."

"They might not feel that way," Emily suggested. "They might want people to be able to see Hailey when she was alive and vibrant."

"Or they may feel her loss that much more keenly. We've downloaded copies of every stream because that's what we used to upload to YouTube, right?"

Rob nodded. "Correct. And YouTube is another issue for them. All the content is there, too."

Krista sighed. "I'm sure they haven't thought about any of this. And God knows it's not my forte. Can I give them your contact info if they need any help with this? Both of you?"

"Of course," said Emily. "I'm sure both of us will help out in any way we can."

"Definitely," Rob agreed. "Whenever they need it."

"Either way, it's their decision, and I don't know how soon they'll be up to making it. There was one other thing I wanted to ask about. I'd like to put up a message on the channel. I mean, everyone knows she's *gone*." Her voice broke on the last word, and she dropped her head, forcing several measured breaths to try to calm herself. When she looked back up again, she steeled herself against the compassion she saw in her moderators' eyes. "Sorry."

"Do *not* apologize."

Emily's compassion snapped over to temper so quickly, it was a reminder to Krista that she wasn't the only one suffering. She'd known Hailey longer, and in person, but online friendships were real and genuine, and these two good people had also been traumatized, not only by her death, but by how she died. "Thanks. It's been a hard day to hold it together."

"I've been weepy all day."

"It's been a temptation to drink my body weight in whiskey," Rob admitted. "I haven't, but it's been a temptation."

"I hear you," said Krista. "Anyway, what I was trying to say is, I'd like to put up a message somewhere on the channel, one that's marked as being from me, but telling everyone that we're shutting down. Somewhere I could say a few short words about Hailey."

"You can do that because you're an editor. Edit the About section of the channel page," Rob directed. "Write a note to the community and to anyone new who comes along because of all the publicity the channel has gotten and is still getting. Talk about Hailey and let everyone know there won't be any new broadcasts."

"Thanks. I'll do that today."

"It's not like the word isn't getting out. Have you seen the subreddit?"

"In the main Twitch subreddit?"

"No, the r/AWFTW subreddit."

Krista winced. "It didn't occur to me to look there. Is it terrible? Should I stay away?"

"No, totally the opposite. It's where the community has gone to remember Hailey as Mortie and to grieve."

"I was there this afternoon," said Emily. "I spent twenty minutes sobbing like a baby and then had to stop. I'll go back in a day or two when I feel a little steadier. But it's wonderful. There were always threads posted about particular questions, but right after you cut the stream last night, one of the Apples started a thread titled 'Thank you, Mortie.' There were thousands of comments about her this afternoon. There will be more by now."

Krista was afraid to ask, but made herself spit it out. "Are they talking about her death?"

"No, the original poster made it clear the thread wasn't to sensationalize her death, but to remember her. And the mods there are deleting any comments they feel are inappropriate. But the comments . . ." Emily turned her face away slightly, blinking furiously, then released a shaky breath. "After months with *AWFTW* and years on her own gaming channel, people felt they knew her and are legit grieving her loss. You should go check it out. You'll have a good cry, but it will also really reinforce what you two did over the last nine months. You made a difference. People are posting stories about how you and she as a team changed lives, or how Hailey specifically said something that spoke to them personally. I know you think this may have all been for nothing and the person who paid for it was Hailey, but you did good. You changed people's lives for the better." Emily swiped a palm over one cheek. "She's being remembered as a hero."

For the first time since the stream started yesterday, some of the tension trickled out from between Krista's shoulder blades. Hailey was getting the recognition she deserved, from the community she loved.

It didn't negate the tragedy, but it made Krista grateful for all Hailey had given to those around her during her short life.

Chapter 30

KRISTA POURED HERSELF ANOTHER CUP of coffee and carried it to Zach's kitchen table, where she'd been sitting reading her email on her phone.

She was going back to work today. Yesterday had shown her that sitting and wallowing wasn't going to be her way of handling the fallout from Hailey's death. Her mind kept circling back to the sight of Hailey's brutalized body and the circumstances that led up to it. Not to mention her well-meaning family was going to drive her over the edge with their constant reaching out—*I just wanted to check in . . . wanted to see how you're doing . . . was thinking of you.* Krista loved them all to the moon and back, but desperately wanted all three of them to take a step back, to give her some space. She needed to breathe.

She'd gotten up at her usual time, showered, dressed, and come into the kitchen to grab some breakfast and a coffee. Thursdays were her late day, which gave her a little time to get mentally into her work headspace. She found Zach putting his coffee cup and plate into the sink, to deal with once he got home, and deftly deflected his opinion that she should take another day. She sent him on his way, telling him she'd check in with him later with an update.

A coffee and a bagel later—in silence because she didn't want any contact with the news—she felt more ready to face her shift. She was in the kitchen, raiding Zach's fridge to put together something for lunch, when Miller called.

She froze when she saw his name on her phone screen, hesitated, but then pushed herself to answer it. *Maybe he's calling to tell you he caught Chase.* "Hello?"

"It's Detective Miller. Have you got a minute? Are you at work?"

"No, I'm at Zach's still. I was off yesterday, but I'm going in today. I'm not on until eleven, so I have a little time. Do you have an update on the investigation?"

"I do. And I have permission from the family to keep you up to date on it."

"I spent some time talking to Hailey's mom yesterday. Honestly, she was more concerned I was hurting than she was about herself."

"She's in shock. It won't last." The weight of experience filled Miller's tone.

"No, it won't." Krista sat back down at the table and picked up her coffee cup. She'd already decided she wouldn't disclose to anyone any of the new aspects she'd learned about Hailey. They might have contributed to her death, but they didn't apply to it. Hailey hadn't even wanted her best friend to know how embarrassed she was by her financial difficulties; there was no reason to share with Miller. She would maintain the pride Hailey worked so hard to hold fast. "Are there any leads on Hailey's killer?"

"Nothing substantial. Though I have some things I can share with you, especially because you need to know what happened."

Krista's heart hammered as she made herself say the words out loud. "Because he might come after me in the same way." She set down the cup, which now trembled in her grip. "That Hailey's death, especially broadcasted on the stream like that, was to terrorize me?" She could hear her own tone of voice ratcheting up and fought for calm. Her gaze shot to the door of Zach's apartment, confirming that the dead bolt remained locked in place.

"You were the one who gave the advice to block him, so we can't discount it. I just want you prepared. Are you alone?"

"Yes, Zach went to work. But I'm locked in."

"I want you to have your cell phone on you at all times. Don't leave it in your bag. Don't put it down at work."

"You want me to have a way of calling for help at any moment." Krista's voice was flat, and she congratulated herself on her outward calm when her hands were trembling and she was fighting to keep her respiration from spiking into hyperventilation.

"Yes. At this point, better safe than sorry."

"Do you have more information about how she died? From the"—she couldn't bring herself to say "blood," couldn't put herself back in Hailey's apartment, with the arterial spray splattered across the wall and the saturated carpet—"crime scene?"

"It's early days, by and large, but I do have some information. I'll say up front, there are no concrete leads. First of all, I heard from my computer forensics team. They've come up empty so far, but they're not even close to giving up. It seems Chase took all the precautions Hailey outlined for us—used VPNs in series, bounced around a number of locations, used an encrypted browser, and disposable email addresses that are untrackable. That doesn't mean they can't trace him backward through the VPNs. They're working on it, but they don't have any answers for us yet. We also know more about her actual death. Now, I normally wouldn't share this much information with someone who was nonfamily. I wouldn't even share this much information, period, but my gut says you need to know this."

"Let me assure you, I don't want to hear it. Tell me anyway."

"We're looking at the trace evidence collected at Hailey's—hair, fibers, prints . . . everything. We have your prints for reference, as well as Zach's and Hailey's. If we're lucky, we'll find some prints that don't match. We're running DNA."

"You still need something to compare it to, though, right?"

"Yes. Someone already in the system, if we're hoping for an in- stantaneous match. Otherwise, we'll have them ready to go for confirmation of anyone who becomes a suspect. But the security camera was where we got some solid information. They'd had some trouble at Hailey's building before—tampering of mailboxes, mostly—so they'd installed a security camera in the front vestibule, which captured everyone going in and out of the building."

Krista's cheeks heated. She could only imagine the footage of her and Zach frantically running in and pushing buttons until some- one buzzed the door open for them. "You caught the killer on the footage?"

"Who we think is the killer, yes. Same getup as when he bought the Visa cash card—ball cap, hoodie, and, this time, dark glasses."

"Because that's not suspicious at night . . ." Krista muttered. "How did he get into the building without making contact with any of the residents?" she asked, her voice raised.

"It looked like he timed it to coincide with someone coming out. The camera picks up a little of the front walk, but not all of it, so the perpetrator must have been standing just out of range, waiting for the right moment. Which makes me wonder if he'd been in the building ahead of time to determine the extents of the security system and knew how to stay out of camera range. Anyway, I made contact with the building owners yesterday, who were ex- tremely cooperative. By the end of the day, they'd sent a copy of all the video footage, which only ended up being the last thirty days. If he scoped the place out before that period of time, we have no record of it.

"However, we have a full accounting of Tuesday. The whole day was pretty typical, with residents and delivery people going in and out. Nothing suspicious, until four forty-seven. Then, as someone is leaving the building, a hooded figure wearing all black comes in. Keeps his head down so there's no clear view of his face, and only a brief flash of light reflecting off his sunglasses. Hailey arrives home, almost an hour later, at five thirty-four, uses her key to exit the vestibule, and enters the building." He paused for a moment as if consulting his notes. "The same hooded figure exits the building at eight minutes after eight. You and Zach entered the vestibule and got someone to buzz you into the building at eight-seventeen."

A shudder ran down Krista's spine. *We missed him by less than ten minutes.*

"I talked to Rob," Miller continued. "He told me Hailey had texted you saying she was late and was going to start the stream remotely. I showed him pictures of what was on her monitors in the apartment, and that's not what happened. The stream was started there on her PC by someone who was familiar with her broadcasting software. He said, once it was started there, it had to be stopped there, which is why you went flying over to get the feed stopped because Twitch hadn't taken it down yet."

The breath Krista inhaled caught several times as grief and rage flooded through her with the memory of the terror and devastation of that night. "That's why Zach and I went. Just to click that single button. So no one could see her like that anymore. We'd all already seen too much."

"Agreed. And while I'm not thrilled you two put yourself in the path of the killer, and only barely missed him, not to mention complicated our evidence collection, I understand why you did it."

Suddenly the timing realization hit her like a slap. "Wait. He went in before five? And then she came home around five-thirty? Did he torture her until he killed her at eight?"

"No. Techs from the ME's office arrived promptly, so we have a solid answer on that. And while I don't have the full report yet, I went down to the ME's office for the autopsy late yesterday afternoon."

"It's already done?"

"Yes. The ME's office is always overloaded, but they bump murder victims up the list because they know the police investigation is waiting on their results. It will be weeks before the full report, which is why I attended the autopsy for the preliminary results.

She was murdered shortly after arriving home, with her time of death between five and seven o'clock based on her body temperature at the time of examination. Because she was found so quickly, the ME could be more accurate with his time of death estimation. But we know she wasn't even home until after five thirty-four. She was killed where you found her; the body wasn't moved. She was attacked from behind, by someone right-handed, using a non-serrated blade. None of her kitchen knives appear to be missing, and most are serrated, so it looks like something he brought in and out with him—possibly some sort of folding knife, like a switchblade, to keep the weapon hidden, as we didn't see a weapon on the video feed."

He paused for a moment, letting all that sink in before continuing. "She may not have even known he was there, and there's no sign of a struggle. Death would have been very quick, and she would have lost consciousness in one to three seconds after the injury." Miller's voice was gentler now. "She didn't suffer long."

Krista was openly weeping, her hand pressed over her mouth, her chest jerking with sobs.

Miller gave her a full thirty seconds of silence before he finally prompted her. "Krista, are you there?"

Krista dropped her hand, swiped wildly at her wet cheeks, and tipped her head back to stare at the ceiling, desperately trying to pull it all together. *"Yes."* The single word was shaky and drenched with grief.

Miller's sigh drifted across the space between them. "I'm sorry to share that much with you, but I want you to be prepared. I don't know why he's doing this, but he's still a threat. He's invading private spaces and killing with no warning. You need to be aware. The other thing to note is that this killing follows the same MO as Shanna—though, notably, there wasn't the same rage aspect. With Shanna, there were multiple stabs to the torso the ME estimates were immediately following the fatal blow. This didn't happen with Hailey."

"She was a means to an end. She was convenient."

"I read it like she also wasn't driving his rage."

"You don't have anything definitive on the killer?"

"Nothing so far. But we're working on it from multiple angles—Shanna, Hailey, and you. In the meantime, I need you to be careful. Be aware of your surroundings at all times. At home, at work. Especially anywhere you're alone. If there's anyone who makes you uncomfortable, someone you make contact with around the neighborhood, anyone, really, be sure to let me know."

"What would I be looking for?"

"Could be someone who seems slightly 'off'. Maybe seems aggressive if he's not masking or controlling his emotions well."

"Actually, I have a client like that. I've only seen him twice, but from the first moment he walked into the clinic, it was clear I was an imposition on his precious time. Micah Lamond. Needs post-op therapy for a broken wrist. I need to see him weekly, which he sees as a cash grab, so he only comes in every two weeks. Each time, he starts off with his attitude dialed up to eleven and we go from there. I was going to have my male partner see him next time because I don't think he likes women. Or maybe just not me?"

"I'd like his contact information. And yes, I know you're a medical facility. I'd need a warrant. I'll tell the judge we need to run all your clients as a precaution, as you're now a target. Leave it with me. But I'd like to learn a little more about this Mr. Lamond. Be sure to bring people you trust into your confidence so they know what's going on in your life. Zach knows, but do your co-workers?"

"Part of it."

"Bring them in. They could also be at risk if you're a target. There's safety in numbers. Be safe. And, as I said, keep your cell phone on you at all times. If anything seems strange, don't second-guess. Call 911. If it's a false alarm, I'll deal with it, but that's how I want you to play it."

"Got it."

"Good. I have to go, but I'll keep you in the loop if I learn any-thing pertinent. You let me know if anything happens that makes you uncomfortable."

"I will. Thanks, Detective Miller." She ended the call.

She sat back, phone in hand, staring at it and wondering if someday soon this device would be the difference between life and death.

Chapter 31

"THANKS SO MUCH, MR. JOHANSSON. Keep up the good work, and I'll see you next week."

Krista watched the older man make his way carefully down the corridor, leaning heavily on his cane. She checked the time on her fitness tracker: 7:02. She was almost done for the day.

Thank God. She was just so tired.

After Hailey's death, more than a week before, Kyle and Melanie had both tried to convince her to take more time off, insisting they could manage the schedule and clients with minimal rebooking, but she'd refused. She needed to be busy. Being idle just made her think about what had happened and could send her into a spiral. Being busy—both her hands and her mind—kept her focused.

Hailey's funeral had been the previous Sunday afternoon, just five days after her death. She'd attended with Zach and had met Emily in person for the first time. They'd hugged, they'd cried, and they'd committed to staying in touch. Part of Krista knew for all her good intentions, she was likely going to want to put this episode in her life behind her forever, which would mean letting go of Emily, Rob, and the Apples, as well as this later incarnation of Hailey.

She suspected once she had time to grieve, to heal, the Hailey that would live on for Krista was the girl she met at eighteen when

SARA DRISCOLL 253

they were assigned a dorm room together. They'd moved out of their dorm at the end of their first year, living off-campus together for the next three years as they finished their degrees. That version of Hailey—fun, whip-sharp, and more than a little irreverent—that was the Hailey that would live on in her mind. But for now, her sorrow and guilt that they'd been clashing, up to the point of her death, continued to weigh heavily on Krista, smothering any chance of her spirits rising.

Sadly, having lived through a crisis like this before, Krista knew the best antidote was time, and she just needed to keep putting one foot in front of the other. Which meant going back to life, as she knew it ten months ago, before Hailey had the idea to create a Twitch channel, back when her biggest goal was to continue to try to find her footing after the loss of Linc.

Now she had to find her footing without Linc or Hailey. Her love and her best friend.

She honestly wasn't sure how much more grief she could handle.

She suspected her family was similarly concerned. Zach wouldn't hear of her moving out, saying his spare room was just sitting there empty and he enjoyed her company. Her parents called every night, her mother texting frequently during the day. They'd always texted each other often—amusing photos, stories about Meatball's latest antics, a sweet sales deal—but the frequency had ramped up over the past week. Krista knew it was her mother's way of not only keeping tabs—every return text was not only proof of life, but proof of safety—but of showing love and support. She couldn't resent her for that. If they couldn't be physically here, it was the next best thing.

She gave herself a shake, knowing her last client of the day was already waiting in the gym. She'd heard Melanie talking to him as they'd passed by, down the corridor.

Just one more. Then you can go home and hole up in peace.

She took a restorative breath, pasted on a smile, then stepped out of the exam room to find Jason Tobin in the gym area, sitting on a treatment bed against the wall, cradling his left forearm in his right hand, his lips folded tight. "Hi, Jason. Sorry for the wait. Ran overtime with the last client." She studied his stiff posture a little longer. "Everything okay?"

"I think I did something dumb."

"Meaning?"

"I overstrained the shoulder last night. Jacquie was lifting a ceramic dish out of the top shelf of one of our cupboards, and she lost her hold on it at the last second. I didn't even think. I just lunged for it." Settling his forearm in his lap, he massaged his left shoulder with his right hand. "To say it hurt would be an understatement." He met her eyes, self-recrimination evident in his expression. "How far did I set myself back?"

"As long as you haven't torn your rotator cuff again, it's nothing we can't fix, though it could add a few weeks to your recovery." She took in his dark expression. "Give yourself a break, Jason. It was a natural reflex reaction."

"Should have reached with the other arm," he muttered. Then he blew out a breath. "Where do we start?"

"Back at the beginning. Let's first see what kind of mobility you have without pain, and we'll go from there. Remember, you've done this before, so it may just mean having to stay with the lower grade of exercises for a little longer. I was going to move you up to the next level, so we might have to hold off on that for a bit. It's okay, everyone gets there at their own pace, and there are often setbacks. All part of the journey. The end goal doesn't change."

"I know. I'm just tired of being on the DL. I want to get back to my job and my normal life."

"Totally get it. And we'll get you there." She patted the treatment bed. "Lie down and let's have a look."

Jason carefully lowered himself to lie supine on the bed. "It's just so quiet in here."

Krista chuckled. "My Bluetooth speaker is in Exam One. Want me to grab it for your Boy George fix?"

"I may need the cheering up. Let's see how bad it is first, then we'll blast the tunes."

"Deal." She took his left wrist in her left hand and cupped her right hand around his left elbow. "Going slowly. You had up to one hundred ten degrees comfortably last time." She eased it up to forty-five, then sixty, then seventy-five. "How's it feeling?"

"Tight, but not really painful." Another fifteen degrees, and Jason hissed through his teeth. *"Stop."*

Krista eased the arm back. "Just past ninety. You're right, it's a bit of a relapse."

The sound of running feet had Krista looking over her shoulder and toward the main corridor as Melanie came into view, moving fast, her complexion pale with lines of stress carved deep around her eyes and lips. "Mel? Everything okay?"

"No. I just got a call from my dad. Mom was in a car accident. She's in an ambulance on her way to RUSH right now." Melanie studied Jason, stretched out on the treatment table. "Dad wants me to meet him there, but you're not done for the day."

Krista was torn. The rule in the clinic was no one worked alone. While the area of town they were in wasn't among the worst of the crime rates, any area in a big city could be unpredictable. And especially now, they were making sure Krista was never alone in the clinic. But if it had been her mother and she couldn't get there, Krista knew she'd be absolutely frantic.

If word had come through before Krista had started Jason's session, she'd have rebooked him for the next day or the next week. But here he was, already on her treatment table, and in pain from an exacerbated injury. She couldn't shuffle him out the door; she needed to offer him aid. That was what she did—what they did—here at this clinic.

"It's your mom. You need to go. Jason and I are already into his session, so we'll finish up here. Can you make sure to lock the door as you leave, and I'll unlock it to let him out at the end of the session? We'll be about forty-five minutes tonight."

"My fault." Jason winced. "Screwed up my shoulder."

"We can fix it," Krista reassured him. "I'll be fine," she said to Melanie. "You deal with your crisis."

Melanie turned her back to Jason and gave Krista a pointed look. "Let me know when you're all wrapped up for the night."

"I can do that. Send your mom my best."

"Thanks." Melanie ran back down the corridor.

"Send updates!" Krista yelled after her.

"Will do!" Melanie's voice was fading.

Krista turned back to Jason. "Sorry about that."

"No worries. Life happens."

"It sure does. Can you sit up, please? I want to test the other planes of movement before we move into some gentle stretching." She caught the disgruntled look on his face. "Then I'll get the music. Sit up."

"Bless you." He awkwardly sat up, pushing off with his right hand and swinging his legs off to dangle over the edge.

Krista tested his lateral motion, nodding in approval. "That's still about fifty degrees, so no regression there."

That perked Jason up a bit. "No?"

"Nope."

The faint sound of the main door closing filtered back from the front of the clinic.

"Baby steps, Jason, we'll get you there. Now, tunes?"

"Yes, please."

Krista jogged into Exam One, grabbed her speaker, and jogged back to set it on a nearby counter. She turned it on, then pulled out her phone, queuing up a Spotify Culture Club playlist. The opening beats of "Church of the Poison Mind" pounded out of the speaker as she slipped her phone back in the side pocket of her yoga pants. "How's that?"

Jason's head bounced to the beat a few times, a grin spreading across his face as the harmonica slid in. "Perfect. How are you going to fix me?"

"We're going back to basics. Back to stretching, rather than strengthening, for this week, at least. Before we begin, I want to do some cold laser therapy on your shoulder. A little now, and then a little more at the end. That will help with inflammation and pain."

"You can do it twice in one session?"

"You can't really overdo it. I'd like to give you some relief before we start and then more at the end so you'll sleep well tonight. If it helps, I'd recommend you coming in early next week for a short session, just for laser therapy, and then back in as usual a week from tonight for stretching, and, if it's feeling better, strengthening. Sound like a plan?"

"For sure."

"Good. Give me a minute. I need to find the laser. It's usually in Exam One, but one of the assistants was using it out here earlier and I don't think it made it back there."

She wound through equipment toward a counter with cupboards underneath. The assistants always straightened this area before they left with Kyle on Thursday nights, but there was always the odd thing still being used. Melanie normally did the last tidying as she waited for Krista's last appointment to end, but tonight, of course, she'd left early. Some scattered free weights and a BOSU ball still littered the floor in various areas, and she steered around them. She'd make a point of cleaning after this session was over so Melanie wouldn't have to deal with it tomorrow, or so Kyle wouldn't have to in the morning, if Melanie didn't come in because her mom needed her.

Crouching down, she opened the cupboard and looked over the contents—medicine balls, stretch bands, stacks of exercise sheets . . . There it was, the portable cold laser consisting of a control box and the attached wand. She was reaching in for the box when she heard the tiniest of sounds behind her, barely audible over Boy George's crooning. Just a tiny *snick*. Like the sound of something snapping into place. Like a lock or a latch.

Or the blade of a folding knife.

She redirected her hands, grasping the medicine ball sitting beside the laser system instead. She was either in a fight for her life or she was about to assault an innocent client.

Spinning in place, she quickly sized up the situation, and her heart rate spiked as she realized her danger. Jason had come up behind her, a switchblade in his right hand. The affable client, the one who was beating himself up because he'd hurt himself, was gone. In its place was a stranger, a man with death in his eyes as he stalked closer.

She couldn't question what was happening. Reacting was all that mattered.

She surged to her feet, flipping her hands around the fifteen-pound medicine ball so she could shoot it out from her chest with minimal movement and maximum force. She launched the ball at Jason, who didn't even try to risk his hold on the knife by blocking it with both hands. He raised his left hand, but what he clearly hadn't counted on was the weight behind the ball. All fifteen pounds hit him in the chest like a lead weight. With a cry of surprise, he staggered backward three paces as Krista slipped behind the recumbent bicycles, putting the equipment between them.

More importantly, he stood between her and the only exit from this space, be it the corridor leading to the front door, or the emergency exit at the back of Exam Two.

She was trapped.

But she sure as hell wasn't helpless. The first thing she needed to do was call for help. Keeping her eyes on Jason, she reached down to the cell phone in her yoga pants pocket, facing in against her thigh. Turning her body slightly so he couldn't see what she was doing, she found the power button with her middle finger and depressed it four times in quick succession, and her phone vibrated against her leg.

She'd done it.

Thanks to Melanie's insistence, she'd set up the Emergency SOS system on her Android phone last week after she'd filled Melanie and Kyle in on what was going on in her life. After fine-tuning the settings, she'd entered in the contact info for Zach, her parents, Detective Miller, and since he had told her to call 911, even if she wasn't sure if it was an emergency, 911 as well. Four pushes of her power button started a cascade, sending out an SOS to all listed contacts, providing the SOS message, her present location with twenty-four hours of location tracking, pictures from her front and back cameras, and a five-second audio snippet.

They'd all receive the message, and Miller and 911 would simultaneously spring into action. Trapped in her pocket, her phone wouldn't be able to send any useful visuals, but she was going to make that five-second sound bite do a lot of heavy lifting to go along with the location, which Miller would identify as the clinic.

"Why the knife, Jason? Is this your follow-up to killing Shanna Garner? To killing Hailey?"

"Shanna was my opening act." The glint in his eye went feral. "Killing Hailey was just to get your attention."

Stay calm. He's trying to knock you off stride. Casual comments about Hailey went a long way to success in that arena, but she bore down, made herself focus on nothing more than the man and the weapon. She grabbed one of the smaller medicine balls, only a five-pounder, and lobbed it at him. With a laugh, he caught it with his left hand and whipped it back at her. She ducked and then stared at him, mouth agape. "Your shoulder . . ."

"Was fine months ago. If you'd ever seen my scars, you'd have known the surgery was two months earlier than I said it was."

"You've been faking your progress all this time. Making it look slow so I'd never think you were a threat." Another thought occurred, one that roiled her stomach. "That way, you'd need more assistance, and I'd be more hands-on with you."

His smile was salacious. "I love having your hands on me. I'm only sorry I didn't get more of it. And now we'll have to finish this. I wasn't going to end it this quickly, but now the situation presents itself, I can't let the opportunity go by. Who knows when my next chance would come...?" His laugh was pure mean. "Too bad about that car accident. You might have gotten a few more weeks without it."

He feinted to his left, so she lunged to her right, but still the knife whistled through the air only a foot away. His arms were too long for her liking.

"Why? Why do we have to end this?" Help was on the way, and that meant stalling for time. Not only did cops have to get here, they had to get through the locked door at the front of the clinic. Nothing a battering ram or a few bullets wouldn't solve, but it would still take extra time and would announce their arrival.

"Because I needed to do this while you thought I was helpless. And now the channel is going off-line, I wasn't going to get my twice-weekly dose of you that way. It's just like Shanna. If I can't have you..." He let his words trail off, his meaning crystal clear.

A shiver of fear skittered down her spine. There was no cold reason here; it was more primal than that. For some reason, he saw her as a possession, one only for him.

"What about Jacquie? What would she think of all this?"

"I'm sure she wouldn't much like it... if she existed. She was all part of the façade."

As he talked, Krista calculated the distance to freedom—about forty-five feet to Exam Two, or about thirty feet to the corridor, but then another forty feet to the front door, which she'd have to take the time to unlock. But they were on a busy street, even at this time of night, which played to her advantage, as the well-lit foyer would be visible to anyone passing by. If she got into a struggle with him there, they might be seen. And while the open carrying of firearms was illegal in Illinois, citizens could carry concealed with the correct permit. She might be lucky enough to find someone who could actually help her. Or maybe the police would be responding by then.

First, though, could she get to the front door? She might have better luck with Exam Two—the only problem being, there was no way to lock the door against him. She'd have to get into the room, around the treatment table, to the door at the back, then out the door into the Starbucks drive-through lane. That could actually be an advantage, as there was constant traffic through there until the store closed at nine o'clock, providing another way to flag down help.

That clinched her plan. Hopefully, law enforcement would arrive before that, but there were no guarantees.

She needed to distract Jason. "I don't get it. Why me?"

His eyes narrowed to slits. "I knew you didn't recognize me."

That gave her a jolt. *Recognize him? I know him?* "And where would I recognize you from?"

"You met me multiple times at Zach's place. I was there because one of my buddies knew Zach from college. You were introduced to me several times."

"I don't remember a Jason."

"That's because I was always introduced as JC. Jason Charles. My dad was Jason, too, so instead of Junior, my family used my initials. Lots of people know me that way." He danced on the balls of his feet. "You met JC a few times. Good to see it made an impression."

Krista didn't remember him by any name, but she wasn't going to tell him that. When she was in college, she went to a couple of parties at Zach's, but she usually thought his friends at the time were a little too into beer for her taste, and she wasn't into sloppy drunks. She'd lumped them all together as "not interested," and had not really registered any of them. Luckily, it was a phase Zach grew out of years ago.

"Zach had a lot of friends. I always considered them out of my league." She didn't add that his premature balding also likely contributed to her not making any connections now, if she'd ever truly noticed him in the first place. Which she doubted.

"Sure you did." His tone conveyed his disbelief. He circled the bikes, walked over a treadmill, to come up on her left side, blocking her way to Exam Two. She countered by skirting the weighted pulley system, keeping the leg press between them. If she could keep him circling, she could get closer to one of the two exits. If one ended up being an open path, she'd take it rather than wait for the other, even if it was shorter. Freedom might never open up in a second direction, and she'd die right here.

Just like Hailey.

"Why Hailey?"

"I met her once at Zach's when she came with you, but she didn't make much of an impression. She was just a geek girl back then. But when I heard about your channel through Zach, I recognized her right away. That blue hair was hot, but she wasn't the goal."

Krista felt the blow like it was a physical strike—Zach was the connection between herself and this man, and therefore Hailey. She knew her brother, and knew when he heard about the connection, he'd think he'd paved the way for not only her misery over the past weeks, but for Hailey's murder. It would kill him. All the online abuse and terror, all the stress, the agony of Hailey's death . . . none of it would have happened if Jason Tobin had never heard of *A Word from the Wise* through her brother.

"You still see Zach?"

"Just saw him two weeks ago. We're in the same fantasy football league. Don't you worry, I'll be sure to offer him my deepest condolences at your passing. I'll come to your funeral and everything."

"No way in hell."

"Exactly where you're going."

"You'll be going to jail. You think you're going to kill me and get away with it? Melanie knows you're here with me. You'll be the first person the cops question."

"By the time they find your body tomorrow, they won't know exactly when you died tonight. I'll tell them you were alive and well when you let me out and locked the door behind me. It's really too bad someone broke in and killed you after that while you were here alone." His grin spread wide. "Sure, they'll find physical evidence that I was here, but I'm supposed to be here. They'll never pin your murder on me. Why would they? Besides the clinic, where you're the angel who's putting me back together, I don't know you at all. I have no motive to kill you. And I'm much too injured to successfully attack and kill you."

Keep him talking. Keep stalling. "You're insane if you think you'll get away with this."

"I'll very much get away with this. I'm too smart to get caught. I was too smart for you." His face took on a smug expression as his tone turned condescending. "You know, I was sorry when you moved out of your apartment. I liked watching you. I liked watching you panic when things went missing or moved around. You thought you were losing your mind. It was fun. Maybe even more fun than watching you panic on-screen during the streams, because you knew you were on camera and tried to tamp it down. But at home, you let yourself be you." His smile disappeared. "Then you left. That was just one of the things you did wrong. The other wasn't listening to me in the chat. You could have saved her. You could have helped me win her over. Shanna's death is on you."

"You're nothing." Krista's voice was cold and detached, with a lip curl to match as if he was a bug to grind under her shoe as she pushed his taunting aside in her head. *Not important. Don't let him throw you.* "You weren't listening to me then, and you certainly aren't now."

Angry color suffused his face. "I'm going to enjoy watching you bleed out, just like the others. I'm only sorry it's always over so fast." He leaped for the leg press, bracing one foot on the angled backrest and pushing off it, reaching out with his left hand to catch her. She jumped backward, but tripped over the BOSU ball, her arms windmilling for balance.

He caught one flailing wrist in his left hand, the crushing pressure and control showing exactly how much progress he'd made following his surgery as he yanked her closer, showing no sign of shoulder pain.

She wasn't a fighter, didn't have any skills in that area, but she was strong from years of managing her clients' physical therapy, and she wasn't about to give up without any kind of struggle. She let him yank her closer, but then used her own inertia to drag him sideways, then down, his left side dropping first.

She fell hard enough to nearly knock the wind from her lungs, twisting to keep from crushing her skull on a ten-pound free weight left on the floor, at the same time ensuring the hold he had on her meant that he landed with his injured shoulder down. He roared with pain and rolled over, trying to pin her.

She caught the flash of the blade and only had enough time to jerk into him, feeling the fiery slice cut across the left side of her neck. She could only pray it hadn't severed a major blood vessel, or she was already the walking dead.

He raised his hand, holding the knife high, readying to strike again. "Tell Hailey and Shanna I said 'Hi.'"

She didn't even respond, just reached out with her right hand for the ten-pound free weight directly over her head. Grasping it, she put every ounce of strength she had left into the equivalent of the forward motion of a triceps extension, hauling the weight up over her head to bring it crashing down against Jason's temple, just as the knife angled in an arc to sweep across her throat, starting under her left ear.

The force of the blow rang up her arm, even as the strike knocked the knife from his hand and his body went limp. She didn't wait to see the damage, but gave him a frantic shove, only vaguely noting the lack of resistance in his body as she scrambled out from under him and rolled to her feet.

One hand clamped over the bloody wound on her neck, she ran for the front door and freedom.

Chapter 32

FOUR HEADS RAISED AT THE knock on Zach's front door.

"I'll get it." Zach set down the coffee mug he'd been cradling, pushed away from the table, and rose, padding in stocking feet to the door. Low male voices sounded, and then he was back, Detective Miller trailing in his wake.

"I'm sorry to bother you at breakfast." Miller scanned the table, still set with the remains of their meal, pausing at the two faces unfamiliar to him. "I'm Detective Simon Miller."

Krista's father rose to his feet and held out a hand. "Zach and Krista have told us about you. Keith and Leila Evans, parents to these two."

Miller shook hands, first with Keith, then with Leila. "When did you folks get into town?"

Keith glanced at the digital clock on the stove, which read 8:11. "About three hours ago." He covered a yawn with his hand. "We got Krista's SOS signal at the same time as everyone else. We managed to get tickets on the red-eye out of Seattle last night, at ten-forty Pacific Time, landed at O'Hare at four-thirty Central Time. Grabbed an Uber and surprised the kids by calling from the front walk of the building about an hour later."

"Yeah, we weren't expecting you to show up out of the blue from two thousand miles away." Zach rolled his eyes. "We also

hadn't gone to bed at a reasonable hour. And there was alcohol."
He raised his coffee cup. "Thus, the large amounts of caffeine, for
multiple reasons."

Krista tipped her head against her father's shoulder. "Unexpected, but very much appreciated."

Keith kissed the top of her head. "We wouldn't be anywhere
else. You couldn't tell us at that point it wasn't safe to come." His
gaze shot to Miller. "It is safe now, right?"

"Yes. Do you mind if I join you? I'd like to update you as to
where we are in the investigation."

Zach motioned him into a chair.

"Coffee?" Leila asked.

"Yes, please. Just black."

She got up, filled a mug, set it in front of Miller, and circled
back to sit in her own chair.

Miller met Zach's bleary eyes. "From what I understand, you're
the connection between Tobin and Krista."

Zach mumbled a curse under his breath, then had the grace to
blush and look at his mother. "Sorry."

"You're not sorry today. None of us are sorry today. Fuck him."
She sat back in her chair, her hands wrapped around her cup, a self-
satisfied smile on her lips. "He terrified my daughter, and he used
my son to do it. Damn right I said that."

Zach touched his mug to hers with a muffled *clink*. "My hero."

"Remember that next time I annoy you by being nosy." She
set her laserlike gaze on Miller. "Anyhoo, what can you tell us
about him?"

Miller turned to Zach. "How well do you know him?"

"Not well, clearly. I met him in college. He was friends with
some of my friends, so he tagged along to some parties and we
bumped into each other now and again. We were never friends,
just connected through mutual friends."

"Apparently, that was enough to bring Krista into his orbit."

"He got in on our fantasy football draft a few years back and again this year in July. We normally do it in August, to account for any last-minute injuries, et cetera, but a lot of the guys were traveling in August and we're really not that serious about it, so we bumped it up. That was the first time I'd seen JC in a long time."

"JC being Jason Tobin?"

"Yeah, that's what we always called him. The guys were giving me a hard time about the fact that Barb and I had just broken up . . . again . . . Neil said I should ask you for advice, someone else questioned why I'd do that, and the story about your Twitch channel came out. I don't remember JC asking anything specific about it, but he was there, so he would have soaked it all in."

"How did Neil know about *A Word from the Wise*?" Krista asked.

"We were just shooting the"—he glanced at his mother—"talking a few months back, and he mentioned he was following some gamer on Twitch, and I mentioned you were on there now. He actually watched a few of your streams."

"Really?"

"Yeah. Anyway, that might be how JC found out. And if he was holding some torch for Krista—"

"That's a hell of a torch," Keith muttered.

"—and started watching himself, that might have been how it all began."

"But this wasn't just watching Krista," Miller stated. "He made it personal and went in as a client. Krista, when did you start seeing him in the clinic?"

"He became a client in September, before Chase547 showed up on the stream. But clearly after he'd been watching, if he knew about it in July. And maybe not just new broadcasts; all our streams are on YouTube, and the most recent streams are on Twitch. He could have watched the whole catalog. That would be hours and hours of viewing."

"Lots of time to kindle an obsession. He clearly had it all planned out," Miller said. "To begin with, you weren't the main attraction. He was focused on Shanna Garner. I showed his picture at the Crooked Barman, and they recognized him right away. He was a regular, usually pretty quiet, the kind that didn't interact much. While most of the time he was alone, he was with someone else occasionally, but he didn't stand out, by and large. Just a guy who talked about having a tough construction job and enjoying a drink after work. Never drank to excess, never caused trouble. But he was served by Shanna on a regular basis."

"Sounds like he tried to stay under the radar," Keith commented. "Not the kind to attract attention. The kind to blend in."

"That's what I thought, too. And when we asked his coworkers about him, they all said the same thing. Everyone kind of nailed him as one of the quiet ones you're not surprised to find out later is completely crazy. He went to you in the clinic, Krista, because he connected to you in real life from your online persona, even if it was all in his head. The injury he told you about was true—he was injured on a construction site, but it was much earlier than he stated, and he was already back to work."

"And that's why I never saw his surgical site. Some clients will show you, but some don't. He always wore a long-sleeved, crew-neck shirt, so he'd have had to remove it completely to show me. And there was never any reason to ask him to do that."

"His being back to work was why he often came to late-afternoon or evening appointments; he was actually working the day job. He was too far along in his recovery to still need physical therapy, so he made it look like he was much earlier in his rehabilitation."

"He was entirely convincing." Krista picked up her fork, pushed her scrambled eggs around her plate for a few seconds, then put it down. "Recovery from a serious injury is different for every person, and we work with them until there's no longer any benefit to treatment. We have to depend on the clients to tell us when they hit a point of pain."

"Recovery can be faked, then," Miller stated.

"Yes. He faked it well. I had zero suspicions."

"Which made you vulnerable when he went after you." Zach's words burned with fury, his eyes fixed on the white gauze bandage on the left side of her throat.

She instinctively laid her fingers against the dressing. It covered a wound about two inches long that a plastic surgeon had stitched closed in the wee hours of the morning. Luckily, it had been a shallow slice and no major vessels had been hit. "Only initially. I held my own."

"You more than held your own." Miller's tone was threaded with glee. "You gave him a grade-two concussion. When the patrol cops who first made it to the scene went in, he was just coming to. He got the treatment he needed from the EMTs, and then we took him in for his interview. His lawyer showed up and he wanted to cop a plea deal."

Fury rose in Krista like lava erupting. Before she could try to form rage into words, Miller beat her to it.

"He's not getting any break from the charges of first-degree murder for Shanna or Hailey. For starters, we have your SOS audio snippet, where he admits to both murders, something he didn't realize was being recorded." He smiled as Krista slumped back in her chair in relief. "They agreed to lower the charge of attempted murder for your attack down to aggravated assault in exchange for a confession of his dealings with Shanna. I know what you're thinking, but we looked at it this way. He's going to jail for a long time, and isn't likely to ever get out, so your charge was icing on the cake. We were more interested in how he'd done what he'd done. His lawyer thought it was a crappy deal and tried to talk him out of it. Tobin seemed to think he'd won some sort of great concession on the charges related to your attack, and they'd never get the murder charges to stick, so he'd be home free in a few years." Miller's chuckle accompanied a satisfied smile.

"Not a chance in hell. When we got our warrant to search his place, we found your missing bracelet and hand massager, as well as Shanna's missing purse. Not to mention his switchblade, which we recovered from the clinic after he attacked you. Forensics has it, and we're hoping to recover traces of DNA in the pivot screw for both Shanna and Hailey. He cleaned it, but it's doubtful he really got in there to get all traces. He's going down on those two counts of murder one."

"What was his story?" Zach asked. "How did he get into Krista's place?"

"That was one of the things we were most interested in. How, and how often, because as opposed to the hack lockpick job he did at Hailey's, there was no trace of picking or any obvious illegal entry. Seems he didn't have to break in. He had his own key."

Krista sat bolt upright. "He had *what*?"

"He had his own key," Miller repeated.

"How did he get that? I certainly didn't give him a key."

"Not willingly. He did it during one of your early therapy sessions. You ducked out of the exam room he was in for a few minutes to find a nerve stimulation device, leaving your keys on the counter. Your work keys, but also your apartment key, which stood out as the only noncommercial key in the bunch. He was all ready with an aluminum casting mold, preloaded with heat-and-set sculpting clay, which essentially made a negative copy of your key in about twenty seconds. He put the keys back so you didn't suspect a thing, hid the mold in his bag, and took it home. He cast the key with a low-melting-point alloy, and voila, he had a copy of your key that he could use to get access to the building. He then used that copy to unlock your front door while you were at the clinic, stroll in, and help himself to your things." He met Krista's eyes. "It's how he swapped your photo and sculpture. How he stole your bracelet, coffee filters, and your hand massager. Which, by the way, we have to hold on to for a bit as evidence, but I'll make sure you get them back as soon as possible."

"Is that how he got access to her master password, too?" Zach asked.

Miller nodded. "He went through every drawer and closet. When he found the note with the password on it, he took a picture of it." He turned to Krista. "He then used it to log into your password manager on your own device and turn off two-factor authentication. At that point, he knew which password manager you used and ensured he could use it anywhere. With that, he got into your Twitch account. When you changed the password, he could find it, because he had access to your password database. And when it became clear that your Twitch account was compromised because he was able to keep unbanning his user ID using your credentials, he beat you to changing your master password to one only he knew so he'd have ultimate control before you locked him out."

"How did he know where she lived?" Zach asked. "He got in to do all this stuff, but how did he know her street address and flat number?"

"That one was old-school. He followed her home one night after a late shift. She almost always walked to work, so he stayed far enough behind that she didn't know she was being followed. Once she got inside, he waited outside, watching to see what lights went on just after she entered the building. She not only turned lights on, she then went to her balcony window to draw the drapes, easily confirming which apartment was hers." He paused for a moment, as if uncomfortable. "There's one other thing. And you're really not going to like it."

Krista put her mug down with a thump. "What?"

"He'd installed a hidden camera in your apartment."

Krista closed her eyes for a moment, fighting the mixture of embarrassment and rage that tangled in her gut. "So that's what he meant. He made some comment about enjoying watching me panic that night as we fought, but I purposely didn't let myself absorb it. He was trying to throw me off so he could overpower me, but I was blocking him out mentally so I could focus on survival."

"Good choice. The camera wasn't installed in your bedroom or bathroom, if that makes you feel a little better."

"It does."

"He replaced the smoke detector in your living room with a fake detector with a built-in Wi-Fi camera he connected to your network so he could watch you from across town. It gave him some jollies to watch you running around looking for things he'd taken." He sent a sly look toward Leila, reading the fury in her eyes. "Fucker."

She toasted him with her coffee cup.

"We have access to that feed," Miller said, "so that will add to his charges. He's not going to get out, Krista. He's going to go away for a long time, even with a plea deal for your charges. You won't have to think of him ever again."

"That would be my pleasure."

"You've permanently shut down the channel?"

"Not yet. That needs sign-off from Hailey's family, but they're going to give it to me." Krista scanned the table, met each pair of eyes in succession. "It's over and I'm not going back to it. Time to close that chapter for good."

Chapter 33

"You're really coming along nicely, Mrs. Bowman." Krista bounced to the beat of George Michael's "Faith" beside the recumbent bike as Mrs. Bowman did some gentle cycling with minimal tension. "How's it feeling?"

Mrs. Bowman's whole body swayed from side to side as she clutched at the handles at her hips. "Not bad at all. Look at me go!"

"There's chocolate in your future, isn't there?"

"Damn straight. How much longer?"

"Aiming for five minutes, but if it hurts at any point, stop right away."

"Here goes nothing." The older woman closed her eyes, bowed her head, and pedaled.

Her client occupied, Krista let her gaze drift across the gym to the leg press machine and the floor around it, where she'd nearly died. Where she might have died if Melanie hadn't been called away, and because of that hadn't been able to clean up the equipment, leaving a ten-pound free weight at hand at the exact moment Krista needed it.

She'd taken the week following her attack off work, flying to Seattle with her parents for a break from Chicago and all its current stressors. When she came back to town, she and Zach spent their evenings combing through rental ads and touring buildings until they found her a new place. No more walking to work. She'd have a daily commute from now on, but it was only ten minutes from Zach's apartment, something that felt right to both of them for now, while they were both still feeling raw.

The Twitch channel for *A Word from the Wise* had been deleted a few days ago, along with Krista's account, as well as Hailey's, at the request of her family. She missed the community, but knew they understood. Otherwise, she had no regrets. Rob had made sure she had a copy of every stream they'd broadcast, right up to the last episode before Chase547 entered their lives, changing them forever. Maybe someday she'd watch them, remembering the fun of the early days, of streaming for just a handful of people, of the lightness and lack of pressure. Given time, she'd appreciate those early days more.

She'd come back to work after her week out West, feeling unusually nervous. So much had happened in that space, even when she hadn't realized she was being manipulated. Yet Melanie and Kyle had welcomed her back with open arms, and had bent over backward to ensure she reclaimed the clinic as her own. It hadn't been lost on her that she was never alone, even in the middle of the workday—there was always one of the two of them, or one of the assistants, checking in to make sure she didn't need anything. Now, three weeks later, she had her feet under her again and realized how shaky she must have been in those first days back. In many ways, she knew she was recovering from trauma, just as her patients were. Hers simply wasn't overtly physical, instead lingering just under the surface.

Time would heal that wound, as well as her physical injury. Her stitches had come out two weeks ago, and her wound was nothing more than a pale-pink line her surgeon had assured her would fade entirely, given time. That made her happy—she didn't want any reminders of what Jason Tobin had done to her.

She realized Mrs. Bowman was speaking to her. "I'm sorry. My mind drifted. What did you say?"

Mrs. Bowman let the pedals rotate to a stop. "That's five minutes."

"How does the knee feel?"

"Good. No pain."

"Excellent. You can get off the bike. We'll do more next week. What about when you're walking? Or on the stairs at home?"

Mrs. Bowman climbed off the bike. "It's good. Not bothering me."

"I think it's time we freed you from wearing your knee brace for everyday use."

"Really?" Mrs. Bowman's grin couldn't have been wider. "You're sure?"

"It's not me who needs to be sure. You do. If you're doing all of this pain free, it's time to remove the brace. But I want you to go back to using it if this is moving too fast and you experience any pain. Alternatively, if you're doing well without it, but have concerns about straining it, you can just wear it for isolated activities that stress the joint. You be the judge. I trust you. Trust yourself."

Mrs. Bowman circled the bike to give her a big hug. "Oh, my girl, thank you. What a difference you've made." She released Krista and reached for her purse. "We both deserve chocolate."

"I'm not saying no to that."

As she nibbled on chocolate and Mrs. Bowman talked about how she'd be able to chase after her grandbabies in a couple of months, Krista reflected on her life.

It wasn't the life she'd intended, one meant to be lived with Linc and the children they'd hoped for. Instead, her life had taken a number of significant turns, leaving her on an entirely different path.

While it wasn't her original vision, it wasn't all wrong.

She had the practice she shared with Kyle, her memories of Linc and their life together, and her family. She had the good work she did, day in and day out in the clinic, making a real difference, freeing people from pain and teaching them how to manage their new lives.

Maybe someday she'd want more, want new friends, a new partner, something different. But not right now.

For now, it was enough.

ACKNOWLEDGMENTS

THERE ARE VERY FEW AUTHORS who can write a novel as a completely solo endeavor, and I am most assuredly not one of those people. For *Shadow Play*, I have been fortunately assisted by the very best:

This book could not have been written without my daughter, Jess. The original germ of the idea of a killer using the Twitch platform to stalk a streamer was suggested by her when I was brainstorming a number of new ideas for a stand-alone novel several years ago. She was instrumental in helping build the story and in teaching me everything I needed to know about Twitch and broadcasting using OBS. We ran private test streams, watched specific streamers as a demonstration of how popular channels function, and she also assisted in making contact with those same streamers so I could ask specific questions as we built our fictional channel. Jess then went above and beyond in designing all the images in this novel, including creating custom channel emotes and subscription badges to match authentic Twitch channels to really give *A Word from the Wise* and the Wise Apples a real-world feel. She also did all the legwork in coming up with approximately fifty original and unused Twitch usernames to fill out our cast of characters. So much appreciation, Jess, for giving this project your all in so many ways. Much of its success will be because of your significant efforts. Thank you!

Many thanks to James Abbate, Kensington editor extraordinaire and my eleventh-hour partner in crime. By this time, James and I have perfected the art of hitting production deadlines by the skin of our teeth. To be clear, we're doing this because of the numerous deadlines I'm juggling, but I'm eternally grateful to James for his unending flexibility, completely nuts work hours, cheerful good humor as he goes above and beyond to bend his schedule to meet mine, and his exacting skills as an editor. To say I'm in good hands is an understatement. This book was definitely no exception, as it had some extra challenges baked in because of the graphics we felt would give this novel an authentic Twitch feel. It created a number of extra hoops for James, and, unsurprisingly, he effortlessly sailed through each one. Thank you, James!

Kensington and I are grateful to Robin Tilotta and the Twitch Brand Assets team for allowing us to use Twitch's custom icons so the chat images included in the story look realistic. They were incredibly flexible around our needs and their efforts go a long way to bringing the authentic Twitch experience to life in *Shadow Play*.

Jake Pfeiffer opened the door for me to the world of physiotherapy, and was generous with both his time and experiences as a physiotherapist. He shared details about his training and his practice that allowed me to ground Krista's professional life and her skills with clients in reality. Thank you, Jake, for sharing your time and talents to allow Krista to really shine as the expert she is!

Twitch streamer Masae allowed me a glimpse behind the curtain into her professional role, and deftly answered all of my questions, usually midstream! Additionally, BrettGB and Katagi were kind enough to cover many issues around moderator responsibilities and tools. Many thanks to you all!

Valerie and Myrna Moretti shared their love of Chicago and helped set the scene for Krista and Hailey, especially in the Rogers Park area. Thank you for adding local color to the story!

Thanks as always goes to my critique team—Kathi Alexander, Jessica Newton, Rick Newton, Jenny Rarden, and Sharon Taylor.

Even under considerable time pressure, your eagle eyes and the way you zero in on issues in a manuscript make for an intense post-crit team edit, but every correction is worthwhile from my perspective. You are invaluable in the logic, look, and feel of the final project, and you are all awesome!

My agent, Nicole Resciniti, is, as always, the woman behind the author. Many thanks to you and the agency for your constant support and for all you do for your authors!

Last, but definitely not least, I'm so grateful to work with such an amazing publishing house. From Seth Lerner's creation of an extremely eye-catching cover that captured multiple angles of the story in a single image, to Robin Cook in production, to Susanna Gruninger in subrights, to the publicity and communications teams—Martin Cahill, Lauren Jernigan, Vida Engstrand, Kait Johnson, Alexandra Nicolajsen, and Andi Paris—every aspect of the book's production and introduction to the world is handled brilliantly. Many thanks for all your support in so many ways!

Jen J. Danna, writing as Sara Driscoll